# ACCL.

### For *Who's the Boss*

"This is a fantastic erotic romance, and Anne Lange does an amazing job at making sure readers get their fill of both with wonderful, believable (and often quite funny) leading lady and man who are both used to being in control. The story is engaging, and the more erotic moments are white-hot!"

—Leigh

"Who's the Boss, is fun to read, well written, thrilling and quite sexy! Anne Lange is one of my favorite authors of erotica romance! If you don't mind steamy scenes, it will surely please you!" —Nicole

### For *Wicked Indulgence*

WINNER OF THE 2016 MÉNAGE ROMANCE READERS FAVORITE CONTEST
WINNER OF THE 2016 CAROLYN READERS' CHOICE AWARD
FINALIST IN THE 2016 AWARD OF EXCELLENCE CONTEST

"I love to read Ménage Romance and this book has it all! Chemistry, passion, love, and forgiveness. This author is truly a magnificent writer. So much so that everything is relatable and has great descriptions. Go one-Click this passionately sensual ménage!"

—Laura and Makayla Redmon for *Cutting Muse Blog*

"A great read! I couldn't get enough! The story line sucks you in and shows you the crazy twists, turns, the sexy fun, the bad, the good and the really really really good! A ménage story that gives you love, emotions and things that need forgiving!"

—Maria York for *Book Boyfriend Hangover*

"Wicked, Emotional, Sensual & So much more. This book had so much going for it I hardly know where to begin. It had the flush of instant attraction when meeting someone that sets your blood on fire, and discovering flames from long ago still burned red-hot and didn't fade over time in the slightest. It had the desire to explore your deepest fantasies and cravings with the man who has always held your heart, along with some help for a super sexy addition. It had the sting of heartbreak that accompanies losing your first love and seeing him again years later along with the fierce longing to make it right. The pace and the story held me captive right from the beginning and the secondary characters were amazing."

—Jenn for *BookwormBetties*

"The BDSM scenes were very descriptive with a visual of what was going on in the club. Nothing was distasteful, it was all written very well. The sex scenes were amazing; they just kept getting better and better. The storyline outside of the sex had me worried and upset, concerned and sad, happy and pleased all throughout the story. This was one of those books I didn't want to put down, I kept turning page after page because I didn't want to stop reading."

—C – *Mama Likes To Read Book Blog*

**For *Hers to Own***

WINNER OF THE 2015 NERFA CONTEST
FINALIST IN THE 2015 GOLDEN QUILL CONTEST
FINALIST IN THE 2015 BDSM CON GOLDEN FLOGGER CONTEST
FINALIST IN THE 2015 BEST BOOK BUYERS CONTEST
A NIGHT OWL REVIEWS TOP PICK

"I really enjoyed reading this book, it was fun and had some thrill. I recommend this book with immense pleasure."

—*Night Owl Reviews*

"The book starts off with panty-melting heat. What a way to kick off a book and get a reader hooked right off! Secrets and drama abound along with scorching hot scenes…"

—*The Book Quarry*

"[W]ell written with a fascinating plot. The main characters and the secondary characters were interesting. This book does a great job of keeping the reader on the edge of your seat as each twist and turn unravel. I had a hard time putting this book down. Overall, this was a very magnificent book and I hope to see these characters again in the future."

—Victoria for *Cocktails and Books*

**For *Friends with Benefits***

FINALIST IN THE 2015 PASSIONATE PLUME CONTEST

"What a nice ménage romance! All three main characters were lovable. I definitely recommend it."

—*Mary's Ménage Whispers*

"The best part about this book? It also has a real story going on in between the sex scenes. Friends with Benefits is emotional, heartwarming, anger evoking, thought provoking, passionate and sigh worthy."

—Robin, *Book Reads and Reviews*

"Ms. Lange's writing is fluid, solid, and incredibly hot. I was fanning myself the entire time I read this...her word choice and narrative had me fully in the moment. There is real depth in the love that builds between Tyler, Angela, and Connor."

—Author Erin Moore

"This story has everything you'd want from a sexy ménage. Smoking hot chemistry, panty melting sex and down-home relatable characters."

—Author Renea Mason

## OTHER TITLES BY ANNE LANGE

### THE VAULT SERIES

FRIENDS WITH BENEFITS
THE PERFECT MOMENT
HERS TO OWN
WICKED INDULGENCE
WHO'S THE BOSS?

### A NEW LEAGUE SERIES

SLIDING INTO HOME
THE FINAL QUARTER

### FAMILY TIES SERIES

HER CHOICE

### THE FOREVER SERIES

FOREVER STARTS TODAY

### STAND ALONE TITLES & SHORT STORIES

WORTH THE RISK
WITH THE GREATEST OF EASE
BLIND TASTE TEST
GAME NIGHT

THE VAULT SERIES
THE MCBRIDE MEN: GABE

# WHO'S THE *Boss*

ANNE LANGE

A|L
hotRom publishing
OTTAWA, ONTARIO

**Who's the Boss**

The Vault Series, The McBride Men: Gabe



Published by hotRom publishing
105 Porcupine Trail
Ottawa, Ontario K0A 1T0
Canada



ISBN: 978-0-9958695-4-7

Cover by Bookin' It Designs
http://www.bookinitdesigns.com/

Book Layout and Design by Ryan Fitzgerald

First electronic publication by Etopia Press: June 2016
ISBN: 978-1-944138-48-6

*Due to the dynamic nature of the Internet, website links contained within this book may be outdated and/or no longer valid.*

## SEXUAL CONTENT WARNING

This book contains sexually explicit content and coarse language, which is only suitable for mature readers over the age of 18, including but not limited to light bondage, m/f/m ménage, and public scenes in an adult club.

Neither hotRom publishing nor the author accept any responsibility for any individual's actions resulting from accessing or reading this story.

Please use your best discretion when considering the contents and always practice safe and consensual sex.

This one is for my mom.
I love the fact that regardless of the type of story I write, she's proud of me.
And she's always the first person who wants to buy a copy.

To Julie
I hope you enjoy.

# WHO'S THE *Boss*

All the best
Ann Lange

# CHAPTER ONE

"JIMMY! WHAT DID I TELL YOU *JUST* LAST WEEK, FOR LIKE the third freaking day in a row?"

Gabe McBride winced. It sounded like the boss wasn't too happy with poor Jimmy. Gabe had shut the door of his black Porsche and rounded the front of the car just in time to catch the tail end of the tongue-lashing some poor soul had the misfortune to receive.

"But–"

"No buts. You need to wear your fucking hardhat and your fucking safety glasses when you're on the fucking job site. Goddamn it, Jimmy. The whole purpose of personal protective equipment is to protect *you* from personal injury. How many times do we have to go through this?" Exasperation laced the boss's words.

"I'll do better, Frankie."

"Yes, you will. If an inspector shows up and catches you without the proper gear, again, we'll get written up, and then I'll *have* to take action. Last warning. Please go to your truck, put your PPE on, and then get back to work."

"Yes, boss."

Based on the number of curse words interjected as adjectives, the boss was fed up with warning Jimmy. Did that raspy voice of command belong to the construction company's owner Frank Stevens?

The growl of frustration that followed reached Gabe's ears and made him chuckle. A rare occurrence these days. But he sobered quick enough. If the man in trouble wasn't following protocol, then he deserved the reprimand, though Gabe personally would have handled it with less colorful wording.

Gabe was a firm believer in rules. When people didn't follow instructions, orders, or rules, accidents happened. Expectations had to be clearly articulated and understood. Consequences were a definite possibility. His goal, like the guy dishing out the directive to Jimmy, was to ensure nobody got hurt while under his watch.

Gabe paused on the sidewalk in front of what appeared to be the renovation of an old restaurant that had run its course. Years old dust and grime coated the windows. Yellow construction tape wrapped the facing and brick like a bow. Sawhorses, toolboxes, two by fours, and sheets of drywall littered the interior. A sign in the window implied the new owners would be ready for business in two months' time and were currently recruiting for wait staff. Judging by the amount of work still to be done, the contactor had better pick up his schedule.

Gabe had stopped at the office to invite his brothers to breakfast, but they'd both been heading out the door in opposite directions, both frazzled and rushed. Gabe overheard Kyle's end of a conversation with a client who needed assistance, but Kyle had been too busy. So Gabe offered to help out.

Gabe guessed the work crew had propped open the front door, and hiked up the windows to allow the slight breeze to filter though. He didn't envy them. He remembered too many months of working night and day, through extreme hot and bitter cold, to get The Vault ready for business. He decided to take a stroll around the building and look at what they might be dealing with before announcing his presence and meeting Mr. Stevens.

Around back, he discovered a parking lot large enough to accommodate about twenty vehicles. Not too bad for a private business in the downtown core. The building itself was two stories of aged red brick, with a rickety fire escape up the back to the second level. Stained cracked windows with boxes stacked in front of them was all he could see. It looked like perhaps an apartment turned storage area existed up there. A door at ground level, probably to the kitchen, stood braced open with a brick.

Gabe surveyed the area around his feet. The pavement required work. Poor patch jobs, weeds growing through open cracks and heaved asphalt made for a very uneven surface. The pressure-treated fence surrounding the lot needed replacement boards and was in dire need of a fresh coat of stain. The whole place, in its current state, created an eyesore for the neighborhood.

On closer inspection Gabe noticed the windows at ground level had no visible locking mechanisms and broken panes of glass jutted out at every angle. The door itself looked like a five-year-old child could kick it in. Security enhancements were definitely in order.

Gabe made his way back to the front of the building. He stopped at the main entrance, his path blocked by the tape across the opening. He could easily step over it, but remained beyond the barrier, respectful of its purpose. He made eye contact with one of the men, and waved him over.

"Can I help you?" the man asked. Obviously he'd been doing hard-labor for some time—he had no need for a gym—but years in the sun had weathered his skin making him appear older than his birth certificate probably stated.

"I'm looking for Frank Stevens." Gabe's gaze swept across the open space. He tried to visualize it filled with diners as staff bustled between tables, and a crowd waiting to be seated, perhaps even lined up down the street.

He looked for a man befitting the name Frank. He pictured an older guy, maybe of Italian heritage, and grizzled around the edges. Years of supervising a construction crew wearing on him, maybe the beginnings of a beer gut stretching his waistband. The man probably grew up in this world, working with generations of family members all doing the same thing to make ends meet.

"You mean Frankie."

Frank, Frankie, was there a difference? Gabe nodded.

"What for?" The older man's eyes changed from friendly to suspicious. He glared at Gabe. "You an inspector or something?"

"No. My brothers and I own a security firm. I came by to discuss some issue Mr. Stevens has been having with vandalism." He probably should have found out a bit more about the job, but Kyle had already been running late. So whatever it was Kyle had yelled out to Gabe as he settled behind the wheel of his car had drifted away in the breeze. "Mr. Stevens should be expecting me."

"Mr. Stevens?"

"That's what I said." Had they not already confirmed that? Why was this man giving him such a strange look? Maybe he couldn't hear well.

The guy started to chuckle, but quickly covered it with a fake cough. "Sure. Um. *Mr.* Stevens is just in the back at the moment. Why don't you wait right where you are? I'll let Frankie know you're here." He shot Gabe one final look, barked out a sharp snort of laughter, and shook his head before he turned away.

Gabe watched him meander his way through the space, avoiding dangerous areas, stepping over tools and chunks of wood in his path.

"Hey, *Mr.* Stevens," he called to somebody out of sight. "There's somebody here to see you."

A couple of other workers stopped what they were doing and glanced in Gabe's direction. There was a response, but from where Gabe stood, he couldn't make it out over the start-up of a saw.

The man he'd spoken with spun on his heel and headed back, taking his time as he retraced his steps. He reached the doorway where Gabe waited, and offered that not-so friendly glare again. Apparently all remnants of humor vanished somewhere between the back of the room and the front of the store. "Frankie will be here in a few minutes. You'd better behave yourself. I'll be paying attention."

After that bizarre warning, the man shuffled over to his workstation and picked up where he'd left off, casting the occasional watchful glance Gabe's way.

Gabe strode over to and leaned against his car. He checked the time and watched a city bus drive by, belching a cloud of noxious exhaust fumes as it passed. It rolled to a stop at the corner, brakes squealing, let off a handful of passengers, and picked up a few more. Inside, the buzz and whir of tools continued amid shouts back and forth between the construction crew. He pulled out his cell phone to skim through his e-mail.

"You're looking for me?"

Gabe paused, his finger hovering over the screen, but he didn't look up. From afar, the voice had been deep and gravelly, immediately conjuring an image of what he assumed Frank Stevens would look like.

But from a couple of feet away, its texture softened and the smoky quality rolled over him, doing something funky to his insides. His cock stirred. It was the first time, in a very long time, that Gabe reacted to a few simple words. Words that offered no sexual inflection, no offer to please, no request for dominance.

Gabe swallowed, and willed his body to regain control. That voice definitely did *not* belong to a man. He raised his head, and his breath caught in his throat.

Before him stood a petite woman. A fucking beautiful-as-hell, petite woman. The top of her head probably only reached the middle of his chest when he was standing. In his current relaxed pose, she looked straight at his neck area. She wore her dark hair tucked up under her construction hat. A few long tendrils had escaped, and those she'd wrapped behind her ears. Ears that held simple gold studs. Man, he hoped her hair, when lose, cascaded down to the middle of her back in glorious waves.

She'd removed her safety glasses and had them dangling from the fingers of her right hand, leaving him with nothing to do but stare into a pair of exotic eyes, the most amazing shade of green. Some might call them plain old hazel eyes. But they made him think of colors he'd find deep in the rain forest. A jungle he'd happily get lost in.

Her waist indented just the right amount. His fingers itched to span it and see if they could meet. He didn't think so, and that unconfirmed guess sent a spike of desire rushing though him because he preferred a woman he could hold without digging his fingertips into her rib cage. One he could grip around the middle while she rode him hard and fast. Then agonizingly slow.

The perfect-sized waist was currently emphasized by a button-down plaid shirt she'd tucked into her dusty jeans and closed off with a light brown leather tool belt. His gaze raked her from head to toe and back again before drifting down to her feet, which were covered in well-worn scuffed work boots. He dragged his eyes back up to her face and zeroed in on those stunning eyes, currently shaded by the brim of her white construction hat.

Holy shit. He must have stumbled across a fault line and precariously straddled both sides.

"You're wasting my time, mister." She rubbed her forehead leaving a smudge of dirt behind. "Who are you? And what do you want? Make it quick because I have work to do."

"Frankie Stevens?" This pretty little thing with the raw,

sexy voice and bedroom eyes couldn't be the guy who'd called Kyle.

"Look, I don't have time for this shit."

And the mouth. His mother would have a field day washing this beauty's mouth out with the dreaded soap she'd threatened him and his brothers with every time she heard them utter a curse word. Hell, he'd love the opportunity to do it.

But Gabe had a better alternative. He pictured those luscious lips wrapped around his cock as she knelt before him, her hands braced against his thighs as she worked up and down his length, over and over, until she learned her lesson. He envisioned plenty of learning opportunities in her future.

"You're Frankie Stevens?" His big head already acknowledged the truth of the situation. His little head stood at attention, anxious for some playtime with this sexy, mouthy, sprite.

She straightened her spine and frowned, but there was a hint of caution in her expression. "I am." She dipped her chin and turned her head slightly, giving him a side-on look. "Who wants to know?"

He finally found his manners and stuck out his hand. "Gabe McBride. My brother Kyle was supposed to let you know that I was coming today. He's tied up with another client." Oh Christ, now he had a vision of her bound to his bed with a scarf of green silk to match her eyes.

Her shoulders sagged, her posture relaxed, and the scowl she'd been wearing disappeared, replaced with a look of relief. His sexual side took a step back and his protective side reared up. She took his hand, surprising him yet again with a firm grip and strong handshake. She had calluses on her palm. Somehow that turned him on even more.

"Thank you for coming. I really hoped to handle this myself, but I'm running into a wall with deadlines looming. I could really use your help."

Gabe, usually a man in control, found he needed to forcibly

stop staring directly at her if he wanted to gain any leverage in this situation. But that was no easy task. He cleared his throat and took a physical step out from her personal space. He immediately wanted to move right back into position and force her to look up at him. He imagined her eyes round and begging for his command. He shook it off.

"My brother didn't have time to give me any details. But I did take a walk around the back of the building. I noticed a few areas that will need to be addressed." Although he was an owner in the security business, his brothers were the true experts in the field. But maybe it was time he stepped up to the plate and took a healthier interest in that part of his revenue stream.

She waved away his remarks. "My men have that under control."

Now he was confused. "I don't understand. I assumed you were having security problems here at the job site."

She shook her head. "Not here. At my construction trailer mostly. I'm hoping it's just some kids playing around, figuring it would be fun to screw with me."

Although he was totally on board for his version of screwing with her, he straightened and tensed, finally getting his head—the proper one this time—back into the game. "I hear a 'but' on the end of that statement."

She sighed and sidled closer to him.

He smelled a mixture of lilac and sawdust and it became his new favorite combination. He barely restrained himself from closing his eyes and leaning forward for a good sniff.

She glanced over her shoulder.

He followed her lead, but not before he let his wandering eyes drop to where her shirt stretched tight. He caught a glimpse of lace underneath. All boyish on the outside, but feminine underneath? What he wouldn't do to get a closer look at the package underneath the wrapping.

Most of her workers were in the shop and hard at work, not paying them any attention whatsoever. That one guy, however, the one who he'd spoken to, watched them with an eagle eye.

She stepped closer.

Gabe could see the pink lacy edge of her bra resting along her ample cleavage bared by the white T-shirt she wore under her button-up shirt. He could smell her shampoo now. That's where the lilac smell came from.

She wore not a speck of makeup, but her eyes, framed by thick, dark lashes, popped and sparkled. Not with fear, or even annoyance, as he would have expected. But good old-fashioned anger.

"I think somebody is trying to put me out of business."

## CHAPTER TWO

"WHY WOULD SOMEBODY WANT TO PUT YOUR COMPANY out of business?"

Frankie looked up at the tall, dark drink of water. And boy she was thirsty. Like trudging-through-the-desert-following-the-path-of-a-sandstorm thirsty.

Her father always told her to stay away from guys like him. According to her dad, the good-looking ones were trouble. And this guy had won the lottery in the looks department.

Taller than her by a foot at least, he had short, dark hair and stunning blue eyes she could happily drown in. His jeans hugged thighs that could crack walnuts she was sure, and she had the strangest urge to rip his shirt off his body and count the size of his pack. Because she'd bet the farm he had an impressive one hidden under there.

Unfortunately, her mom hadn't been around long enough to either contradict or agree with such sage advice, or pass along any other words of parental wisdom. But Frankie was certain her mom would have thrown up at least a few red flags. Because this guy looked like sin with a capital S.

"Ms. Stevens?"

People pictured construction workers slaving away shirtless in the hot sun, muscles bulging, beads of sweat trickling down their washboard abs as though competing in a moguls race. And of course, they wore nothing but frayed cut-offs, work boots, and a red bandanna tied around their head.

Perhaps somewhere, but not on her job sites. She'd haul their ass to the table for lack of industry-approved personal protective equipment. She had rules, and they were there for a reason. Frayed shorts and topless workers had no place at a construction site. And her men most definitely couldn't compete with the caliber of eye candy of one Mr. Gabe McBride.

She sighed and rubbed at her right temple. "I'm beginning to think it's not my business, but probably more specifically, me."

A crash inside the restaurant startled her, followed by a curse and a muttered apology.

"I don't understand. What would somebody have against you?" the very handsome Gabe McBride asked, completely ignoring the chaos behind her.

Frankie assessed Mr. Sex-on-a-Stick. He looked rather adorable with his forehead all wrinkled and confusion marring his GQ-model face. The guy could rock the dark, brooding look. Dark hair, dark stubble, a dark look, and piercing eyes. Built like a professional body builder, the man packed muscles like she packed her laundry into her hamper—tight.

Even leaning against his car, he towered over her. Normally she tried to avoid being in that position. She didn't like giving anybody an edge that could be used to intimidate. For some reason, though, she didn't feel threatened by this man in the least. But he sure as hell was one of the few specimens she'd seen of late who could tempt her focus away from the job for a few hours.

"Did you not meet somebody's schedule or something?" he asked.

Damn. How disappointing. She felt like somebody had let the air out of her balloon. The poor guy must not be too bright. She'd have to spell it out for him.

"I've got boobs." She tucked her hands under her breasts and lifted, drawing his gaze straight to the offending pair of D's.

He blinked, and his top lip twitched like he was trying to hold in a chuckle. He looked rather uncomfortable. It was cute as hell.

"Well, they are nice," he stated deadpan.

Wow, no drool or jerk comment. She released the treasures, oddly pleased at the compliment that typically pissed her off and had on occasion garnered a slap across the face. "I suppose. But they don't have anything to do with construction," she explained. "They know nothing about concrete, steel girders, wood, or crane operation. They don't know how to estimate a job or manage one to make sure the project is completed when it's supposed to be. They have no clue which trades to hire when, or what permits are needed before work can begin or be approved for occupation." She tapped a finger lightly against her aching temple. "All that knowledge happens to be in here." She waved a hand in front of her breasts like a model on a game show. "Not here."

He looked down at her, the oddest expression on his face. Then he smiled. And when those stunning lips curved up, the heavens opened and the angels sang the sweetest melody.

The man had the most amazing smile. It absolutely made her giddy, and for some strange reason she had the insane urge to fall to her knees, wrap her hands around one muscular thigh, and rub her cheek against his flesh.

*What the fuck?*

"I'm sure your breasts have nothing to do with whatever you believe is happening," he said.

She gaped at him while he stood there all confident and knowledgeable-like. She'd homed in on the way he said breasts and immediately her tired brain filled with images of him hovering over her as he licked every inch of her naked body before he trailed his fingers down her spine, over her ass, only to tuck two of them deep inside her pussy, making her squirm and beg for release.

She shook her head and pushed the picture aside for consideration later tonight when she ultimately dropped, exhausted, into her lonely bed. Hey, it would be nice to have new fodder for her dreams. "What I believe is that somebody doesn't like the competition. They don't like the fact that I know how to build things and they don't like the fact that I'm now running the show instead of my father."

Did he have to look so fucking hot? Maybe it was the car. Any guy would look stellar leaning against a Porsche, wouldn't they?

"Where's your father, if I may ask?"

She sucked in a breath, the pain of losing her mentor and the man she'd loved most in the world still too fresh after a year. "He passed away."

"I'm sorry." He paused. "Could it be one of your own crew?"

She didn't want to believe that but couldn't deny the thought had crossed her mind. She shrugged. She truly hoped not. That would be a total blow to her ego, which was fragile enough these days when she found herself behind closed doors with the drapes closed tight.

"I don't think so. At least I hope not. I think somebody is angry my father left his company to me. Unfortunately for them, I intend to see it flourish."

"And can you do that?"

Frankie opened her mouth, ready to blast him. But then she looked into his eyes and realized his question contained honest curiosity. He wasn't belittling her ability to be successful in a predominantly man's world.

She took a deep breath, calming her heart rate and stifling her rush to jump to conclusions. "Yes, I can. I've been living in this world since I could walk. I've been doing this work since I could lift a hammer." Tears sprung to her eyes, but she willed them away. "I've been running this company solo since the day my father suffered his first stroke." The second one had killed him. She paused and then looked up into Mr. McBride's face again, focusing on those compelling blue eyes. "I know construction, Mr. McBride. It's my life. I love it. And I'm good at it."

She shut down the sales pitch, tucked her trembling fingers into the back pockets of her jeans, and dropped her chin. *God, she missed her father.*

She loved hard work. She liked being in control. But she hated spilling her guts.

"Then I guess we should have a chat about what's been going on so my brothers and I can ensure you have a company to keep running."

# CHAPTER THREE

Gabe followed the lovely Ms. Stevens and her battered Ford pickup as they drove back to her office, which was actually no more than a construction trailer that had seen better days propped up on cement blocks on a large rural lot just outside of town.

During the drive, he pondered the sexy, petite woman with the mouth of a…well a construction worker. The complete opposite of the women he typically found himself attracted to, and he couldn't explain the draw. Lust probably. It had been a while since he'd played with anybody. Even longer since he'd been in a relationship of any length. Hell, he couldn't remember the last female in his life he'd attached the label of girlfriend to.

Gabe couldn't put his finger on why this one tugged at him like a fish on the end of a hook. He'd always gravitated toward soft-spoken, girly-girls. Women who liked to dress pretty, liked pretty things, wanted a family, and would maybe consider being a stay-at-home mom for a few years. Those women tended to submit to his particular expectations rather easily.

Frankie embodied none of those things. And he sure as hell could not see her willingly falling to her knees or bending over his lap. Though, the vision of her in those positions… Fuck. A rough groan worked its way up his throat. He usually had more control. He prided himself on his control. Gabe reached down and adjusted himself.

Over the years, his brothers had ribbed him about his fantasy life partner. His mother often told him she'd taught him better. His father would no doubt roll over in his grave. Gabe wasn't a chauvinist—far from it. He loved self-confident, self-sufficient, strong women. Hell, to put up with a man like him, she had to be able to hold her own. But he equally cherished the softer side of them. The side that wanted to be with a man like him. A man who liked to show women how special they were.

After his father passed away, Gabe watched his mother work her ass off keeping things together for him and his brothers. She did what was necessary and ensured they never wanted for anything.

When he was old enough, he got a job. He wanted to remove at least some of the burden from her shoulders. He was extremely proud of what she'd accomplished being the sole provider in the family for many years. But now, as an adult, he worried she'd missed out on opportunities for happiness because she had three little boys depending on her. And he felt his father would have not wanted that for her.

Gabe didn't want the woman he eventually settled down with to feel as though she *had* to work to support herself or their children. Likewise, he wasn't a man who thought women had it easy. But he dreaded the thought of his wife returning home after a long day at the office and forcing a smile for him or their kids. He wanted her to have the freedom to spend as much time as she wished with them, not to only see them a few hours each day in the mad rush to get dinner on the table and homework completed before bedtime. His brothers teased him about being born in the wrong generation.

Gabe pulled his Porsche in next to her truck. He climbed out from behind the steering wheel and took in his surroundings. In addition to the trailer, which was sheltered from the sun by two large maples, there was a large dump truck, a backhoe and a couple of pickups, all sporting her company logo.

About twenty-five yards down the drive was a large multi-vehicle garage. Another twenty-five yards or so beyond that sat what he assumed to be the original farmhouse and a large red barn behind that. Even from where he stood, it was clear somebody with a loving touch had cared for the home over the years. All the buildings could use a coat of paint, but they were far from run down. The wrap-around veranda looked inviting with its swing and Adirondack chairs. Potted plants were scattered around the area, and pink and white rose bushes hid the porch skirting and added splashes of color. A flagstone path led the way to the porch steps. Lush green grass covered the property.

Opposite the string of buildings, a washed-out white fence stretched from the very front of the property where it edged up to the road, all the way to the line of trees at the back. He easily pictured horses grazing in that enclosure. Wildflowers sprang up here and there along the fence and the tree line.

Frankie joined him. "Sorry you had to drive to the job site. We could have actually just met here."

"No worries."

"Come on inside," she beckoned. "Everyone is out on job sites, so we can talk in private."

He nodded toward the house. "Is that where you live?"

She glanced up the road. "Yeah. I grew up here."

"It's a nice home. Just you?"

"Me and my sister."

"Do you manage the upkeep yourself?"

She cocked her head as she stared at him, her stance rigid. "I do." The challenge, in her eyes and in her tone, rang clear as a bell. She turned away. "Follow me."

Had he imagined the hitch in her voice? The barely there shimmer of tears in her eyes before she gave him her back? Rather than make her feel awkward, he refrained from saying anything more and simply trailed behind her. Besides, the view was anything but boring.

The inside of the trailer looked like any other trailer he'd been in, only cleaner. Did that mean she liked order? Preferred neatness, even in an environment prone to dirt and chaos?

Inside her small office at the back of the trailer, she slipped past a vertical filing cabinet and moved around a steel-framed desk to sit in her high-backed chair, pointing to one of her two guest chairs, indicating he should sit.

"Do you work with your brother often?" she asked, fingering a small bouquet of purple and white flowers perched on the corner of her desk, probably picked from her own field.

Gabe nodded as he fit his large frame into the small arm chair. "Brothers, and yes. We actually have two businesses. Kyle and Kade generally take the lead on the security side of things, while I tend to manage our other one."

She pursed her lips. A look of frustration crossed her face as she leaned back. He half expected her to cross her arms over her generous chest and huff.

"Are we wasting time here?" she asked. "If you can't help me—"

He raised his right hand. "I didn't say I couldn't help. I simply said they tend to take the lead on this side of the business. But I'm perfectly capable of helping you with whatever security issues you have."

She didn't look convinced.

"Listen, tell me what the problem is and if it's not my area of expertise, I will happily," *not,* "get one of my brothers on the job." For some reason the mere thought of Frankie Stevens sitting across from Kyle, or even Kade, just rubbed him the wrong way.

She chewed the inside of her cheek for a long moment.

He waited. He was good at waiting, though the dominant

in him reared up, ready to scold her and tell her to stop doing that.

"Fine." She relented and slumped a bit in her chair. She weaved her fingers together and settled her hands in her lap. "After my father passed away, I took over the company. Things were going OK for the first couple of months, but then I started noticing a few things that didn't seem quite right."

"Like what?"

"We weren't getting jobs."

"Don't you bid on work like any other contractor? The process should work fairly if you meet the requirements, are qualified to do the work, and provide the lower bid."

"Exactly. That's how it works for larger jobs. And I happen to know we should have been the winning bid on many occasions."

"But—"

This time she stuck her hand up.

Even though she tried to look like one of the guys, the pink nail polish definitely took her out of the running. Did she wear the same shade on her toes?

"Large or small, these are people my father worked with for years. Contracts that he would have won with ease. I'm not trying to be egotistical, because we certainly didn't get every job we bid on when he was alive. And I don't expect to win every project now. But we got enough work then that when we're now suddenly getting much fewer, it begins to look suspicious."

He'd grant her that as a possibility.

"Then there are the break-ins."

He straightened in his chair. "Somebody's been breaking into your job sites?"

She shook her head. "No. At least not yet. They've been breaking in here."

He automatically looked around, alarmed that somebody was trespassing on her property, getting close to her home. A home that two young women lived in alone. "Have they stolen anything?"

"A few small tools. Nothing major or not easily replaceable, so far. But it's still a nuisance. What's worse is the equipment they damaged." She shook her head. "Whoever's doing it knows something about what they're doing."

"How long has this been going on?" he asked.

She glanced out the window and then dropped her gaze down to the photos on her desk. One, a black and white of a married coupled he assumed were her parents, and the other a pair of young girls smiling. The younger one sat atop a chestnut horse. The older girl stood next to the animal's head, holding the reins, both beaming for the camera.

Gabe realized the flowers and the two photos were the only personal touches in the room.

She sighed and returned her attention back to him, reaching out to brush her thumb down the glass of the photo of the married couple. "As far as the break-ins go, I didn't think anything of it the first time or two. And yes, I did initially chalk up it up to kids pulling pranks."

"But?" Gabe pressed. She had said initially. So something changed.

She hesitated and he could see the conflict in her face.

"But what changed the playing field for me was after the brakes failed on one of the trucks. My godfather was moving it for me. He could have been seriously hurt. I started taking it a lot more seriously then."

Now he felt her concern. "Somebody took out the brakes? You're sure?"

"Yes. Positive. Somebody bled them almost dry. Thankfully Lawrence was on the property and not going fast when they actually failed. It could have been one of my men out on the main road where he or somebody else could have truly been hurt." Her eyebrows furrowed in worry, and her eyes turned a shade greener in anger.

"When did all of this start happening?" Gabe asked.

"The first time was about eight months after my dad died. They waited another month before they tried something again. The more serious ones have been in the last month or so. That's why I decided to call McBride Security. This isn't something I can handle on my own anymore."

"You probably should have called us sooner." From the sound of it, she was lucky nobody had been hurt or around when the vandals decided to make an appearance. He shuddered to think what could have happened if she or her sister were here and inadvertently walked in on something.

"It pisses me off more than anything," she said. "What angers me most though, is they seem to get into the trailer with ease, and they've gone through my things."

"How do you know?" he asked.

"They move my stuff around." She cocked her head toward her desk. "My family picture is moved. My plant. Things in my drawers and filing cabinets are sifted through. Nothing obvious to anyone other than to me. But I feel violated. They've been in my personal space." She sighed heavily. "A couple of weeks ago, they ripped up drawings for a new project I was bidding on."

"Why would somebody want to do that?" It seemed rather childish or stalker-ish, depending how you looked at it.

"To fuck with me?" She shook her head. "I don't know. I like control. I like my office and the trailer to be neat. Just because I work in construction doesn't mean the place needs to look like a construction site."

"Maybe it is just kids, at least some of it." He remembered sneaking onto job sites as a kid. Standing next to large equipment was thrilling, making a young boy feel so much smaller.

And who could resist seeing a little boy's toy in real-life size? His father had caught him and his friends once, not long before he died, and it was the last time. But, to be honest, this didn't feel like the work of a group of boys looking to get into trouble.

She started to roll her eyes but stopped. "I don't think so. Kids would be random. The first time that's exactly what it seemed to be and why I disregarded it."

"Could still be random vandalism," he commented.

"If the drawings had been on top of the pile or in the pile at all, or my personal things clearly moved around I'd agree. But these were filed in my desk. They had to look for and find them, when that pretty stack out on the conference table could have sufficed."

Gabe remembered seeing the neat stack of drawings she referred to. Easily visible and available to anybody walking through the door. Kids out for a good time would be more interested in a grab and dash. They wouldn't stick around to look for something specific and risk being caught.

"And the damage to the vehicles, and Lawrence's near miss just doesn't convince me it's a bunch of boys out for a thrill."

At least she was smart enough to ask for help when she needed it. "Any trouble with any of your crew? Infighting among the guys?"

"No."

"What about other companies?"

"Not that I'm aware of."

"Anybody showing a professional interest in your company?" Gabe asked.

"Um…"

He stilled. "Somebody looking to buy it?"

She shifted in her chair. "Yes. A few months ago, I turned down an offer to be bought out by a larger company."

* * *

She had his full attention now. The look in his eyes intensified, the angles on his face hardened giving him an even edgier and more brooding look than before.

"Who tried to buy you out?" He'd taken his phone from the holster attached to his belt, punched a few buttons and looked up at her expectantly, his thumbs hovering over the keypad.

"Diamond Construction." She waited while he typed that information into his phone.

"Was it a generous offer? Perhaps something too good to be true?"

"It was more than reasonable," she said. "But I wasn't interested."

He glanced up at her. "Why not?"

She looked at him pointedly. "Because I have no plans to sell my company."

"OK. About this Diamond—"

"I don't think it was them," she cut him off.

He paused and raised his head, his gaze pinned to hers. Never mind his eyes, the man had one hell of a sexy mouth. Damn, what would those lips feel like brushing over hers? Or even better, other parts of her body that hadn't experienced the touch of a lover's tongue in far too long?

"Why not?"

She licked her lips and cleared her throat. Was it hot in here? "I've known Lawrence Diamond since I was a baby. He and my father grew up together and were best friends."

"And competitors," he noted.

"Yes. But it was never a problem for them, and there was plenty of work to go around." Her father and Lawrence often recommended each other to clients when they had too much on their own plates. They even shared some jobs during slow times over the years.

Gabe's insinuation fell flat. Lawrence would never try to

push her out of the business. He loved her as if she were his own daughter.

"But now your father is gone. Maybe he wants to sweep in and pick up the extra work," Gabe suggested as he shrugged one massive shoulder. "He is a businessman with employees and bills to pay."

"He wouldn't do that to me. He's my godfather, he loves me. I spent my childhood going between my father's construction sites and his. He's taught me half of what I know."

"Then why offer to buy you out?"

"Because he knows how much I loved my father and how much it kills me to keep working without him by my side," she said. "He thought it might ease the pain if I didn't have to face everything my father worked so hard to build every single day." She paused and took a deep breath, her gaze drifting to the picture of her parents. One of the few photos she had of her mother.

"But he also knows how much I love this work. And that, because of how much I loved my father, I would do everything I could to keep the company going in his name. He's as concerned as I am over what's been happening. He even offered to hire a couple of full-time security guards for me."

She waved away Gabe's doubtful look. "He just wanted to give me the option. He's always looking out for me and my sister. Besides, he knows if I ever did decide to sell, it would be to him anyway. Hell, I'd *give* him the business."

She'd shocked him. But he didn't understand. She enjoyed the work, the freedom of being her own boss and creating new homes or businesses or refurbishing broken or damaged buildings. Watching a client's eyes light up when they saw the finished project—that was proof positive she'd done her job well.

But even more than that, her best childhood memories were those spent with her dad as he patiently allowed her to tag along behind him, peppering him with questions every few minutes. He'd stop whatever he was doing to explain the tools, the process, and the safety measures. He took the time to show her how everything worked, how to drive the heavy equipment, how to read drawings, prepare estimates and run the business. Hell, she could drive the loader before she could drive a car.

Looking down into the casket that day and saying goodbye to her father had been hard enough. Walking away from everything he'd built would be walking away from his heart and soul. And that, she refused to do.

Gabe typed a few more words into his phone. "We'll check him out anyway, just as a matter of course and to cover all of our bases."

"Fill your boots." If he wanted to waste a couple of hours looking into people who she considered family, he could go for it.

"Who else might want to sabotage you?"

She snorted. "It's beyond sabotage, Mr. McBride."

"Gabe."

Her cheeks warmed. "Gabe. Somebody is trying to put me out of business. And if they can't scare me into selling, then they'll simply begin by destroying my equipment. Maybe eventually my job sites, knowing that I won't have the immediate collateral to fix or replace everything. Which means I'll lose any contracts I have in play because I won't be in a position to finish the job. I'll be forced into breach of contract which comes with its own set of problems and costs." And she'd lose the very thing her father had built from the ground up. That wrenched at her heart.

"We won't let it come to that, Ms. Stevens."

"Frankie."

He angled his head to the side and stared at her until she started to fidget. His unblinking gaze sent tendrils of something warm and tingly through her body. She felt alert and alive for the first time in ages.

"What's your real name?" he asked, a hint of that delicious smile tilting the corners of his mouth.

She narrowed her eyes. "Why?"

He chuckled. "Because you may sound like a Frankie, but you don't look like a Frankie."

Any other guy and she would have given him an earful for that remark, or an uppercut to the jaw. She'd been Frankie since she could talk and realized she hated dresses and skirts. The only dress she owned was the black thing she'd worn to her father's funeral. If she could have gotten away with her jeans and work shirt, she would have. But her sister had insisted she show proper respect and dress appropriately. Her father would have understood, but in the end she'd relented to make her sister feel better.

She could argue, spit, and fight with the best of the boys. The only thing remotely girlish about her was her nail polish and her underwear. For some insane reason, she loved to wear pink nail polish. Pink! Pink was so not her thing. Frankie could only fathom that it was linked to one of the strongest memories—really the only memory—she had of her mother. Her mom used to paint her tiny fingers and toes pink. After her mom died, she'd continued the tradition.

"Only my mother called me by my real name," she confessed.

"And why is that?"

"Because I want people to call me Frankie."

He appeared to consider her statement. "Tell me anyway."

She rolled her eyes theatrically. "Is it necessary?"

"For the invoice," he replied. Did more than professional curiosity sparkle in his eyes?

She sighed while she tried to ignore the sensation his possible interest stirred in her body. "Francesca," she said, her voice low as though spilling the secret would bare everything to him.

His eyes widened and a look of appreciation crossed his face. He almost smiled. "That's a very pretty name. And it suits you."

She laughed so hard she choked.

He waited her out, studying her, a slight curve on his lips, but delight danced in his eyes this time. "You don't believe me." He looked amused as he leaned back and crossed his arms over his chest, drawing her eyes to his biceps as they bulged.

"No. I don't. I'm as much a Francesca as you're a Gabriella."

Horror replaced the amusement, and she laughed again, but this time she was the one amused.

Once she regained control, she took a final, calming breath and canted forward. "So, can you help me, Gabe McBride?"

He stared at her. What was going through his mind?

"Put together a list of anybody you can think of that might want to see you out of business. Competitors. Anybody with a grudge against your father or you. Give me a list of your employees and any subs you hire on a regular basis." He paused. His shoulders tensed and his mouth thinned to a firm line. He unfolded his arms and glanced down at his phone as he typed something. "And your husband's name."

"I'm not married."

He stilled but didn't raise his head. "Your boyfriend's name then."

"I don't have a boyfriend."

His head came up, slow as he rolled his neck to a straight and tall position. He zeroed in on her face with an intensity that shocked her. "A current friend with benefits? A potential boyfriend? A best friend who happens to be male?"

She swallowed hard but couldn't look away. "No, no and no." Was that surprise or relief in his eyes?

"How about past boyfriends?"

That broke the spell. She blinked and turned her head. He'd find out anyway. "John. He's one of my employees." He continued to stare at her. Did the man not blink? "He's a pain in the ass, but I don't think he's behind this either."

Her one clusterfuck of a relationship, and the reason she'd sworn off men for the time being. Many days she questioned why she even kept him around. At least he'd backed off over the last few months. He came to work, did his job, and went home. He wasn't her best employee, but he wasn't her worst either. And Lord knew she couldn't afford to lose the men she had because very few tradesmen, or guys in the construction industry period, would willingly work for a female.

"We'll see." Gabe stood, stretching those long legs.

The move drew her gaze directly to his crotch since it was now closer to her eye level.

"Any others?" he asked.

"No." She gulped at the defined ridge behind the zipper of his pants. She clenched her thighs together.

He coughed and she jerked her head up catching his twinkling gaze. Oops. He smirked.

She dropped her chin, heat dancing over her cheeks.

"No other boyfriends? I find that hard to believe."

"I don't have time for men, Gabe. I have schedules to keep on the jobs and a company to run."

"Put anybody you know on that list, friend or foe, and we'll at least check them out. Can you remember the dates of any of the incidents?"

Gathering her wits about her, she rose, rubbing her sweating palms down the fronts of her jeans. She needed to look at him without blushing. And ogling everything below his waist wasn't helping at all. "I have most of them. Once I realized there was something going on I started taking notes and pictures."

"Great. Give all of it to us. We can match up people's activity with the dates and see if anything or anybody suspicious rises to the top."

Relief flooded her. He believed her. Or at least he was going to help her. "I'll get everything together tonight and send it over tomorrow. Should I send it to you or your brother?"

"Send it to me." He reached into his back pocket and pulled out his wallet, retrieving a business card that he handed over to her, stretching his long arm across the desk.

As soon as their fingers connected, sparks of awareness shot up to her shoulder. She pulled back, her gaze darting up to lock with his. Had he felt it too?

But he shifted, hiding whatever reaction he might have had. He stepped back toward the door, his expression giving nothing away. "While I'm here, do you mind if I take a look around?"

"Sure. Give me a minute or two to make a call and then I'll give you the grand tour."

"I'll just wait outside." He turned to walk out of her office but hesitated at the threshold and looked back over his shoulder at her.

Good lord, women probably fell over themselves to get this man's attention. She'd certainly consider doing his bidding. Right after she feasted on his scrumptious body of course. Staring too long into those blue eyes of his and she'd be a puddle on the floor at his feet.

"I can promise you one thing," he said in a gruff but confident tone.

"What's that?"

"I won't let anyone hurt you or take your company away, Francesca."

## CHAPTER FOUR

FRANCESCA. GABE LOVED HOW IT ROLLED OFF HIS TONGUE. The name of elegance, of sophistication. A beautiful name fit for a gorgeous lady.

He was also a good judge of character. And he suspected she hid behind the male form of her name.

Ms. Francesca Stevens concealed her vulnerability behind denim and power tools. Gabe's sudden desire to unveil it surged to the surface with a vehemence that surprised him. What about her called so strongly to him? He didn't know her, had never even seen her before today. His past relationships all developed over time, so his instantaneous reaction to this woman made no sense.

Lust. And no warm body next to his for months. It was the only explanation.

He waited for her outside the trailer, hands resting on his hips as he gazed around the property, zeroing in on the barn. As he sauntered in that direction, he looked out over the field. Fresh country air infused his senses. How did she and her sister manage to stay on top of things with a property of this size? The footprint was huge and her job kept her busy most of the week. She obviously took great pride in things she cared deeply for. The grounds alone required full-time attention.

Gabe caught movement in one of the second floor windows and slowed his steps, squinting, trying to make out the person. Too far away to make out who it might be, he assumed it was her sister. Altering his course, he circled the perimeter of the barn before arriving back in front and trying the door. Locked.

The crunch of gravel from behind warned him of her approach. But he'd known before that. The warmth on his back hadn't been from the glare of the sun.

"I used to keep it open during the day," she said, "but since the break-ins, I've had to resort to locking everything away. Unfortunately, I don't have room in there for the larger vehicles."

He turned and was once again overwhelmed by her slight stature but large presence. Or maybe it was just him. He couldn't seem to shake the vision of her strapped to a spanking bench while he paddled her pretty ass until it flared rosy red and heated his hand.

She'd removed her plaid shirt, giving him a much-improved view of her upper chest profiled by her white T-shirt, the lace edge of her bra enticing him more now than ever. He licked his lips. Another image took front and center in his brain. This one of him crawling up her body, teasing her every inch of the way with his tongue, torturing himself by not stopping anywhere for long, completely avoiding the areas he ached to spend lengthy moments worshiping until she writhed under him, begging him to stop. Imploring him to keep going.

"How many people have keys to the buildings and the vehicles outside?" he asked, fighting to dispel the mental sex he currently engaged in. He was used to planning out scenes down to the last detail, so he wasn't typically prone to daytime fantasy fests like the explicit collage that had been dancing through this head since he'd met the pretty brunette.

"My sister and I have keys to everything of course. My foreman, Randy, has keys to the trailer, barn and vehicles. The guys have keys to the barn and vehicles."

"That's a lot of keys," he admonished, already considering the amount of effort required to check up on everybody. Good thing his brothers had people they could contract that out to.

"Can't be helped. Otherwise somebody has to be here all day to let everybody in. Normally either me or Randy are the first here, and we typically get everyone going. But there's certainly times one of the guys has to stop by during the day for more material or different equipment."

He nodded toward the barn. "Why don't you show me around inside?"

She stepped around him and pulled a ring of keys from her pocket attached to a long black lanyard splattered with what looked like blue paint. Quickly locating the one she wanted, she unlatched the lock and slid the large barn door to the right.

Gabe stepped inside, his eyes taking a moment to adjust to the dim interior.

"I keep extra supplies and material in here, as well as the smaller equipment. When we order material specific to a job ahead of time, it's stored in here until we need it at the job site." She snorted, the sound somehow very endearing. "Thought, maybe it would be safer here."

Stalls that at some point housed horses had been converted to compartments of material. Total order and cleanliness. Another thing she had in common with him. Not that he was counting.

"There's a small kitchen and a make-shift conference room down to the right. On bad weather days, it gives the guys a place to hang out, and I can use it for meetings when I have more people in attendance than what can fit in the trailer."

"Do you have a security system?"

She nodded. "It's an old one that my father installed years ago." She led him over to a panel to the right of the large sliding door. "I'm sure it needs to be updated."

One quick glance and he agreed. That make and model expired long ago. Hell, the distributer went out of business years ago. "Do you have the budget to install a new one?"

She grimaced. "I can swing it. In the meantime, I have my sister's dog who can play guard for a few days if necessary. She wouldn't hurt a flea, but she looks mean."

"What kind of dog?" A nice large dog could hold the fort until he arranged to have the installers pay her a visit.

"A bulldog."

Gabe just looked at her.

"She's ugly," she added, deadpan.

Gabe reached into his pocket for his phone. "I think I can help there. Hang on a minute." He called Kyle.

"Hello?"

"Hey, it's me. Can you or Kade contact one of the companies you recommend for security system installations?" He looked around. "I've got a barn, approximately sixteen hundred square feet, and a construction trailer that need updated systems ASAP. Something not necessarily top-of-the-line, but not bottom of the pile either. It's got to be reliable and we need to have quick access to the security tapes when necessary."

"Sure," his brother said, drawing out the word for a couple of beats. "Is this for Steven's Construction?"

"Yes."

"Just get the basics, Gabe. I can take a run out there later today and get everything I need. I'll make up the contract and bring it with me."

Gabe turned his body slightly to the right. "No trouble. I've got it."

Kyle's harsh breaths filled the line telling Gabe his brother was running.

"Don't you have work to do at the club?" Curiosity weighed heavy in Kyle's question.

Gabe lowered his voice and turned further from Francesca. "Nothing important. I don't mind. It's been a while and I know you guys are busy."

"Gabe? What's going on?"

He stiffened. "Nothing."

His brother chuckled in his ear. "How come I don't believe you?"

Gabe pulled his free hand out of his pocket sending his keys tumbling to the ground. He bent over to pick them up, but a strangled sound from behind had him spinning around only to find Francesca staring wide-eyed at him, a faint blush staining her cheeks.

"Just get on the phone and line somebody up to come out here later today to scope the place out, and then they can come back tomorrow to do the work. I'll oversee it myself."

"That's not necessary, Gabe," Francesca cut in.

"Hey, I heard that. That was definitely a female voice. A deep, very sexy voice, I might add. What's up big brother? The truth."

"I'll explain later." He locked his gaze onto hers. The startled look in her eyes and the strange feeling rolling around in his gut precluded him from saying anything further to either his brother or the pretty Ms. Stevens. "I'll meet you guys at the office first thing in the morning."

"Why not later today?"

His brother was intent on pushing for more details. But he wasn't going to get them until Gabe had time to think them over. Never one to rush into anything, he needed the evening to step away from this instant attraction he was experiencing and see if it was just a response to being celibate for too long.

"I'll see you in the morning, Kyle. You can let me know then what your security guy plans to do, and I'll let Fran… uh, the client know. See you in the morning." Gabe hit end and shoved his cell phone into his pocket before Kyle could attempt to cajole more information out of him.

He had no clue what stopped him from telling his brother about Francesca. It wasn't like Kyle was looking for a love interest. His younger brother was even more private than he was. And Kyle's twin, Kade, was a newlywed.

Gabe's hesitation confused him, but he wouldn't deny it. He had learned years ago to trust his instincts. And green flags were waving brightly before him. If he were entering a department store, the friendly smiling greeter was welcoming him in.

Although, right now, his instincts advised him to keep his mouth shut until he figured a few things out.

* * *

Frankie killed time stubbing the steel toe of her work boot into the gravel, pretending to check through her mail on her phone while she discreetly watched and waited as Gabe finished his conversation with his brother. But when he'd dropped his keys and bent over to pick them up… Holy hell that man had a luscious rear end. She'd almost swallowed her tongue. Nice, tight, and round, only made more mouthwatering by the stonewashed denim covering it. The pocket on the right had been worn smooth and bulged with the shape of his wallet.

For most of the drive from the job site to here, she'd wondered who'd smiled down on her today to send her such a divine specimen. Did his brothers look like him? If Kyle McBride had found her this morning instead of Gabe, would she be standing here wondering what his skin tasted like?

She shook her head, angry that she'd let a good-looking guy distract her. She'd made that particular mistake before and had no plans for a repeat. After her last disastrous relationship, she'd committed to no more distractions. Being a woman in this business was hard enough. She didn't have time to be all ditzy over some sexy hunk.

Frankie zeroed in on his boot-covered feet and worked her way up his long, lean legs to his—swallow—waist, passing over his chest to land on his chiseled face. Maybe she should consider another security firm. One with men her father's age, married for fifty odd years and a grandfather. Maybe a beer gut and two chins. It would really help if he belched or something.

She stretched and rolled her neck as Gabe wrapped up his conversation and walked over to join her.

"Kyle will get in touch with one of his suppliers and have somebody sent out today. You can probably expect him later in the afternoon."

"Sounds good. I need to check on my other jobs, but I'll plan to spend the afternoon here catching up on paperwork."

He just stood there, gazing at her.

She wished like hell she could read his expression. She hoped her face wasn't as flushed as it felt.

He seemed to be pondering something

"Is everything OK?" she asked.

"Yeah." He blinked and ran a hand through his short hair. "I'll give you a call later to confirm they showed up and got everything they need."

"OK." She tucked her hands into her back pockets. Wouldn't want to risk touching him, even accidently. She might never stop.

"Guess I should get going." He didn't move.

She rocked back on her heels.

He frowned, gave her a terse nod and then strolled toward his car.

Frankie watched and drooled over each strong stride until he dropped his sexy-as-hell ass into the driver seat and started his car.

He sent her one last smoldering look that only fanned the flame, and then he turned the vehicle to face the road and drove away.

Unsticking her tongue from the roof of her mouth, Frankie spun and trudged up the few stairs into the trailer, closing the door behind her.

Coffee. She needed her mid-morning fix. She needed to put Gabe McBride from her mind and get her head back on the job. After she completed her rounds of the job sites, she'd come back here and pull together the info he needed. That should give her enough time and space to clear her head.

Standing at the counter, staring absently out the window while she waited for the coffee to brew, Frankie wiped her mind clean of her troubles and her distracting new security expert. The slight scent of vanilla and hazelnut wafted up to tease her. She listened to the liquid drip through the filter and pour in a single stream into the mug, the only sound other than her breathing in the cramped workspace. Maybe she should bring a radio out here.

The backside of the trailer looked out to the property line dividing her farm from Mr. and Mrs. Sunder's place. Though it wasn't their place anymore. They'd retired and moved to Florida to be near their daughter and grandchildren. The new owners had purchased the land and the livestock. In the distance she could make out the shape of grazing cattle.

Frankie wished the trailer had a few more windows to let in more light. What she'd truly prefer was actual office space. That was one of her goals. With Lawrence's help, she'd even gone so far as to scope out a few of the available units over in the industrial area on the West end of town. More central would be better, with easier highway access and more visibility, but at the moment it was out of her price range. Technically, she could afford it, but she wanted to be certain of the company's future before she made any major moves or purchases.

Over the years she'd often tried to convince her dad to get real office space, but he had always chosen the trailer. Every single time. Said he liked running the business but still wanted to feel like one of the guys.

She'd understood her father's stance while he was alive, but now that he was gone, she'd been rethinking it. For a while, she'd wanted to maintain status quo for the sake of the crew and her father's memory. But after talking with her Godfather, she'd come to the realization that no matter how ingrained she'd been in the entire operation since she was a kid, she wasn't one of the guys. When she'd been a child, they'd looked at her as an endearing nuisance. As she got older and grew breasts, they regarded her differently. The boss's daughter became just that.

Only John had risked her father's wrath by asking her out. Too bad she'd said yes.

Though she wasn't really one of the girls either. When she was little, she played with trucks and toy loaders, not dolls. She'd never had girlfriends, didn't do the BFF thing. The girls in her classes growing up didn't like to get their hands dirty. Hell, they didn't even know the difference between a Philips and a Robertson screwdriver.

She'd secretly envied her sister and her circle of friends, their sleepovers and shopping excursions. Though, how anybody could spend hours upon hours roaming a mall and not buy a single damn thing was beyond her. She might be able to toss a decent spitball, but she did miss having somebody special to confide in. She had her sister of course. But some things you couldn't tell even your sister.

Frankie had simply always been more comfortable around the boys than the girls. She spoke their language and understood their need to know how things operated mechanically. However, professionally, when competing with other contractors, she needed to appear as the owner of a company. She needed to make an impression, an important one—that she was here to stay, and could and *would* work just as hard as them. She deserved to be treated as fairly as any of the others in the industry.

That's why she hoped Gabe could help her. Somebody wanted her to fail. For some reason she intimidated or threatened them.

"Frankie? Hey there you are. Why haven't you been answering your phone?"

Startled at the unexpected interruption, or more specifically, her sister's appearance at the trailer, Frankie turned to see Sophie poking her head inside the door.

"You can come in, you know. Nothing in here bites."

Sophie's disbelieving gaze swept the length of the trailer. "Well, it is cleaner than Dad used to keep it. But I'm still not coming in."

Sophie despised the trailer. Ever since she was a little girl, she'd refused to set foot inside. Frankie used to think it was simply the state of cleanliness that had kept her sister out. Their father had not been the neatest person, and the guys didn't know the meaning of the word organized or clutter-free. Some days she seriously questioned whether they were born in homes, caves, or barns. Even when her dad was still alive, the barn had been cleaner than the trailer.

When she took over the business, one of the very first things she did was scour the trailer. It had taken a full day to clean it out and clean it up.

And yet, her sister still refused to step over the threshold.

"You're being ridiculous, Sophie."

The young woman staring back at her was no longer a little girl. Five years her junior, Sophie could pass as the same age or older than Frankie. She had their mother's looks but their father's height.

Sophie shook her head, her long dark waves of hair, the one thing they did share, swaying back and forth. "That rat I saw was huge. Like big as a cat."

Frankie rolled her eyes. "That was ten years ago, and it was a mouse."

"Don't matter. Rat, mouse, it was a rodent. I don't like rodents."

"You live on a farm," Frankie pointed out.

"What I don't see can't hurt me. And if I stay out of the places where rodents generally reside, I won't see them."

Frankie wanted to yank out her big sister card and wipe that smug grin off Sophie's face. She could have told her about the mouse she'd found in the house last month. A small trap and a bit of peanut butter had dealt with that furry little baby. But she feared if she gave away her secret, her sister would be packed and moved out by nightfall. Frankie had no other family left. She couldn't afford to lose her sister.

"Obviously you were looking for me."

"Yeah. But you weren't answering your phone."

Frankie pulled her phone from her back pocket. "Sorry, it's dead. Again. I charged the damn thing just last night. I didn't notice earlier either." She dropped the useless phone on the table. "I'll charge it while I'm catching up on paperwork this afternoon. What did you want?"

"Who was that cute guy I noticed from the house?"

Frankie barely resisted rolling her eyes a second time. Of course. How typical. Sophie didn't really want to talk to her. Sophie was all about the cute guys.

"That was the security specialist I hired."

She leaned against the door frame and crossed her arms over her chest. "Well, from a distance he looked pretty freaking hot. I'm interested in knowing what he looks like up close and personal though."

"Why?"

Sophie shrugged. "Curious. I like hot guys and I haven't found one worth dating in a while."

A funny feeling settled in the pit of Frankie's stomach. She clenched her teeth, realized what she was doing, and forcibly relaxed her jaw. "Maybe he's married," she ground out. Though she hadn't noticed a ring on his finger. Not that she looked, once or maybe twice. "Or has a girlfriend."

"That would be one very lucky lady," Sophie declared.

Frankie frowned. The idea of Gabe with a girlfriend didn't sit well with her either.

"Regardless," her sister continued. She shrugged with casual indifference and a cocky grin. "Doesn't hurt to flirt."

Unless Frankie hit her. That would hurt. OK, she wouldn't really hit her sister. Pinch her maybe. Hide her favorite shoes, probably. But she'd never hit her sister. In fact, she'd beat the crap out of any person who tried to hit her baby sister.

"Maybe he's not the flirting type." Frankie wished she could flirt. The skill came to her sister naturally, but Frankie had to work at it. And even then, it only came across as weird and uncomfortable for both parties.

Sophie grinned and wiggled her eyebrows. "Never know until I try."

The idea of Sophie flirting with Gabe soured Frankie's stomach. Worse, if he fell for it, and reciprocated... Now she wanted to hit him.

"He's too old for you." Frankie pushed away from the counter, walking toward her sister, edging her out of the trailer and back into the safe zone.

Sophie's shoulders relaxed as she moved away from the trailer, and Frankie immediately felt a bout of sympathy for her. Sophie never had a close relationship with their father. She'd never taken an interest in the family business. And although their dad tried time and again to find something he could enjoy with his youngest daughter, he was as uncomfortable around dolls as Sophie was around tools.

"Gabe will be here to do a job. I don't need him distracted. I need him to figure out who's got an issue with me." She needed *him* not to distract *her*.

Sophie studied her, eyes narrowed, expression thoughtful. Then she stepped back and gasped. "Oh my, God. You like him."

"Don't be ridiculous. I don't even know him." Frankie spun on her heel and began fast walking toward the house.

"You think he's cute."

He was drop-dead gorgeous.

"You want to fuck him."

Ten ways to Sunday. And when did her sister adopt such a dirty mouth? Oh yes, a trait they shared.

"Did you flirt with him? Find out if he's single?"

Yeah right. "Nope and nope."

"Why not?" she demanded, sounding totally affronted as she hurried to stay in step.

Frankie rolled her neck back and forth on her shoulders but didn't miss a stride. Her goal—reach the front porch. Then, her bedroom. She was almost there, but her sister could be damn tenacious when she wanted something.

"Frankie! Are you telling me you had a hot stud within your grasp and you didn't get the goods on him?"

"I know his name and where he works. I know what he does and what I need him to do."

"Not those goods," Sophie growled through clenched teeth, exasperated as she tended to be when she didn't get the answers she wanted.

"Yes, Sophie, I'm well aware of the goods you're referring to." Another set of goods popped into her mind, bulging and trapped behind soft well-worn denim.

Up the porch stairs, door open. Almost there. She just needed to get to her room.

"You need to find a man, Frankie. It's been way too long. This just might be your lucky day."

Frankie ducked into the powder room, slammed the door shut in her sister's face, and leaned back against it.

"Frankie," her sister called through the door. "You know I'm right."

Yeah, that was the problem. And now, thanks to her little

sister, she'd be fantasizing about a distraction she didn't want and practicing her flirting technique in the mirror so she could put it to the test the next time she saw Gabe McBride.

# CHAPTER FIVE

"WHAT DO YOU MEAN, YOU WANT THE CASE?" KYLE asked. "Since when did *you* get in the security business?"

Gabe bristled. "I *am* one of the owners." Actually, he'd expected the question. But he hadn't anticipated it being flung at him heavily loaded with sarcastic disbelief.

"I think what Kyle is not so eloquently stating," Kade, always the mediator of the three of them, interrupted, "is that you typically focus on the club while we take care of McBride Security." He cocked his head and scrutinized Gabe. "What's up, bro? Why do you want to handle this one personally?"

Gabe shoved his hands into the front pockets of his jeans. He strode over to the small bank of windows overlooking Main Street. At this time of the morning, the coffee shop across the street bustled with patrons stopping in to get their caffeine fix before they began their day.

Yesterday, when he'd offered to help his brothers by taking one of their meetings, he'd had every intention of simply gathering the basic intelligence, handing it over to them, and then heading home to catch up on club paperwork. He had shipments scheduled to arrive later this week, bills to pay, and payroll to complete.

Yet, after he'd left Frankie's yesterday, he'd gone straight to the club where he'd tried to spend a few hours working, but he hadn't been able to shake her from his mind. More than once he'd found himself ready to jump into his car and drive back out to her place. He tried telling himself it was just to watch over the men Kyle had hired to install her new security system. Generally, he wasn't in the habit of fooling himself.

After hearing that rough smoky voice cursing the poor worker out, and then discovering those sexy vocals belonged to a petite fireball, he couldn't fathom placing her in the hands of his brothers, no matter how capable they might be.

Francesca had a vulnerable side she worked hard to hide. But it called to him like a siren and lured him in so close he could see the dark specs in her green eyes. He could watch her pulse throb in her throat. He could smell that lilac and sawdust scent she wore so well.

His natural protective instincts screamed for him to tuck her under his shoulder and shield her from whoever was causing her trouble. Though he suspected she'd only stomp on his foot and poke him in the chest while she gave him a piece of her pretty mind. How he'd ever heard a word while watching those succulent lips curve and stretch and shape each syllable coming out of her mouth was beyond him.

One of his brothers cleared his throat. Gabe cursed, then twisted and stared at Kade. "Where's your wife?"

"What does Brienna have to do with anything?"

She didn't. Gabe just blurted that out to keep from responding to his brother's question. He'd never felt so unbalanced before. He just needed the focus to be not on him. And normally Kade loved to dish some pretty purple prose about his bride. They'd been married for almost a year now, and Gabe's gut told him they were attempting to make him an uncle.

The more conservative of the three of them, Kade had found the love of his life after reuniting with a girl he'd liked from afar back in high school. And in the process, he managed to rid himself of the blame he'd harbored over the death of his best friend all those years ago. Threats from a girl from his past almost ruined his and Brienna's chance at happiness, but they'd survived it. And his brother was happy now.

Gabe wished Kyle would find somebody to take his mind off *his* troubles. He'd worried about his younger brother from the moment he'd decided not to reenlist for another tour in the military. Gabe knew something had happened over there that last time. Since his return home, Kyle had been a virtual safe about his time overseas. Their mother worried about each of her sons, but she watched Kyle with a particularly keen eye. Gabe continued to assure her that one day Kyle would be ready to talk. And when that day came, they'd all be there to listen.

At the moment though, his twin brothers gaped at him like he'd just announced he planned to kick them to the curb and take over their business.

Gabe rubbed a hand across his face before he walked over and dropped into one of the visitor's chairs. Kade and Kyle watched him, their faces a mask of identical curiosity.

Kade's held a hint of concern as well. "Gabe," he said. "You're always a man of few words, but this is pitiful even for you."

"Fess up about *Mr.* Stevens, Gabe." Kyle crossed his arms. He had a particular glint in his eyes. He'd heard Frankie over the phone yesterday, and apparently he hadn't forgotten about it.

"Frankie," Gabe confirmed, though he preferred to call her by her given name, especially in private. She might consider herself all tomboy, but he saw what she hid beneath the work boots and plaid shirt. The occasional peek-a-boo of lace revealed the beautiful woman aching to be recognized.

"Did he do or say something that insinuated he didn't want Kyle or me working for him?" Kade looked insulted that anyone might consider their work inferior.

"No."

Kyle just smirked.

"Then, I don't get it," Kade continued, obviously the only one in the room who didn't have a clue about what was going on. "Why would you want to take on this case? What's it about?"

"It's about a woman," the ever-helpful Kyle supplied. "And I'm guessing she's somebody our big brother wants to get to know better."

"What woman?" Kade tossed confused looks between him and Kyle like a penguin watching a tennis match.

Kyle's grin grew until Gabe wanted to smack it off. "The e-mail I received didn't say much except confirm the time and a location. Although, the client did give another meeting spot in the voicemail he, she, left but there was so much noise in the background it was kind of hard to get all the details."

Usually in control of his emotions and his actions, Gabe had the common sense to admit this woman, whom he'd only spend a short time with, wound him up like no other had before. Would his brothers understand something he barely understood himself?

"But I'm thinking there was much more to the meeting with Ms. Stevens. And Gabe's about to tell us all about it." Kyle, the jackass, leaned forward to make his point. "Aren't you, big brother?"

All his life he'd planned on finding the perfect partner. Somebody he could settle down and start a family with. Somebody who would rely on him to protect and provide for her and their children. It was a role he'd stepped into when their father died, and he'd taken it very seriously. Everything he'd learned from his father, he'd applied to the way he chose to live his life and plan for his future.

Not that he needed to protect his brothers. Both were strong, mature, and capable, but he was still the oldest. His mom was self-sufficient. She'd barely paused after she'd lost her husband. Instead, she turned to her three children and together they'd continued on.

And yet, he considered it his duty to watch over them,

something his father would have wanted. Gabe remembered listening to his mom cry at night after she'd thought the boys had gone to sleep. After that very first time, even at such a young age, he'd taken it upon himself to do everything he possibly could to make things easier for her.

In his role at The Vault, he watched over his staff and their guests, ensuring nobody stepped out of bounds. He made certain nobody got hurt. People had their roles, they had rules to follow, and he guided those who asked for help.

He'd always been in control. But now this feisty cute-as-a-button woman with the dark wavy hair, big green eyes, and the mouth of a long-haul trucker caused him to misstep.

He wanted her. Bad.

He wanted to taste her, touch her, send her into a tail-spin until she puddled at his feet exhausted but satiated. He wanted to listen to her moans, her whimpers, her pleas as she begged him to let her come.

He wanted to bury his cock as deep as she'd take him until she drowned him in her essence, snuggle his face between her pillowy breasts, and feel her hardened nipples graze his palms like sharp spikes.

He'd never had such an over the top reaction to someone before.

And she needed him. Every single protective instinct in him rose up, ready to charge forward and be her knight in shining armor. Though he also had a distinct feeling, she'd be racing neck to neck with him into battle.

Gabe raised his head and speared his brothers with a look, ready to come clean with them. After all, he was a man of action. In every move he made, whether in business or in play, he assessed the situation, he deliberated, he made decisions, preferably on facts presented to him, and then he took action.

Well, Francesca Stevens had a problem. He could help. He'd spent hours last night considering the potential threats and taking the first stab at reviewing the list of employees, friends, and competitors she'd emailed to him late yesterday afternoon.

Then he'd spent a few more hours assessing the sparks of desire that seemed to fling between them. He couldn't let that go unexplored. So he'd decided over his morning coffee that he'd do something about that too. And he'd help her find the person behind the threats in the process.

He had a plan. "Her name is Francesca Stevens."

The twins stared at him blankly for a long moment, blinking like owls blinded by a sudden bright light, before they turned and looked at each other, looked back at him, and then burst into gales of laughter. Hard, bent-at-the-waist, hands-on-their-knees, laughter.

"I'm not sure what's so funny," he stated, his voice tight.

When they eventually started to gasp for breath, Gabe coughed to regain their attention. "Finished?"

"Well, now it makes perfect sense," Kade struggled to speak while wiping a few tears from his eyes.

"She must be pretty fucking awesome if you're willing to spend a few days away from the club looking after some helpless female," Kyle added.

His brothers had nailed his "type" long ago. He looked forward to introducing them to Frankie. "Francesca is far from helpless." Emotionally vulnerable perhaps, but a far cry from weak or powerless.

"But I'd bet she's gorgeous and needs a big bad protector," Kyle quipped.

"She may be a foot shorter than me, but she's got more balls than some men I know, uses more curse words than you do, and she's not afraid to stand up for herself." But she was also smart enough to know when to ask for help. And for one who preferred to be in control at all times, stepping back to let somebody else step forward and run the show took courage.

He would know. And that, probably more than anything, was what sealed the deal for him.

"So what does she need from us?" Kade asked.

"She's inherited her father's construction company, but somebody apparently considers her viable competition. From the sounds of it, they're doing whatever they can to scare her out of business."

"Scare her? Has she been threatened?" Kade asked.

"Not personally." At least not yet. "But somebody who started out causing serious mischief has upped their game. Stealing tools, tampering with the vehicles, and breaking into her office."

"I assume she's ruled out teenagers having fun at her expense?" Kyle probed.

Gabe nodded. "I asked her to send over a list of employees and anybody else she can think of who might want to see her shut down. I got it last night." He'd chuckled over how neat, complete, and organized it was. She'd even grouped and prioritized them in what she thought would be a helpful manner and put their names in alphabetical order by last name. Something he would do without thought.

Kyle straightened, his amusement at Gabe's expense passed. "That's a good start. I can get Melissa to begin making a few calls and we'll split up the list and do the same. If we need to chase anybody down, I'll give Deacon a call to lend a hand."

"I also want you to check into other companies that may have lost bids to her in the past six months. One of them is Diamond Construction."

"Who's that?" Kyle asked.

"Should we start with them?" Kade wondered.

"Owner's a close family friend and not somebody she considers a threat."

"Then why check them out?"

"Because they're somebody who has a vested interest in her

failure. She may not think Lawrence Diamond would ever do something to take her father's business away from her, but I don't know the man from Adam. As far as I'm concerned, he's simply another contractor who bids on the same jobs she does and sees an opening now that her father is gone."

He knew his brothers wouldn't question his logic. Though they might question his sanity.

"So, you're going to be the point man on this case, I take it?" Kade crossed his arms over his chest and leaned back against the desk, his long legs stretched out in front of him. He'd worn this stupid glow since his wedding and it had only intensified over the last few weeks. Gabe wanted some of what his brother had.

"I think it's about time I tested out this side of the family business," Gabe said in response.

"What about The Vault?"

"Nothing will change there. That place almost runs itself these days." A picture of Francesca splayed out over the spanking bench, with each limb tied down and her ass stinging from his hand appeared before his eyes again. Like the previous day, the images were so vivid he could almost reach out and touch her. Smell her. Taste her. His mouth watered.

He hadn't played in public for quite some time. Would Francesca be aroused if he put her on display while he flogged her? No. He didn't think so. He suspected she would feel exposed in front of people she didn't know. She'd need privacy to relax and let down her guard. To let go.

And Gabe had every intention of giving her what she needed.

# CHAPTER SIX

"HEY, FRANKIE, DID YOU LEAVE THE BARN DOORS OPEN?" Sophia called up the stairs.

Sitting on her freshly made bed, Frankie paused in the middle of pulling on her jeans. Dread filled her. Damn it. Not again. She was getting fucking tired of this. Why couldn't this person just face her? Why did he have to sneak around and try to frighten her?

She crossed her fingers. Let this time just be a lock that didn't latch, the wind, a forgetful moment by one of the guys. Maybe Randy came by early this morning. Hell, maybe she forgot to lock it herself last night.

Though she clearly remembered doing so, as well as spending an additional twenty minutes verifying that every damn window and door on both the trailer and the barn were secured nice and tight. She'd even checked every point of entry on the house, not willing to risk anybody coming into their home.

An icy chill skated down her spine. She'd received what she'd thought had been a prank call the previous night. Her caller hadn't said a word, but she'd heard him breathing on the other end and sensed his frustration. Because of her conversation with Gabe earlier in the day, her gut now screamed at her that this person might escalate. She'd even discussed it with Lawrence when he called during dinner. He'd offered to help, but she'd declined. He hadn't been pleased with her refusal, but she needed to handle this her own way.

"Frankie? Did you hear me?" Sophie called again.

"Yeah," she responded. Frankie quickly finished dressing

and then headed downstairs, trying her best not to appear too concerned. She didn't want to raise alarms with her sister. Knowing Sophie, she'd just charge into trouble without thinking it through first, and Frankie would not let any harm come to her last living relative.

She found her sister in the kitchen, an empty cereal bowl and a half empty cup of coffee in front of her while she scoured the classifieds. Regardless of how many times Frankie offered Sophie a job, she'd refused, intent on doing her own thing. Whatever that was.

Beside her bowl, she had stacked a small, colorful mound of discarded cereal pieces. "Sophie, you're the only person I know who doesn't like marshmallows in her cereal."

Her sister didn't spare her a glance, just waved a dismissive hand in her direction. "Those are not marshmallows. They're tiny sugar cubes and they're gross."

Frankie chuckled. They were complete opposites. Where Frankie could name every maker and tool in her sleep, Sophie didn't know Craftsman from DeWALT. But she knew about twenty or so shades of pink and could create the most awesome braids without the aid of a mirror. Frankie could manage a slightly off-center ponytail. And she never could catch every strand of hair.

"Were you out in the barn before your shower?" Her sister glanced up, picking up her coffee cup to take a sip. "I didn't hear you leave the house."

Sophie may not have shown any interest in the family business but Frankie knew damn well she was aware of what was going on. She just didn't know all of it.

"No. I wasn't out there."

Concern clouded her sister's face. "One of the crew?"

Frankie shrugged and took a clean mug from the cupboard. "Maybe." She didn't want Sophie to worry. "I'll check with Randy to see if one of the guys stopped in early. You didn't go out there did you?" The mere idea of her younger sister coming across vandals in the act of whatever they had planned for her this time scared the crap out of her.

"No. But I heard a loud noise. It sounded like someone banging on something. When I looked out the window, I noticed the barn side door swinging open in the wind. It's banging against the lock."

"Are the trucks in the yard?"

"Yes, from what I could see. That's why I thought maybe you had been out there."

So it wasn't one of the guys. "Did you hear anything else?"

"Besides the door, no."

And neither had she. She hadn't heard anything the other times either though. Maybe she should have her hearing checked. Or the dog's. Apparently she was deaf too. Speaking of the ugly mutt…

"Where's Beauty?" Frankie filled her coffee cup, added some cream and sweetener and then headed toward the back door.

"Sleeping out on the back porch."

Figured.

"Do you want some company?" her sister asked. The offer to join her, to actually step foot inside the barn where she might see a mouse, spoke volumes.

"No. I'm fine. Hey don't you have a couple of interviews today?" Sophie had been job hunting since she graduated from college, but she hadn't found anything steady yet. She currently worked a couple of part time jobs to make some cash, but Frankie knew discouragement was setting in. "You probably should be preparing for those."

"I have one with a legal office downtown this afternoon, and one with a doctor's office tomorrow morning."

"I'll keep my fingers crossed. Start the dishwasher when you're finished and throw in a load of laundry before you leave, will you?"

The kitchen door slammed closed behind Frankie as she made her way down the stairs of the back porch, effectively keeping her sister otherwise occupied. Not knowing exactly what she was walking into, she refused to put Sophie at risk.

The early morning sun was drying the dew on the grass. Birds sung in the trees. She shifted her gaze to the barn and the side entry door that swung in the breeze, every now and then banging against the padlock that hung through the latch on the left side.

Other than the padlock hanging precariously from the latch, everything seemed untouched and unharmed. She strode toward the doors, her footsteps sure and confident, her heart beating at a frantic pace, and her palms sweaty. The pick-up and loader were parked next to the barn just like any other day. She glanced across the yard to where the trailer stood. No light shone through the windows. Not that she expected there to be. Most of the guys drove straight to their job sites in the morning unless they needed the truck to transport material. Only Randy made a habit of stopping in to check on her and receive any special instructions for the day.

Frankie slowed her steps as she reached the barn and with only a moment's hesitation she yanked the door open, permitting the sun's rays to cut through the dim interior and crush the darkness.

She stepped inside and stopped. "Hello. Is anybody in here?"

Silence. She looked around trying to see beyond the obvious, looking for something, anything that could explain the creepy tentacles spreading out along her skin and wrapping around her, chilling her to the bone. Nothing appeared out of sorts, and not one to delay the inevitable, she continued further into the building.

Half way down the center aisle the stench hit her. What was that smell? Covering her nose with one hand to try and stop the burning sensation working its way up her nasal passages,

Frankie moved toward where she thought the stench originated from. She passed stacks of drywall and lumber, shelving that contained boxes holding an assortment of nails, screws, electrical supplies, and spools of wire in various widths and types.

The next area contained their storage of paint and stains, both interior and exterior. A few more steps and it quickly became obvious she'd reached the source of the smell. She rounded the end of the shelving unit and found four cans of turpentine upended and spilled across three large roles of carpeting, effectively ruining the entire lot. Carpeting she'd had to special order for a project on the other side of town. A project where her crew was scheduled to lay the flooring in two weeks' time. Carpeting that had a six-week lead time.

"Fuck!" She pulled out her phone.

* * *

As Gabe drove toward Frankie's home, he couldn't disguise his sense of satisfaction that Francesca had opted to call him before she called the police. Only a hint of anxiety had filled her voice, but it was enough to pluck at his inner protector, and he'd left the logistics of the night's schedule for The Vault in Wendy's capable hands.

His hostess might appear to most as nothing more than a pretty face in a sexy gown when patrons entered the club. But in fact, she could run the place just as well as he or his brothers could, and he hoped she would one day take a more active role in managing The Vault. Occasionally, he'd like to enjoy the benefits of the club like any other member. But he couldn't do that unless he could turn over control to somebody he trusted. And other than his brothers, that list was very short.

He couldn't ignore the fact that he would like nothing better than to take Francesca to The Vault. His gut told him that she needed a safe place to release her control. He wanted to give her that extra sense of security, and the experience that went along with it. Regardless of the fact he'd just met her, intuition suggested she would be the one to beat when it came to looking for life-long companionship. She was everything he didn't think he'd want in a wife, but he had an inkling she was everything he needed. And he'd learned long ago to trust his instincts. Only one small detail, now he needed to get to know her.

Gabe turned off the main road and drove along Francesca's drive, passing the trailer and stopping in front of the large barn. He climbed out of his black Porsche and rounded the hood just as she emerged through the doors, stepping from the dark interior into the sunlit yard.

Anger hardened her facial features. She clenched her jaw and fisted her hands. Stress lines bracketed her kissable mouth.

He waited for her to reach him. When she stopped within about a foot, sixteen inches at most, his gaze drifted down to her lips. He stood transfixed while she licked them. The scents covering her body from her morning shower drifted off her and landed on him. Today she wore a light blue scoop-necked cotton T-shirt tucked into her jeans. Her breasts pushed up and presented him with a nice view of her cleavage.

"Hi." An empty mug hung from her fingers, and her hair looked like she'd been shoving her fingers through it.

"Good morning." She hadn't given him any details on the phone, only indicated that she needed to see him right away. "I take it you had more trouble." The only information he'd gotten from her was that her vandal had struck again. Gabe glanced around, but there was no obvious damage. So it must be inside the barn.

"The police are on the way." Her eyes, when she raised her head and captured his gaze, sparked. She was pissed.

But the stiffness in which she carried herself portrayed her fear as well. He didn't like seeing that. He didn't want her to be afraid. More importantly, he didn't want her to feel the need to hide it from him.

"My sister noticed the door on the barn was left open. I clearly remember locking it last night."

"You've already been inside." It wasn't a question, since she'd been on her way out as he arrived. "You know you shouldn't have done that." He felt like a parent scolding a child, but she had interfered with a potential crime scene. The police would not be pleased. More importantly, she could have been hurt if the intruder had been waiting inside.

"I did. I needed to know if the open door was an honest mistake or something else."

She looked straight at him. He could see by her stance, with one hand on her hip and the gleam in her eyes, that she was challenging him to give her shit. He liked that about her. And although he understood—he would have done the same—the cops still wouldn't be happy that she had traipsed all over the scene and possibly destroyed evidence. He battled against the need to punish her for putting herself at risk and hauling her into his arms to comfort her. Or perhaps himself.

"Honey, the police generally prefer you don't walk all over their crime scene."

"Don't 'honey' me, and it's my barn."

"I thought you wanted to find out who's behind this." For good reason she wasn't in the best of moods but she'd have to lose the attitude before the cops showed up.

"Of course I do." She huffed.

It was cute. Though he didn't tell her that.

"But I needed to know what they'd done."

"And what did you find?" he asked.

"Turpentine."

"Paint thinner?"

"Yes. Poured all over the carpeting I need for a job.

Carpeting that has a long lead time, and now replacing it is going to push me a few weeks behind schedule."

"And your client will not be happy about that."

She dropped her gaze to the ground, scuffing the toe of her boot in the dirt. "No. No, he will not be happy at all. And he was a difficult client to get."

"Why?" Gabe asked. "I assume you had to submit a bid like anybody else."

Francesca shuffled closer.

The lilac blend of her shampoo made him think of fields and sunshine. Early in the morning. Which made him think of breakfast. Which made him think of having breakfast with her. Which of course lead him to think of spending the night with her before breakfast.

He shook off the imagery before things got out of hand.

"Of course. I submitted a fair bid and I won the job. But the client wasn't too pleased with a woman winning the job. Fortunately for me, there wasn't anything he could do without risking a potential lawsuit. But he's been watching every move I make and this will give him grounds for claiming I'm not competent. He could try to terminate the contract."

"I'm sorry."

She straightened and lifted her chin. "I'll be fine. I'll make some calls and find a supplier who can expedite the carpet. I'm sure I'll still lose a couple of weeks, but hopefully no more than that."

Gabe swallowed. She stood inches away. He couldn't take his eyes off her mouth. He watched her lips move as she spoke. He imagined them painted with red lipstick and wrapped around his cock. When he caught a glimpse of her tongue and imagined it dragging up the length of his erection he suffered through smothering a groan.

"Too bad they didn't wait a few days," he said, his voice husky to his own ears.

She glanced up. Her eyes widened, their color darkening. "Why's that?" Her words came out on a shuddering breath.

He found himself swaying toward her.

She shifted slightly in his direction.

"We could have had the new security system completely functional by then and caught them on camera."

Her lips came much closer, close enough that if he leaned in just a bit, he could taste them.

Her tongue slipped out to run along her bottom lip, moistening it. "Um, maybe the old cameras caught the guy."

Fuck. He raised his right arm, his fingers twitching in anticipation. If he cupped her cheek would she tilt her head into the palm of his hand?

Gabe was close enough to feel each puff of breath from her mouth. His own watered.

Her eyelashes fluttered and drifted toward her cheeks as she closed her eyes.

Now. He was going to kiss her now. He lowered his head. Only a very short distance to go. Fuck this was going to be so good.

The crunch of tires on the driveway gravel broke the bubble of intense silence that surrounded them.

Francesca blinked once. Twice. She gasped and jumped away from him.

# CHAPTER SEVEN

REGRET AND ANNOYANCE AT THE UNTIMELY INTERRUPtion filled Gabe, but he let his hand drop away as he spun to meet the police officer who climbed out of the cruiser.

He cleared his throat. Behind him, Frankie breathed deep. He could hear each inhale and exhale. The heat coming off her body in waves warmed his back.

"Sir? Did you call the police?" The officer, a stern-looking man with a military haircut streaked with gray, addressed Gabe.

Francesca stepped out from behind him and moved forward before he could say a word. "No. I did. Thank you for coming, officer."

"Officer Peters, ma'am."

She didn't look so vulnerable now. Back straight, chin up, determination shone in her eyes. She was back in control. A part of Gabe wanted to push her back and let him handle the situation, but he knew that would never fly with her. And truth be told, this side of her turned him on.

"You indicated there was a break-in?"

"Yes. Somebody broke into my barn and tossed turpentine all over carpeting I have set aside for a job."

Peters put his hands on his hips and did his best to stare her down. "Ma'am. How do you know somebody ruined your carpeting? I'm sure the dispatcher would have advised you to remain outside until we arrived."

"Because I went inside before I called you."

Gabe coughed to disguise his laughter. He never had the

urge to laugh as often as he did when he was around Frankie.

"My sister noticed the door was open this morning," she continued. "But I remember quite specifically locking it last night. I came out to check, thinking perhaps one of my men was in there."

"You should have called the police first and then waited for us to arrive to check the situation out. Someone might have been waiting inside."

"You're probably right. But I thought one of my employees left it open."

Gabe cringed at the possibility of Frankie walking unprotected into the barn unaware of somebody hiding in wait. Given the current events, had she even considered the possibility? She probably had and then ignored it. Once he introduced her to his lifestyle choices, he would take great pleasure in giving her a spanking for putting herself in harm's way.

Officer Peters scowled but apparently decided not to push the matter at the moment. "Why don't you show me what you found, ma'am?"

"Frankie Stevens." She indicated Gabe with her right hand. "This is Gabe McBride, he's a security expert I hired just yesterday."

Gabe shook hands with Peters.

The man acknowledged her with a sharp nod of his chin. He followed Frankie, stopping for a moment to investigate the clearly broken lock. "Did you touch the lock, Ms. Stevens?"

From a distance it would appear as though the lock had simply been opened. However, on closer inspection, Gabe noticed the metal had been cut, probably with a large set of bolt cutters.

"No."

"Good. When the tech gets here, I'll ask him to check for prints." Officer Peters paused every few steps to shine his flashlight around, aiming the light into corners and between crates. Nothing turned up.

Gabe trailed behind them as they continued into the barn. Walking down the center aisle, he took the opportunity to take a good look around the inside of the barn. Francesca liked order. The interior was neat, clean, and highly organized. Though as they moved further down the barn, the stench of turpentine filled his nostrils.

When they rounded the end of a long row of shelving, he saw three oversize rolls of carpeting. The plastic wrap had been pulled back to bare more than half the length of each roll. Although potentially only the outer layer had been destroyed, Gabe knew that the damage was extensive enough that Frankie would be forced to replace all three rolls. Considering their size, the cost would be significant.

"Who had access?" Peters walked the length of the rolls, stepped over to the opposite side, and bent down to look at the split plastic covering.

Even Gabe could see it has been neatly sliced open.

"Myself, my sister, and my foreman, Randy Owens. But all of the guys on the crew know where I keep the spare in the trailer."

"That's a lot of people, Ms. Stevens." He admonished her, just like Gabe had yesterday.

And just like then, she didn't back down. "I can't be everywhere at once, Officer. And I trust my employees."

"Nobody else?" he asked.

"To the lock, no. My sister rarely comes out here. My foreman sometimes comes here first before heading over to one of the job sites. The other guys typically go straight to their assigned jobs. They would only come here to pick up equipment if necessary."

She cocked her head and Gabe noticed how the sunlight streaming in through the open door highlighted the different shades in her hair. He slid his gaze down the curves of her body. In profile to him, he lingered on her torso. She had a magnificent shape. He dragged his eyes back up in time to see her squint when she shifted because the glare had hit her in the eye.

"If the lock was cut, what difference does it make who has a key?" she asked.

Peters glanced up. "Just because it was, doesn't mean they didn't have a key. They could have wanted you to think it was a stranger."

Gabe watched as the frown that crinkled her brow line eventually transformed as she scowled. He guessed she really hadn't considered that the person doing this could be somebody close to her.

He glanced back toward the carpeting. "I guess these are ruined."

Frankie sighed heavily. "Yeah. And I doubt I'll be able to get more in time."

This close, the strong smell of the turpentine was beginning to give Gabe a headache. He looked up and saw Francesca rubbing between her eyes. She was probably experiencing the effects as well.

"Officer, maybe we could go outside. I think the strength of the solvent is beginning to give Ms. Stevens a headache."

Francesca looked ready to argue, even though the pain dulled the light in her eyes.

The cop looked up at him. "Of course." He rose to full height. "There's really nothing more I can do in here at the moment anyway. The techs will salvage any fingerprints and take some photographs." He walked around the end of the carpeting and headed toward the door. "Do you have a security system, ma'am?" he asked just as they stepped out into the fresh air.

"A very old one. I'm not even sure the cameras still work.

Mr. McBride has already made arrangements to have a new one installed for me."

"What about the trailer? Have you checked to see if it's been broken into?"

She jerked her head around. Gabe realized the thought hadn't even crossed her mind. She took two steps in that direction, but he stopped her.

"Let Officer Peters go first, Francesca. Just in case."

She nodded, but judging by the tightening of her lips she didn't like being held back. She handed the officer the key and they walked over with him, but waited outside while he went in to investigate. He wasn't in there long before returning. "Everything seems to be fine. The lock was still intact and nothing seems to be out of place, but you'll need to check yourself, Ms. Stevens."

Frankie dashed inside the trailer and Peters turned to Gabe.

"Do you have a firm lined up to do the installation?" he asked. "If not, I can recommend a few."

"Yes. I had somebody out here yesterday doing the initial estimate. She should have a new system in place within the next few days. I'll be putting in a call after we're finished here to try and expedite that."

"Good. It doesn't help that so many people have access to the keys. She'll need to change the locks and get better control over who has keys to both the trailer and the barn."

"Yes, sir. I'll see that she follows through on that."

Frankie returned and joined them. "Everything seems to be in place."

"I recommend you get your locks changed as soon as possible, Ms. Stevens. And only give out two or three keys at most. You need to severely limit who has access to your property and your buildings."

"Yes, sir. I'll call Randy to see if he lent his to anybody. But

I can't see him doing that. I know I didn't and I doubt Sophie did, but I'll ask her, just in case."

"I'll file a report and once the technicians finish up I'll send you a copy. It will take a few days. If anything more happens or you discover something is missing, please give me a call." He handed Francesca a business card.

They were just wrapping up when an old pickup pulled up the drive and came to a stop not far from where they stood. The cop lifted his chin, silently asking who the newcomer was.

"That's my foreman. We can ask him right now about his keys."

Gabe remained near the police car while Francesca and Officer Peters headed over to talk to the older man he'd met the previous day. While he waited, a young woman came out of the main house and sauntered over to join him. She had the same hair color as Francesca's and their facial features were similar. But where Francesca's eyes were the green, her sister's were brown. Where Francesca was five foot nothing, her sister was a good six inches taller. And where Francesca hid her curiosity, the sister gave him a blatant once-over. Twice.

"Hi." She added a flirty smile, tossing her hair over her shoulder as she stuffed her hands into the front pockets of her jeans, stretching and leaning back so her cropped top rose up and bared more of her mid-riff.

He cocked one eyebrow. Pretty ran in the family, but she was too young for him. And she wasn't her sister. "Hello."

"Are you a friend of Frankie's?"

He lifted one shoulder. "Sort of." They'd only just met, but he hoped to be much more than that. Soon.

"How do you know her?"

"She hired me."

She narrowed her eyes, as she studied him for a moment.

She had to be the one sneaking a look out the window yesterday. And he'd hazard a guess she'd already grilled her sister for details. But he watched, amused as feigned surprise lit up her expression.

"You're the security guy she hired to find out who's been threatening her."

His body tightened. "She's been threatened?" She hadn't mentioned any verbal or written threats. Was this new or information she hadn't yet given him? And why wouldn't she? So far she'd been very forthcoming with the details he and his brothers needed to try and find whoever was behind the vandalism.

"I'm talking about the break-ins. They scared her."

"She looked angry to me," he said.

The girl shook her head. "I know my sister. She likes to hide behind her 'I need to be in control at all times because I'm a woman in a man's world' attitude. But trust me, her nerves have been strung tight since the second or third time it happened. The first time pissed her off. The second she became a little more cautious. But after that, she's known it was more than just some obnoxious kids causing trouble." She stuck out her hand. "I'm Sophie by the way."

He took it. "Gabe."

She reluctantly released his hand and crossed her arms over her chest. "Hello, Gabe," she purred. "My sister didn't mention how cute you are." She pulled her head back a bit, angled it, and squinted her eyes. "And to be honest, the fact that she talked about you at all is very unlike her." Sophie twitched her lips back and forth. "I think she likes you."

Gabe snorted. Matchmaker much? Or sibling rivalry? "We've only just met. A little early for that, don't you think?" As the words left his mouth, his own thoughts from earlier smacked him in the chest. Pursuing a woman he hardly knew was not his normal protocol. But something about Frankie was different, and it was good to know she might be feeling something similar. Though he highly suspected she would prefer he didn't know.

He coughed and glanced over to where she stood with her foreman and the police officer. They appeared to be just finishing up, so Gabe decided it was time to push a few buttons with Ms. Stevens and see how far she might be willing to go with him. At least for tonight.

"Excuse me. I think I'll go talk to your sister." He left Sophie and wandered over to Francesca. He passed the officer on the way, and they acknowledged each other with a slight nod. When he reached Francesca, she was wrapping up the day's priorities with her foreman. The man barely spared Gabe a glance before he climbed in his own truck and left.

"Would you like to have dinner with me tonight?" He tossed out the invitation before she could even take a breath between ending her discussion with her foreman and beginning one with him. His unexpected request appeared to knock her back on her heels. He liked keeping her off kilter.

"Um..."

"Don't think about it, Francesca. We can talk about your situation and decide how we want to move forward."

A look of dejection fell over her face, but she masked it quickly. "Oh. It's a working dinner."

He didn't like the feeling that settled in his gut when she thought he didn't want to take her on a date. "That's not what I..."

"No," she interrupted. "That's good. We need to discuss work. I hired you to do a job for me. I don't date the people who work for me."

A sense of rejection rolled over him. He didn't like it one bit.

"Since it's a working dinner, how about we grab some pizza and we can talk in the trailer." She jabbed her thumb in its direction. "I'll even pay."

"No." He stood firm, hands on his hips as he glared down at her.

She jutted her chin out and glared back. "Excuse me?"

She could justify this in any way that made her comfortable, but as far as he was concerned, it was a date. Their first date. He had every intention of taking her to a nice restaurant, buying her a nice meal, and if luck were with him, he'd end the night by getting a nice taste of her lips. That, in his definition, was a date. And she was one hell of an attractive woman who he found himself very interested in. Regardless of what he thought he'd been looking for.

"I'll pick you up at seven. And dress nice." With that, he turned on his heel and walked to his car. Behind him, she huffed out her displeasure. Placing his sunglasses over his eyes, he cast her a quick final glance, climbed into his car, and drove away.

As he turned onto the road at the end of the drive, he congratulated himself. But it wasn't with pride.

For the first time in his life, he'd had to get away before *he* lost control.

## CHAPTER EIGHT

FRANKIE STOOD IN FRONT OF HER CLOSET, WRAPPED IN A towel, and looked at each potential outfit. He'd said to dress nice. Did that mean *dress* nice or dark jeans nice? Because she could do dark jeans nice.

"You need to wear a dress."

Frankie turned to see Sophie leaning against the door casing, a grin on her face. Their father had always commented on how much Sophie looked like their mother. Sophie always brushed the compliment off. She hated hearing it, and he'd said it often enough.

Their mother had died giving birth to Sophie, leaving only a handful of pictures and bedtime stories told to an infant and a five-year-old child by a devastated husband, a man used to dealing with guys on the construction site. Their grandmother had helped out for a few years before she passed away, and then from that point, there'd been a handful of housekeepers slash babysitters.

The babysitters eventually disappeared and she became both big sister and pseudo mom to Sophie, who hadn't been too receptive to the idea of being bossed around by her older sister. Though neither she nor their father ever blamed Sophie, they'd always suspected she harbored guilt over the death of her mother. Frankie had a handful of memories still ingrained in her mind and the imaginings of a five-year-old. But those were more than what Sophie had.

"Should I pull out my 'I told you so' sign now?" her sister asked.

Frankie glared at Sophie over her shoulder. "Other than

for Dad's funeral, I've never needed a dress before tonight."

"Didn't John ever take you somewhere nice?"

Just the mention of her last boyfriend sent a trail of disgust through her. He still worked for her, against her better judgment, but he'd begged to keep the job, and she couldn't very well fire him just because they'd broken up. Her father had warned her about dating somebody she worked with, but she hadn't listened. The one time she'd actually ignored her father's advice.

"No. We usually went to a pub or for pizza."

"Well, Gabe told you he was taking you somewhere nice, so you need to look the part." She turned and crooked her finger over her shoulder. "Follow me."

Frankie trudged along behind, stepping into her sister's bedroom and plopping down on Sophie's bed. Where Frankie preferred blacks, blues, and greens in her choice of décor, Sophie preferred various shades of pink and purple. Frankie's room didn't have an unmade bed or clothes littering the floor either. Sophie's looked like a hurricane had blown through.

Sophie threw open her closet door, stood back and swept her arm wide. "Pick something."

"Um..."

"Fine. I'll do it." She spun back to study the choices, her long hair swinging out around her neck. "You can't go wrong with a little black dress."

"I have one of those."

"That was for Dad's funeral, Frankie. It's not date material."

She perused the numerous outfits before her while Frankie slouched on the edge of the unmade bed.

"What about red? You'd look pretty hot in red."

"This isn't a date. It's a working dinner. I don't need to look hot."

Sophie cast her *that* look. "Yeah right." She turned her attention back to the rack of clothes and began rooting though them, pushing aside the ones she apparently found unworthy, stopping to critically assess those with potential. With a sharp flick of the wrist, she pushed aside item after item, until she stopped at a black number that had white piping along the sleeve and collar lines and a thin belt of the same color around the waist. She pulled the hanger from the rod and held it up. "This one."

Frankie looked at the short black dress. It was pretty. She guessed. "That won't fit me."

Sophie raised her perfectly shaped brows into a skeptical arch. "Of course it will. We wear the same size. It will just be a little longer on you than it is on me. Which means it will fit you just right." She shoved the dress toward her. "Try it on."

"Do I have to?"

"Yes."

Frankie rolled her eyes but stood and removed the towel while Sophie removed the dress from the hanger and handed it over. Frankie slipped it over her head and the soft cool material slid sensuously down her body, flowing over her hips and settling into place.

"Perfect." Sophie twirled around and dropped to her knees to dig through the crap on the floor of her closet. She backed out on her hands and knees with a pair of strappy heels clutched in one hand. "Here, put these on."

It was Frankie's turn to look skeptical. "I can't wear those. I'll break my neck."

"You can practice."

Frankie looked at her watch. "I've got an hour."

Sophie grinned. "Then practice fast."

"Soph..."

"Finish getting dressed and then I'll fix your hair and makeup."

"What's wrong with my hair?" Frankie patted her wet ponytail.

"Get those on your feet and I'll meet you in the bathroom in five." She crossed the room but stopped just before leaving. "And put on some sexy underwear and a cute bra." Then she gave Frankie a devious grin. "Or not."

Her sister left her standing in the middle of the bedroom while she went and gathered her stuff to make Frankie look like date material. Even though this wasn't a date.

Sighing heavily, Frankie padded back to her own room. She dropped the shoes on her bed and rummaged through the neat stacks in her top drawer looking for clean underwear suitable to wear under the dress.

Her fingers grazed a lacy, black thong that she'd never worn. Sophie had given it to her for Christmas last year with the matching demi bra. Frankie preferred her boy shorts and simple but lace-trimmed bras. They were pretty but functional. Sophie suggested she wear something sexy. Would Gabe want her to wear sexy?

What was she thinking? Gabe wouldn't even see them. She started to put them back, but paused, her hand hovering over the open drawer. Screw it, she'd wear them. They'd probably fit better under the dress anyway.

Slamming the drawer shut before she changed her mind, she tossed them on the bed next to the shoes. She removed the dress so she could step into the thong and pulled the bra into place. Then she slipped the dress over her head for the second time, enjoying again how it slid down over her body. As she twisted side to side looking at her reflection in the mirror on the back of her closet door, she couldn't deny how the sexy undergarments made her feel more attractive. Pulling up the hem of the dress, she perched on the edge of her bed and pulled the dangerous pair of shoes onto her feet. Then she stood and toddled back to her full-length mirror.

The dress hit her mid-thigh. It was sleeveless, with decorative buckles on each shoulder, and a matching one between her breasts that scrunched the material together, shaping the top to her breasts and showing plenty of cleavage. It nipped in just enough at the waist. She added the belt. The silky material hung and hugged in all the right places. The heels, though too high for her, suited the dress.

She looked nice.

"Frankie. Get your ass in here," Sophie called from the bathroom they shared.

Frankie turned carefully on the shoes and walked, slowly, to the bathroom to find her sister sitting on the edge of the tub, the curling iron plugged in, and a display of makeup spread out on the counter like she was preparing to perform her artistry on a dozen women.

Thirty minutes later, Frankie's hair hung in heavy waves over her shoulders and her eyes were a smoky gray, looking wide and sensuous. Amazed at how she'd gone from pretty to really pretty, Frankie waited in the front hall, biting her nails and watching the clock.

Gabe said he'd pick her up at seven. It was five minutes to the hour.

This felt too much like a real date now. Only she'd never been this anxious about any date she'd been on in the past. Her palms were clammy. Her stomach somersaulted. Wasn't one of the guys sick this past week?

She was just about to call Gabe and cancel this working dinner when his sleek black Porsche pulled to a stop in front of her house.

Her not-date was here.

Gabe climbed from his car and strode up the walk to her porch, his natural swagger showing off his casual confidence. He looked gorgeous in his dark, double-breasted suit, obviously made specifically for him. He wore a light gray dress shirt with a black silk tie.

She stared at him through the screen door. She probably

shouldn't be standing there like a teenaged girl eagerly awaiting her date, but nothing could pull her away.

He jogged up the steps and came to a stop. He looked right back at her through the black mesh. His lips swung up into a full, dazzling smile. His eyes glittered.

Her sister was right. The man was fucking hot.

"You look beautiful," he said.

"Thank you. You don't look so bad yourself."

He stepped back and she pushed open the door.

"Do you want to come in for minute?"

"We have reservations for seven-thirty downtown at Clementine's."

Wow. She'd always wanted to try that place. People who could afford to eat there spoke very highly about it. Reservations were difficult to get, which meant that if Gabe managed to get them in on such short notice, he knew somebody who knew somebody.

"Then I guess we should go."

Just then Sophie joined them, wolf-whistling from halfway up the stairs. Gabe ducked his head, but not before Frankie caught the slight blush to his cheeks. Oh my God, the man had a sweet side to him.

She waved her sister off and stepped out onto the porch to join him, thinking about all the things that could go wrong on this not-date. She took two more steps and caught one heel on a chip in the wood and almost did a header down the stairs. That one hadn't crossed her mind.

Gabe grabbed her elbow. "Whoa. You OK?"

"I don't wear heels very often." This was such a mistake. She wanted to slink away in embarrassment.

He chuckled. "Then maybe you should hold on to me."

The rich smoothness of his voice flowed over her like good whiskey. She was in trouble. Big trouble.

Gabe held out his arm. She didn't like the idea of letting him take the lead, but she saw no other way of getting down the stairs without tripping and breaking an ankle. She wouldn't be able to work if that happened.

Taking his offer of assistance, he led her to the car without any further careless missteps. Before she knew it, he had her settled on butter-soft leather seats, strapped in, and they were roaring down the driveway toward the road.

They didn't speak much for most of the trip. Frankie was a mixture of nerves and a surprising amount of excitement. The man sitting next to her handled the vehicle like it was an extension of his body through every shift, turn, press of the gas or brake, making each seem like an effortless maneuver. He guided the car through traffic as if everyone else knew he was coming and simply moved out of his way.

"Nice car," she said, breaking the silence.

He glanced her way, gave her an almost-smile, and then returned his attention to the road in front of them. "Thanks."

"So, you have a brother, right? The one I talked to when I called?"

"I actually have two, Kyle and Kade. They're twins."

"Really? Identical?" If they looked anything like him, the women were probably lined up.

"Yep."

"Older or younger than you?"

"Younger by a couple of years."

"All three of you work in the same business?" She wished her sister had an interest in the construction company. Having somebody to share the workload with would be nice. Being able to discuss problems and brainstorm solutions or just have somebody you could come home to and bitch about the day with would be nice. Like it used to be when her father was still alive.

She missed that. She missed him.

Gabe nodded. "We own two businesses actually."

She stared at him. "What's the other one?"

He darted a quick look in her direction, but didn't hold her gaze long at all. "A club."

"Cool. What kind of club?"

Rather than answer her question, Gabe turned the car into the private parking lot behind the restaurant and parked the car. Ready to open the door, she paused at the last second. Proper date protocol dictated she wait for him to round the car and help her out. But this wasn't supposed to be a date.

The car door opened, and Gabe waited with his hand held out. She placed her palm in his and a tingle of awareness danced through her. She swallowed hard and peered up at him through lowered lashes. God he was sexy. And so out of her league.

With a firm hand at her lower back, he guided her across the small parking lot and into the restaurant. Every step was beautiful torture because he rubbed his thumb along her skin and it drove her insane. When she stepped through the doorway, his touch fell away. Even though she felt the loss, she breathed a sigh of relief. She barely knew this man, yet he made her feel something she'd never experienced before. It confused her.

Immediately, the sweetest stomach-rumbling aromas assaulted her. Garlic, tomato, and oregano, mixed with perfectly cooked beef. A few floral arrangements scattered throughout the dining and entry area added their fragrance to the blend. The low murmur of diners already enjoying their evening out filled the space, while classically dressed wait staff moved among the candlelit tables.

They were seated near the front window. The round table, dressed for two, was covered in starched white linen over black. A bud vase holding a white day lily rested on the end nearest the glass. Blinds were drawn on the windows, preventing outsiders from intruding on personal moments, but allowed the people inside the restaurant to see what was happening out on the street.

After they ordered a bottle of wine, Frankie tried to relax as she studied the menu, though she continued to be distracted by the man sitting across from her. She could smell his cologne. He looked so handsome she wanted to crawl onto his lap and nuzzle her nose against his neck.

"You look very pretty tonight, Francesca. You should dress up more often."

She felt heat creep up her face. "I don't have too many occasions to dress up on a construction site."

"I suppose not. But hiding such beauty is definitely a waste."

# CHAPTER NINE

GABE COULDN'T TAKE HIS EYES OFF OF HER. HE COULD tell the attention made her uncomfortable. His comment certainly embarrassed her. He knew she felt out of sorts not covered by denim, work shirts, and wearing steel-toed boots. He figured she didn't realize how beautiful she looked in her normal everyday clothes. But she looked absolutely stunning tonight. Every man in the place, young and old, turned to appreciate the view as she passed by him on her way to the table. She was totally oblivious to the admiring glances.

She'd looked adorable trying to navigate the stairs and gravel driveway in shoes he guessed belonged to her sister. She'd look fucking hot as hell in nothing *but* those shoes and strapped to a St. Andrews cross.

But he had no desire to see her uncomfortable tonight. At least not when it came to her choice of footwear.

"So how come the handsome Gabriel McBride doesn't have a wife tucked away somewhere?" she asked, a teasing glint in her eyes as she sipped her wine.

Her question jogged him back to the present. He shrugged. "Never found a woman I wanted to fill the part, I guess." And he hadn't really been looking, he realized.

"And what does the right one look like?"

Nothing like what he'd thought. "I've always envisioned a woman who would be happy at home taking care of me and our kids."

She laughed. "I'm not sure I can picture a *Leave it to Beaver* home life for you."

Neither could he anymore. "What about you?" he asked. "Tell me the kind of man it will take to tie you down."

She shook her head. "Not happening anytime soon. I'm too busy. Besides, I can be mouthy, more like one of the guys. I'm certainly no housewife."

No, she wasn't that. But something told him a life with Francesca Stevens wouldn't be mundane.

"So, you said in the car you have a club. What kind of club do you and your brothers own? One of the bars downtown?"

What would she think if she knew the truth? Would his other source of income or sexual preferences be a turn-on or a complete turn off? He'd never lied about who he was or what he did, and he had no intention of beginning now. If his choices aroused her, they could have a wonderful time together. And if she considered him a pervert, well, then he'd make sure he found whoever was trying to run her business into the ground and ensure she felt as secure as possible before he moved on.

Though that thought distressed him more than he liked.

"No," he finally answered. "It's not downtown."

She frowned, her forehead wrinkling into a cute dip.

He hadn't planned on getting into this discussion here. He'd rather show her. "We own an adult club," he replied, keeping his tone low, conscious of the other diners.

"Adult club?" She shook her head. "I'm not sure I understand."

She picked up her wine and took a delicate sip. Gabe focused on every movement she made, on each expression that crossed her face or flitted through those gorgeous eyes of hers, trying to entrench each as a memory, just in case she sent him packing in the next thirty minutes. For somebody who loudly and happily proclaimed herself a tomboy, she moved like a ballerina, spoke like a phone sex goddess, and smelled like a bouquet of fresh springtime flowers.

Sometimes with a little lumber mill thrown in for good measure.

He suddenly realized he wanted more of everything she had to offer. He'd been teasing himself with fantasies. But as he sat staring across the table at her, all rational thought fled his brain. He wanted to know everything about Francesca Stevens. Right down to the sounds she made when she came.

He cleared his throat and drank from his glass, a burst of ripe melon coating his taste buds. He preferred to kick back with an ice-cold beer, but when formality called for it, a nice crisp white Pinot Grigio did the trick. He'd gone with formal tonight, thinking she'd enjoy being wooed. But as he sat across from her, drinking in her beautify, he realized that although she currently looked the part, Frankie wasn't a wine girl either.

"Gabe?"

He placed his glass on the table, and wrapped his fingers around the stem. For the first time ever he hesitated. He really didn't want this evening to end before it even began. But he needed to know where she stood on what he did for a living. He cleared his throat and lowered his voice given the close proximity of the other tables.

"We have a club. It's called The Vault. It's a place people come to experience an evening out with their partner where, should they choose, they can engage in…more."

She scrunched up her nose. "More what?"

A knot formed in his throat. He'd never been this nervous before. "A few years back, my brothers and I bought an estate home and renovated it," he continued. "We offer a safe environment for people to spend an evening and be as erotic as they'd like."

Her eyes widened.

"There are rules, of course. Everything must be safe, sane, and consensual. No means no, regardless of who says it."

"Ah...does that mean they're nude?" she whispered.

He chuckled and relaxed. She didn't appear appalled. That was a start. "Some. But not generally in the ballroom. Though the outfits may not leave too much to the imagination."

"Why?" she asked.

He frowned. "Why what?"

"Why would you own such a place?"

He shrugged, not sure if she had moved onto simple curiosity or now found herself disgusted. "Why not? It's a perfectly legitimate business. People who enjoy that lifestyle need a place they can go to without fear of discrimination."

The waiter appeared with their meals, so Gabe held his tongue until the young man had deposited the plates, filled their water glasses, topped up their wine, and left them alone.

She sat across from him, not moving, not picking up her fork to eat or taking a drink. She waited.

Gabe started to sweat, not sure how much information to convey. Not sure if she was judging him. Finally, he recognized her total silence and the expression on her face as not one of disdain, but rather one of interest. For the first time in his life, he worried that a woman he was attracted to would be unable and unwilling to accept him. So he mentally crossed his fingers and continued. "We have three floors. The main floor is more like a typical dance club. The second floor has some public and private rooms."

"What happens in those rooms?" Her cheeks glowed, and she licked her lips, drawing his gaze like a bee to honey.

"Anything within the rules that's not hard-core BDSM."

"BDSM."

"Bondage—"

"I know what it stands for." Her throat moved up and down in the most seductive dance as she swallowed.

"Well, we have an area in the basement where the more serious people in the lifestyle can play."

"The basement?"

"Yes, The Vault. The club is named for it."

"Oh." She cocked an eyebrow. "Catchy."

He had no clue where her mind was at. She gave him no indication whatsoever of whether he had to gobble down his food and take her home or if they could linger over dessert and think of games they could play in The Vault.

She still hadn't touched her food or drink. She trained those green eyes on his face. "Tell me more about those rooms on the second floor."

Encouraged, he offered a friendly smile and relaxed a little more. "Sure. There's a handful of bedrooms that are just that. They're available on a first-come first-served basis, but there's a fee for using them. The other rooms we modified a bit. We put in some two-way windows so people can watch from the hallway. We took one room, knocked out the wall to the adjoining room, and created a theater of sorts."

"Sounds big. Lots of rooms to—" Her lips twitched. "—play with."

Relieved that she didn't seem ready to kick his ass to the curb, Gabe felt the tension he'd been holding on to leave his body and acknowledged her pun with a smile. "Yes."

She picked up her fork and dug into her pasta.

As she twirled her fork through the noodles, Gabe cut into his steak.

They'd each swallowed a few mouthfuls before she spoke again. "What do they do in those rooms? The ones where people can watch."

"Depends," he said. "Sometimes it's just couples or threesomes—"

"Wait, threesomes? As in three people?"

"Yes, Francesca. That's the definition of threesome."

She blushed. "You didn't let me finish."

"I knew where you were going." He paused to taste the

garlic mashed potatoes. The chef here used some secret ingredient that Gabe had yet to figure out. They were delicious though. "Some put on public displays, meaning they like people to watch them."

"They have…" She suddenly paused and looked around the room, guilt stamped all over her face, as though she just remembered they were in a public place. "…sex in front of other people?" She leaned forward and whispered the word sex so low, he had to read her lips.

Gabe tried to make light of their discussion and leaned forward himself. "Yes. If they want to. Not everybody wants to."

They both sat back. But when she bent forward again, so did he. To hear her better, sure, but also to smell her. And just to be that much closer to her.

"Have you? Do you like to do…that…in front of other people?"

He didn't answer immediately, not quite certain how to. Was this a test? Would his response send her running?

She shifted back in her chair and blocked all emotion from her face, waiting for his response.

He resolved to be as honest as possible. "I have."

She stiffened.

"But not often."

As her shoulders relaxed, so did Gabe. "My brothers are more into public demonstrations than I am. I can certainly appreciate the appeal, but my time with a beautiful woman is not something I'm generally interested in sharing with others."

"What else?"

"Excuse me?" What more did she want to hear? Or what more did he care to share in a full-to-capacity restaurant.

"Why that type of club? What do you get out of it, if you don't do the same things that your guests do?"

Good question. Smart lady. But then again, since the moment he met her, he'd never questioned her intelligence. "I didn't say I get nothing out of it, Francesca. I simply said I don't often have sex in front of my guests."

"Oh." She blushed hard, her cheeks flaming red.

"I tend to use the facilities on off nights," he clarified. "When the club is open, I'm managing it. It's my job. I make sure everyone is having a good time and playing safely. I don't have time to indulge myself when I'm working."

She picked up her fork and resumed eating her meal, taking two mouthfuls, plus one of the side salad, before she asked her next question. "Can anyone go to this place...The Vault?"

He paused with his own knife and fork ready to slice through his fillet minion. "The club or the playroom in the club?" Talking about the club always left him with a sense of pride, regardless of what others thought. Tonight there was one difference though. Tonight it mattered.

"Either."

He took his turn to eat a few bites of the mouthwatering meal that was becoming more tasteless with each swallow before providing an answer.

Talking about the club with Francesca sitting across the table from him, looking sexy in a dress and fuck-me shoes she clearly didn't feel comfortable in, aroused him. He wanted to show her the club, not talk about it. He needed to see her reaction first hand. He needed to experience it.

"We are open to the public, but it's by invitation or referral. Although we don't unreasonably deny people. I guess you could say we're fairly exclusive. Anybody visiting has to have a background check completed. And it's more exhaustive if they wish to be a full-fledged member or use the basement on a regular basis. Everybody has to sign a non-disclosure agreement."

"Why?" Her eyes lit up.

"The members expect utmost discretion. Most are professionals with families. They don't want their personal or public profiles tarnished simply because they like to experience the more sensual side of their nature."

She pursed her lips into a sexy pout. "Makes sense." She paused. "Do members pay lots of money to visit your club?"

"Memberships are not too steep to be totally restrictive, but are high enough to make most people seriously consider their objectives for being there before making a commitment."

She nodded and twirled another forkful of noodles through some sauce before placing it in her mouth. She washed it down with a sip of wine. "So, tell me. What *exactly* happens in The Vault?"

*In* the Vault, not *at* The Vault. His cock swelled. He shrugged and then selected a slice of warm bread from the basket in the center of the table. He spread some creamy butter on it. "It's usually much easier to show somebody who's interested rather than tell them about it. Don't they say a picture's worth a thousand words?" He bit into the bread and chewed.

She narrowed her eyes the slightest bit. "Why don't you give it a try anyway?"

Gabe's body went on full alert. He rubbed one suddenly damp palm, a first for him, down his thigh. Christ, for a man always in control, every ounce of it fled.

"Well, usually the people who play down there are more interested in bondage, flogging, spankings, maybe some wax play."

"Spankings? Seriously? People really do that?"

Gabe wanted to chuckle over the look of disbelief on her face. "You should try it some time, Francesca. I happen to think you'd like it."

Her eyes widened further. "Why would you think that?" She dropped her voice to just above a whisper at the last second, as she glanced around the room. "I'm not into that sort of thing. I'm not weak. I refuse to let any man rule over me, control me in any way, or lay a hand on me."

"It has nothing to do with control in the way you're using the word, and everything to do with power, Francesca. *Your* power, I might add."

She scoffed. "What kind of power does a woman have if she's bent over and some guy is whacking her behind?" She chewed on her lower lip for a moment. "By the way. How does it happen?"

"What do you mean?"

She blushed and fidgeted in her chair. She took a chunk of tomato from her dish and shoved it into her mouth.

Although he knew his meal was cooked to perfection, Gabe had to admit, he had no recollection of what he'd shoved in his mouth so far. And he hadn't even asked her about the pasta. He focused totally on his date, fascinated as she squirmed on her chair, darted glances around the room and twisted her napkin. His brave date wasn't giving up. She wanted to know. He watched her face, fascinated as she searched for ways to ask the awkward questions tactfully.

"Exactly how does a man spank a lover?"

"He swats her ass."

She rolled her eyes. "Does he use his hand?"

"Sometimes a paddle will be used. Or any implement with a flat edge." A thrill roared through him when the color in her cheeks deepened. "I prefer to use my hand."

"And what, she just drops her pants and bends over?"

"Normally, she'd lie over a spanking bench or her partner's lap."

"Your lap?"

His body's reaction to her slip of the tongue was instant and rock hard, and now he couldn't stop himself.

It no longer mattered that they sat in a crowded restaurant. As far as he was concerned, they'd been ensconced in a bubble. She'd given him two openings. Could he take this one? It was a risk. One where any chance of him developing a relationship with this woman could fly out the window in the next few minutes. But he was willing to risk everything, including her storming out in the middle of their date. Gabe refused to ignore his gut. This woman was important to his future. And he was a risk taker.

Gabe canted slightly forward. He reached one hand across the table and grabbed the tips of her fingers. He lowered his voice an octave or two and stared deep into her eyes, seeing every fleck, excited to watch her pupils grow.

"I'd love nothing more than to shim that silk dress up to your waist and lay you over my lap, Francesca. To feel the heat of your skin through my pants. My mouth waters with the image of your bared ass rising to meet the palm of my hand. I can already imagine the rosy glow of each cheek. I can even imagine the sweet smell of your arousal."

She gasped.

He stopped and made a show of inhaling nice and deep. The faint scent of her excitement teased the air with a slight perfume, enough that, close as he was to her, it created a pleasurable torture within him. "And I know if I slip my fingers between your legs, your pussy would be nice and wet."

He watched the long column of her throat move up and down as though over a hard lump. Did she realize she'd raised one hand up between her breasts? Or that her breathing had become labored, her nostrils flaring ever so slightly. Or that beneath the black silk of her dress, her nipples were rigid points.

If they'd been at the club, he would have her spread out on the table before him and she'd be his dessert. He didn't think she'd appreciate him giving her a live demonstration of just a how good a naughty spanking could be. Or how much of a sweet tooth he had.

At least not here.

Above them, a throat cleared loudly, but he couldn't pull his gaze away from the expression on her face, the yearning in her eyes.

"How are your meals?"

They both blinked, and while Francesca grabbed her fork, ducked her head, and feigned absolute interest in her now lukewarm meal, Gabe addressed the hovering waiter. "They're just fine, thank you."

Francesca was shoving bites of pasta into her mouth between rather large sips of water. Her blush had spread down her neck and up to her ears. Was that sweat glistening on her brow?

He looked up at the young man standing next to him, politely waiting for further instructions, his face a blank slate. If he'd heard a word Gabe had said, he gave nothing away.

"Actually," Gabe said, "if you could please package up a few choices of your best desserts and bring us the check, that would be most appreciated."

Frankie's head shot up, her water glass held in such a tight grip that Gabe feared the thing would shatter.

"Of course, sir. I'll have the chef prepare a selection for you." He hurried away in the direction of the kitchen.

"I hope you don't mind. But I'd much rather finish our meal in private. Would you prefer my place or yours?" It was time for Gabe to take control. It was time to find out just how much Frankie was willing to, or interested in integrating herself into his life.

"Ah…"

"The choice is yours, Francesca. But those are the only two choices you have."

"Um…"

He waited. He allowed his patience to show by picking up his own fork and taking two more bites of the food from his plate. He lifted his wineglass to his mouth, swallowing back a healthy mouthful. He'd surprised her. But he believed, or rather he hoped, his date wasn't yet over.

Francesca shifted in her chair.

Gabe glanced across the table at her. She'd placed her utensils and napkin on her plate, signaling she was finished. She'd dropped her hands to her lap, but considering they were hidden from his view, he couldn't tell if they were relaxed or gripped together, her knuckles white with nervous tension. But what interested him most was the look of determination on her face.

"I gather you've made your decision," he said.

She nodded. "Your place."

His surprise must have shown because she gave him a shy smile.

"I'd like to see The Vault."

# CHAPTER TEN

THIS WAS A BAD IDEA. FRANKIE WRUNG HER HANDS IN HER lap. She pressed her knees tight together. She should have told him she wasn't interested and asked him to take her home. And then he could leave. But she didn't want him to leave.

She should have reminded him she didn't take orders from him or any man and she actually had three choices. So why had she picked his place? Now he'd have to take her home when their date ended. Unless she spent the night with him.

But damn it, spending even more time with the man and getting to know him beyond a professional acquaintance wasn't part of the plan. She needed a new plan. She needed to stay away from him. She didn't need a man. She was surrounded by men every single day.

And yet she didn't utter a word. In truth she was very curious about The Vault. What enticed women or men to give up control to another person. What benefits did it provide them?

Gabe drove to an older, long-established part of town, not far from the downtown core. Ten years ago, the area had seen better days. Now, aging, rundown buildings and lawns littered with past-their-prime vehicles and forgotten bicycles were no more. In their place, new, modern estate-sized homes stood regal and proud. But they fit. Old architecture blended with new and somehow it all worked.

Gabe turned into a gated driveway. After pressing a remote to open them, he steered the car through the ornate gates and then closed the massive things behind them. All she could do was stare wide-eyed. Ahead of them she saw a large fountain, and beyond it a very large home. She'd have to ask who his landscaper was. The whole place belonged on the freaking cover of *Better Homes and Gardens*.

"This is The Vault? I didn't see any signage." And it looked nothing like any club she had ever gone to. Not that she'd been to many. One actually, years ago.

"This is it. I don't openly advertise. I get more than enough business by word of mouth."

There was a guesthouse, which resembled the main house, off to the left and surrounded by a group of maple trees.

"Does anyone live here?"

"I live in the guest house. We have an apartment on the third floor, but that's normally used by my brothers on nights when things run late and they don't feel up to driving to their own homes."

She sat in silence as Gabe continued along the drive, finally coming to a stop near the main door of the mansion. And that's what it was. It was a fucking mansion. "I thought you just said you lived in the other house?" she asked.

"I do. But you said you wanted to see The Vault."

His quiet tone made her nervous. Not a scared nervous. A "holy shit is this really happening" nervous. Gabe was going to give her a tour of a club where people came to have sex. In front of other people. *With* other people. Sophie would eat this up with a freaking spoon.

Sophie finding out about this was a horrible thought. She could never know. Although, Frankie wouldn't be a bit surprised if her sister already knew about The Vault. She had a circle of friends. They did things together. She went on dates. She knew things. Things Frankie had never experienced because she was the tomboy, not the princess. She didn't hang out with other girls dishing gossip on the men in their lives. The only men in her life received a paycheck from her.

She glanced around, shifting and squinting through the

glass and the darkness beyond to the limited reach of the floodlights. "This whole place is…wow. Who did the remodel for you?"

He tossed her a pained look. "Sorry, not your father's company."

She laughed. "I know. My father never would have taken on a project like this even if you'd asked him to. This would have been too big for him."

"We used Thompson Construction."

She nodded with appreciation. "They're very good."

"We're pleased with the end result." Gabe drew the car to a stop and turned it off.

The ticking of the engine became the only sound inside the car. Until she focused and detected the faint in and out of his breathing. And the thumping of her heart. Could he hear how it pounded against her chest? If her energy came with sound waves, they'd be bouncing off the doors.

Gabe opened his door and got out. He closed it and rounded the hood of the car to her side. She followed every step he took, swallowing hard as he neared her side. Normally she would have already been out and maybe waiting for him, or even finding her own way to the door. *That* was the kind of girl she was.

But Gabe treated her differently. He treated her like a…a woman.

Frankie lifted her right hand, ready to bite a nail. A bad habit her sister gave her shit for about as often as Frankie gave Sophie hell for drinking orange juice straight from the carton.

Gabe opened the door and offered his hand. With the low profile of the Porsche and her little black dress, she'd need every bit of courage she could muster and all the help he could provide. And then some, if he was willing. And if she had the guts to ask for it.

The main house, built entirely of stone, stood three stories tall. It looked old. Meaning Gabe and his brothers had the means to restore such a place amid applicable heritage requirements. For a place of this size, that wouldn't be cheap, nor an easy task.

"Was the building in good condition when you bought it?" She strove for blasé when casual was the last thing she felt.

Standing next to her, he put his hands in the pockets of his pants, and the flaps of his suit jacket flipped back. The pose stretched his dress shirt tight across his chest. What did he look like underneath? Smooth? A sprinkling of hair? She liked a little male hair. Frankie closed her eyes. She'd gone there again. She needed to stop doing that. This was just a tour of his business.

"We were lucky. The previous owners took good care of the place. There was some work required to bring the attic and the basement up to code, mostly because we had specified uses for those areas. I mentioned we did some remodeling on the inside, but the outside really just got a cosmetic update. The grounds needed the most work, actually. The owners were elderly. The husband had suffered a stroke and couldn't maintain the property any longer."

Frankie felt her gut clench at the reminder of what she'd been through with her own father. His first stroke had left him disabled. Watching the pain, anger, and humiliation in his face every day when he tried but couldn't do the most basic things damn near gutted her.

Gabe paused and Frankie glanced at him. In her heels, she'd only gained three inches, which put her staring straight at his shoulder area. She tilted her head back to peer up at his handsome face. She thought he'd be watching her, but his attention was glued to the building. She followed his line of sight. Large smooth stones of varied shades of gray covered the exterior. The windows, framed in white, stood out against the stone façade. No lights appeared to be on anywhere in the building.

"Isn't anyone here tonight?" As she asked the question, she cast her gaze around the area. There were no other cars, unless they were parked somewhere else.

"We're not open Sunday through Tuesday. Wednesdays are for newcomers. Thursdays are often restricted to certain members. Like any club, Fridays and Saturdays are the busiest nights." He took her hand and led her to the front door.

Rose bushes bloomed along the front wall, their fragrance almost cloying in the humid evening air. Gabe strode with purpose up the steps and, taking a key from his pocket, he unlocked the front door and stepped aside so she could enter. He leaned in, ran his hand along the wall next to the door, and flicked on a light.

Frankie stepped into a huge entryway. It was like walking into a home most people only saw on television or in the movies.

"I'll show you around."

Straight ahead, on the opposite side of a round table that held a vase with a beautiful bouquet of red and white roses, was a set of double doors. A hallway to the right led to another part of the house and a circular staircase on the left led to the second floor. She glanced up. There was a railing where anybody up there could peer down on the entry hall. Impressive.

Gabe ushered her to the right, turning on lights along the way and as they passed an elevator. He pointed to closed doors in a very non-emotional way and stated their purpose. "That's a powder room, and next to it is a change room." He looked over to the opposite side of the hallway. "The parking at the side brings you in through that mudroom."

She paused and poked her head into the room he pointed at. She nearly swallowed her tongue. "This is a mudroom?" The floor gleamed. Beautiful oak cabinets with intricate scrollwork in the doors covered one wall. A small crystal chandelier hung from the ceiling. "Damn." There was actual mud in hers.

He chuckled. "Well, I don't have children leaving mitts, hats, and dirty boots. And I have cleaning staff in almost every day." He took her hand again and gave it a gentle tug. "Follow me. We need to talk about a few things before we go any further on this tour."

He led the way through a doorway at the end of the hall and switched on the light. It was an office. A very nice office. She could work in an office like this. A massive, very orderly, dark cherry desk sat to one side and comfortable looking seating was laid out near the large, curved window that overlooked the backyard. She wished for more light so she could see beyond the glass.

Pausing near the desk, she spun around to face him. "What made you decide to buy such a grand home and turn it into a sex club?"

Immediately after the words crossed her lips she regretted them. She didn't want to insult Gabe or his choices, but saying her curiosity was piqued was an understatement. What made a man and his brothers decide to run a club like he'd described? A place people came to for the purpose of sex? Who did that?

Thankfully, he didn't appear offended in the least. In fact, his beautiful blue eyes twinkled, but she did notice his posture had changed. With his hand, he indicated she take a seat in one of the two guest chairs.

He perched on the edge of the desk. "First, it's not like people come here just to fuck." He grinned.

If he thought being crude would turn her off, or piss her off, he had much to learn about her. In her world, the f-bomb was used regularly as an adjective. It wasn't a hammer, it was a fucking hammer. "Then why the exclusivity and the secrecy?"

He tipped his head to acknowledge her questions. "Many of the people who come here hold prominent positions in the city or in the organizations they work for. They don't want to risk their reputation, or that of their loved ones. And I certainly don't wish to risk mine either. My members expect privacy, discretion, and security. They come here to have fun, to experiment, to do something others would possibly condemn them for. But here, they can do all those things without judgment."

He had become very professional, almost stern, very different from the man she'd been dealing with thus far. She wasn't sure if she liked this side of him. "How do you make sure you can do that?"

"Memberships are high enough to keep out the people who only plan to come here to screw around. And please don't misunderstand. People do have sex while they're here. And they do fuck. But there's a difference. Of course there's no absolute guarantee assholes or persons with an agenda won't get in and even try to cause trouble. We have security on-site and cameras throughout the building. We take every reasonable precaution we can."

"So there's somebody watching what people are doing?" she asked, incredulous. "Including when they're having sex?"

"There are discreet cameras in the rooms, yes. And I have two men I trust implicitly keeping tabs on the guests. I have to take that measure, Francesca, to ensure everyone's safety. When they detect questionable behavior, they alert me or my brothers and other members of my security team."

"And do your members know they're being watched?" She wasn't sure how she felt about that.

"They do. It's one of the items in the contract they sign before they are allowed to come here. But rest assured, my staff is extremely discreet. We respect the privacy of our members, but we take their safety and security very seriously. That's our priority." He paused. "The biggest element to meeting the membership requirements, in my opinion, is confirming that all parties are on board for what The Vault provides. I talk to both the husband and the wife for instance, to make sure they both want this. It doesn't work if one is being coerced to come. This type of club doesn't fix problems in a relationship, but it can sure as hell end one."

"Contract?" She held up her hand before he could explain. She had lots of questions. One on the top of her list being how Gabe and his brothers kept out men or women who had anger issues or over the top control issues. "Later. Define 'questionable' for me, please."

"Everything and anything that happens within these walls must follow the rules of safe, sane, and consensual. No means no. That is my number one rule, and it's non-negotiable in every scene, public or private. I truly don't care if the person being told no is a partner or a stranger, or even a spouse. I don't care if they're in an official relationship or not. If you say no to whomever you are with, and that person doesn't respect your wishes and cease whatever they are doing that very moment, my men will step in."

"Wow. And what happens to the aggressor?"

"They will be removed from the premises and depending on the circumstances may not be permitted back."

"Even if they're a paid member?"

He nodded, the movement firm and decisive. "Even if they are a paid member."

"OK. Now, what about this contract?"

"There's actually two." He got up and rounded the desk. Opening a drawer, he took out a piece of paper and laid it on top of the organized and polished-to-a-shine surface, face-up, then spun it around so she could read it. He retrieved a pen from the black holder on the corner of the desk and placed it beside the single page.

"I know you understand contracts and terms, Francesca, so I won't bore you with the details because I fully expect you'll want to read it yourself. Which I would of course encourage you to do."

She still wasn't sure about this side of him, so formal, but she had to admit, it was calming her nerves. And for some strange reason it was sexy as hell.

He returned to his spot on the corner of the desk. "This one is the non-disclosure agreement. In a nutshell it states you can't and won't share any information or photographs or video of anything you see or hear within this building and on the premises."

She picked up the sheet and glanced at him. "You want me to read this now?"

"Yes. You need to sign that before I give you the twenty-five cent tour."

One sharp nod from him and she read the page. Straightforward. Cameras and video equipment were not allowed. No discussing details of the rooms, furniture, equipment, people or goings-on.

He handed her the pen and she signed.

"Good. Now I will take you on that tour."

"One thing first," she said. She bent down and slipped off her shoes. Her toes and heels gave a huge sigh of relief.

Gabe's quiet laughter sent a warm feeling rushing through her.

"You said this was the first contract. There's more?"

He nodded. "That comes later and only if you want to visit the club as a member. It covers more specifics around expectations, limitations, and medical requirements."

She gave him a questioning look.

"I'll explain later if you wish to come back. Maybe become a member?"

Her? A member of a sex club? "Oh, no. I don't do clubs."

Was that a look of regret on his face? He turned away too quickly for her to say, tucking the signed form back into the desk drawer, but she had a gut feeling she'd disappointed him.

He stood and held out a hand, beckoning her. "Come on. I'll show you the rest of the place now."

They walked side by side, hand in hand down the hall back toward the main entrance. She expected him to release her, but he'd only tightened his hold, enfolding her small fingers within his large ones. She kind of liked it.

The décor was stunning. Soft colors, heavy woodwork on baseboards and crown molding—probably all original. The flooring years ago would have been hardwood, but somewhere along the way the wood had been switched to ceramic that resembled marble.

"How much does a membership cost?" Curiosity, that's all. Who wouldn't be? She knew nothing about this sort of thing. She didn't understand it, and wasn't certain she even wanted to. But she also couldn't forget the arousal Gabe's description of being spanked had built. A few more words, privacy or not, and she would have combusted right there in the restaurant.

"It depends on the type of member or how frequent you plan to attend. A Gold membership is five thousand a year per couple, Silver is twenty-five hundred, and a Bronze is one thousand. The Bronze is a limited membership. And we have a Platinum membership for clients who frequent The Vault itself."

Wow. That was a hefty sum. And all for the purpose of having someone take command over another person. She'd never ever been into a man controlling her, and the whole idea of having sex in a public place while other people watched and judged her performance made her feel totally exposed.

Gabe peered down at her. "What's going through that pretty head of yours?"

"I'm not sure you want to know."

He stopped and turned so that he stood in front of her. He placed one hand under her chin and lifted. "Of course I do. In a place like this, living this type of lifestyle, it's critical to understand what people are thinking and feeling. Open and honest communication is the cornerstone to any relationship, but certainly in this one. People get hurt otherwise."

"OK. I will admit that maybe I'm interested," she said. "I'm nervous about what I'll see, what I'll think." What she'd feel.

"And I fully expect that," he said. "It's fine to be nervous. But I need you to be honest with me, Francesca. I need to know if you're comfortable or not with what I do here. That's very important to me."

She didn't know why her opinion mattered, but she laughed, trying to lighten the suddenly serious mood. "No worries, there, Gabe. I'll tell you exactly what I'm thinking." Well, most of it anyway.

He nodded in agreement. "Thank you."

"I get it. I understand the reason for secrecy."

He shook his head. "It's not secrecy. It's discretion and protection. I don't want my guests to wake up in the morning and find a picture of them having sex with somebody who's not their partner or spouse on the front page of the morning newspaper. I don't want an employee to lose their job because their boss doesn't understand that they like their sex with a side dish of kink."

"I have my own business problems too. It's hard enough being a female working in a man's world. I already have one person trying to shove me out of it. I don't want them getting more ammunition and ruining my reputation right along with my business." Another good reason she should be asking him to take her home.

Gabe gripped her shoulders and bent at the knees so he could be at eye-level with her. "I'm going to find who's doing this to you, Francesca. You won't lose anything."

Frankie gazed up at him. Gabe was drop-dead gorgeous. She'd never met a man so good-looking. He made her feel all gooey inside with one warm look. He made her feel like a woman who'd never considered herself "girly." Hell, even using an adjective like gooey made her want to chuck this dress, slip on her jeans and work boots, and hammer some nails. Hard.

But it was the only word that came to mind that described the feelings she had going on inside. It was the reason she was still here.

From the moment she'd found him leaning against his sexy car waiting for her, she'd had to bite her lip to keep from licking his chest, clench her hands to keep from running her fingers through his short dark hair, and clamp her thighs together to squash the tingling of arousal created by just being near him. These were new sensations for her. Her dates in the past had to spend time during foreplay to get her good and hot for them. This guy just had to look at her and sweat licked at her brow, her heart started thumping, and her entire body tightened in anticipation.

He wasn't her type. The man was tall. He had to be six four. Demanding. And serious. He looked thoughtful at all times, like his brain never took a break. And his smile was one that said he didn't offer it often, but he smiled plenty with her. She liked that.

Right now he was all business as he gazed down at her, his eyes conveying the promise of his words. The grip of his fingers on her shoulders offered comfort, security, and strength.

She could count on him. "I know."

# CHAPTER ELEVEN

FRANKIE LOOKED UP AT HIM WITH GRATITUDE SHINING in her eyes, and Gabe vowed he would do everything in his power to keep his word. Removing his hands from her shoulders, he continued the tour. "My security office is on the other side of the building. During the nights we're open, I have one man situated there and another in the basement."

Leading her back to the main entrance, he paused to point out the security office and staff kitchen. Then he took her to the ballroom. Gabe pushed the doors open, flipped on the lights, and moved aside so Frankie could enter and get the full effect.

"Wow," she exclaimed.

Her bright smile pleased him. Not many homes contained a ballroom these days, so its size and elegance impressed most people.

"I can only imagine what this place looked like in its day."

"Well, not much different, actually. We refinished the hardwood and added the lights in the ceiling, but other than that, we didn't change much."

She looked at him, a wide, teasing grin on her face. "Oh, they had stripper poles back then?"

He laughed. "OK, so we added a couple of those."

Gabe stood back while she wandered around the room. Tonight the space almost echoed with its emptiness, but tomorrow night it would be hopping with adults of all ages dressed in whatever made them feel sexy. They'd be dancing to sensual beats, maybe with their partner, maybe *for* their partner. Sometimes in groups of three or more.

The most important thing was that they could relax and let their desire for the people they were with speak through the movement of their bodies. Something they couldn't or didn't feel comfortable doing in a typical nightclub.

He looked around, seeing the ballroom through Francesca's eyes. From the day he and his brothers first toured the building, it had become one of his favorite rooms. They'd never considered using the space for any other purpose than its original intent. The one thing they'd agreed on from day one was to preserve as much of the heritage and spirit of the building and the grounds as they could. They'd brought it up to code, and made changes to some of the bedrooms, but the rest of the house, the basement aside, had received facelifts, not much more.

Frankie ran a hand along the top of the bar. "Why a club like this?" She'd raised her voice so he could hear her from the across the room.

She'd asked him that earlier and he hadn't answered her then. He still wasn't sure he was ready to divulge his reasoning.

Gabe removed his jacket and hung it over the back of the nearest chair. "It seemed like a good idea. And it seems I was right." As he strode across the dance floor, he undid the button at first his right cuff and carefully and methodically rolled up his sleeve. He did the same to the left. Above him, the lights embedded in the ceiling lit up the room like twinkling stars.

She'd turned to watch his progress. "I mean, what made you decide to open this club, here in this city, and run it with your brothers?" Her voice had dropped. Her chest rose and fell with each shallow breath she took, her hands twitching at her sides as she strummed her fingers against her thighs.

"I wanted something a little different." He closed the gap between them. "I visited something similar a few years back and it intrigued me."

She moved toward one of the poles. "Are you in it for the sex?"

"I'm in it because I think it's a good investment. Personally, it called to something inside me."

"Does that mean you're...what is it called?"

"A Dominant. I prefer to be the dominant one in a relationship. Especially when it comes to the person I'm having sex with, yes."

She paused and peeked at him from below her lashes. The lights played with the shades of her hair, making some strands appear very light, the others very dark. "What about having sex with more than one person?"

Did she entertain ménage fantasies? Didn't matter, he needed to be honest with her. "No. I'm not into sharing." If she were his, he'd never let another man touch her.

Relief blossomed on her face.

"Some people only come here to dance, Francesca. It's just a night out at a very sexy, uninhibited club. Others are looking to explore their wilder side."

"How wild do you get, Gabe?" She'd cocked her head at an angle and fluttered her lashes. Was she flirting with him?

"I'm not hard-core if that's what you're wondering, and I'm not into submission on a round-the-clock basis." Though people who didn't know him assumed the complete opposite. They didn't understand or respect the fact that he simply liked his privacy. "I like to take control in the bedroom. I like to play around with some toys, maybe try a spanking or a flogger. I'm pretty good with one of those." She'd look awesome wearing his stripes.

She licked her lips.

He moved closer.

"How do you stop things from getting out of control?" she asked. "In a bar they drink and become assholes quite often."

"I hope the cost deters them from that. And our two-drink limit helps."

"Why allow alcohol at all? That would significantly reduce the risk."

He shrugged. "Perhaps. But frankly, sometimes people need to relax in order to have fun. A drink or two can do that. Every member is very clear on the expectations and the rules. There is zero tolerance." Mere inches separated them. "The Doms are not permitted to drink at all, however."

"Why's that?" she asked, her breathing hitched. She tried to escape by edging closer to the poles.

He changed course to intercept her. "Because they have to be in control at all times, both for the safety of their partner and the others around them. They also monitor the activities and serve as extra security when necessary."

She arrived at her destination. She wrapped one small hand around the pole. Like most people, she appeared too shy to attempt a twirl.

"Go ahead, Francesca," he urged. "Test it out."

She dropped her hand, stepped away, and shook her head slowly. "No. I don't know how. I'd just make a fool of myself."

"There's nobody here to see you, sweetheart. I know you want to."

Her grin was shy but eager. She reached out again and wrapped her fingers around the pole. Then, she leaned away from it and used the forced momentum of her body to swing around it without lifting her feet from the floor. The always-confident Frankie looked a little lost at the moment.

Gabe moved in behind her. He bent his head down to her neck, closed his eyes, and inhaled. "You smell divine. Did I mention that earlier?" he whispered along the column of her neck. He grazed the bottom of her earlobe with his teeth.

She shivered. "Ah, no. I…um…don't think so."

Private booths ringed the perimeter of the room. Round tables that accommodated four comfortably were scattered throughout so the open floor didn't appear overly large. Tonight there was just the two of them. In a heartbeat he could have her bent over one of those tables, her dress up around her waist, and his cock buried balls-deep inside of her. It twitched in excitement at the prospect. He fought against the desire to grind his pelvis against her behind. The gentleman in him scolded the horndog.

He'd argued with his brothers over the two stripper poles. They'd wanted them; he hadn't. But he had to admit, they were a nice addition. Especially if he could get Francesca to dance around one again.

A mirrored ball hung from the ceiling. On club nights, it reflected the laser lights controlled from a small room creatively concealed in the back corner where they also housed their disc jockey.

He spun her around. "Are you ready to continue the tour, Francesca, or would you like to stay here and dance for me?"

Her eyes widened, and she tugged her bottom lip between her teeth.

"Don't do that." The endearment flowed easily off his tongue and felt far too natural.

"Do what?"

"Bite on your bottom lip."

"I can do—"

"My place," he interrupted her, "my rules. And I say no biting your pretty lips." He stepped into her personal space, pressing her back to the pole. He leaned down, his chin almost touching her shoulder. "Or I may have to spank you," he whispered in her ear.

Frankie gasped. Red bloomed across her cheekbones, and her lips were puffy from where she'd bitten. The lighting in the room shone down over her, highlighting the column of her neck and her upper chest. He could see her pulse throbbing under her skin.

Gabe, keeping his face straight, his gaze serious, dipped his chin and waited her out. When at last she broke eye contact, he wanted to fist-pump the air. Oh, her submission would be the sweetest thing he'd tasted in years. And he was starving. For her.

"How about we continue the tour?"

Surprise, and arousal, lit up her eyes.

He held out his hand, palm up, a spark of lust and satisfaction racing through him when she placed her hand in his.

As they crossed the floor to the door and then to the stairs, he returned the conversation to where they'd left off. "We actually have many members who never move beyond the ballroom and the main floor. They simply like a night out where they can talk with other adults."

"They can do that in any bar," Frankie responded, her voice husky. Then she swung her head and gazed over her shoulder. "They clearly come here, and pay much more to do so, for another reason."

"True," he said. "But here, no matter how old they are, who they are, or how they look, they can dress and behave in a way they can't in those other bars. Nobody judges them here."

He led her up the stairs and guided her down the hallway, flicking on lights, and allowing her to peer into the empty rooms. "On the nights we're open, it can get pretty busy up here. The private rooms are in the other wing."

Gabe paid close attention to her face and body language as she checked out each room, her gaze sweeping from side to side. If she wondered about the king sized beds, the odd-shaped chairs or benches with cuffs or straps, the swing hanging from the corner in one room, or the stage and love seat theatre seating in another, never mind the occasional two-way window, she didn't say. Though her eyes grew wider as they moved further down the hall, and her cheeks seemed to be permanently pink now.

"You said earlier that these rooms are for public demonstrations and public play. What's the difference?"

"Demonstrations are put on by experienced staff or guests. Generally they display a certain skill. Sometimes they are used for teaching a sub a specific lesson."

She raised her eyes to his, a question clear in them, but the words didn't pass her lips.

He hesitated to allow her time to ask, but she didn't so he continued. "Some people conduct a scene in one of the rooms and permit others to watch from a safe and quiet distance."

"Sex should be a private act between two people."

He paused. Between two people? That happened to be his preference. Private? She hadn't yet experienced the thrill of voyeurism. He spun on one heel. "Come, on. I'll take you to the dungeon."

Francesca followed him back down the stairs across the ballroom and to the elevator. They rode to the basement in absolute silence but she wore a thoughtful expression on her face. He wished he knew her thoughts.

On the nights they were open, one of his security team, Josh, would have greeted them as soon as they stepped off the elevator. Gabe rarely came down here on the quiet nights, because, well, it was kind of creepy being down in the basement all alone. Though tonight he wasn't all alone. And it wasn't eerie at all. In fact, it was rather…private.

"So this is The Vault?"

He glanced back at Frankie who had wandered into the old wine cellar while he'd been getting the key from its storage spot in the podium next to the door.

After inserting the key into the appropriate keyhole, he reached behind the podium and felt around for a second before he found and pressed the button that opened the pocket door. "No, *this* is The Vault." He stepped back and motioned to Frankie.

She moved past him, her steps cautious as she crossed the door frame and entered the namesake of his club. "Holy shit."

He chuckled.

"Is this what a real live dungeon looks like?"

"I personally prefer calling it by its name or simply referring to it as 'playroom.' Like I said, I'm not into the hard-core stuff, Francesca, so I'm sure there's plenty of equipment you'd find in a dungeon that won't be in mine." He made a mental note to never show her Kyle's personal playroom.

"Looks like you've got quite the collection though. What is all of this?" She wandered further into the room, pausing at the first station she came to, a table usually used for wax play. A favorite for Jamie, one of the Doms.

"Everything down here is for giving and receiving pleasure. It's for people to experience sensations and emotions they might not reach during normal interactions. It's the tools that only those with complete trust in their partner should be using."

She'd watched him while he spoke, her gaze pinned to his face, darting back and forth between his lips and his eyes. He saw the pulse in her neck flutter and her pupils enlarge. Every now and then her jaw dropped open as she scanned the room, and it looked like she was talking to herself. He'd love to hear the play-by-play happening inside her head.

Giving her the lead, Gabe trailed behind as she roamed, pausing to point out a swing, two St. Andrews crosses, and a stockade—a new addition at Deacon's request. She stopped near one of the spanking benches.

"That looks like something I'd see in gym. A weight bench of some sort," she said.

"Similar idea." He settled on the bench to demonstrate. "One person leans over the bench like this and then they are in the perfect position for the other person to spank them." Gabe returned to an upright position. "This is a basic bench.

We have a couple of more elaborate ones that include cuffs."

"Huh. And people go for that? It surprises me. I'm not judging, but I'm just not sure why somebody would want to let another person do that to them. Why would they want to give away their control?"

"Because it feels good."

"How? I don't understand. Letting somebody else take the lead is either a sign of weakness, or that person is simply a team player and has no interest in leading the team." The look on her face clearly conveyed her confusion.

"Quite the opposite actually," Gabe told her. "The person who gives away control is far from weak. It takes great strength to trust another individual with the responsibility of your pleasure. Or pain. On the flip side, that other person has to trust that you'll let them know your likes and dislikes, and more importantly, when they've gone too far. They need to trust that you'll say stop when you truly need them to stop."

"I..."

He stood and took her two hands in his. Gabe dipped his head so they were at eye level. "Francesca, you've had to take care of your sister from a very young age. You took care of your father when he fell ill. You take care of the business he worked hard to establish, which includes taking care of his employees. Sometimes, don't you want to let go and let somebody take care of you?"

He paused and watched as her pupils dilated and she licked her lips. Lips he wanted to taste but wasn't sure she was ready to go to that level of intimacy with him yet. Instead he focused on her current need.

"When you're with me, Francesca, you're safe. You can hand over the reins. You can put yourself in my hands. I promise, I won't let you get hurt. Let me take care of your pleasure. Let me make you feel like every woman should be made to feel."

She blinked. "And what's that?"

"Sexy. Beautiful. Adored."

She gulped. He could see she struggled with making the decision.

"Want to give it a try, Francesca?"

# CHAPTER TWELVE

FRANKIE STARED AT HIM, HER JAW HANGING OPEN. He placed a finger beneath her chin and closed her mouth. "You can trust me, Francesca."

She ran her tongue over her lips, moistening them, then she swallowed. "Um…"

"I know what I'm doing."

God, that deep, sexy voice of his did funny things to all kinds of places on her body. Areas she'd never really felt so alive in before.

"I don't know," she whispered. She was terrified. Crazy though it might be, not of what might happen. Her "I'm not into this" meter had already begun shifting to the opposite side. The danger was in how easily she could get in over her head with this man.

She was so fucking turned-on right now, she couldn't breathe. A few well-chosen words and he'd nailed it. After years of having to be the strong one—the big sister, the stand-in mom, the dutiful daughter, the caregiver, and now the employer—people came to her with their problems and she fixed them. Quite literally in many cases. Was it so wrong to want a reprieve from that? A short escape, a brief interlude where somebody else ran the show for a little while. Where she allowed somebody else to make the decisions and she just had to go along for the ride?

Frankie focused on Gabe again. When she'd turned around and saw him stalking her across the dance floor, rolling up his sleeves to bare his muscular forearms, she'd almost done a girly thing she wasn't even sure was possible. She almost swooned for fuck's sake. Who the hell swooned outside of damsels in distress? That alone indicated she needed to do something. Or she needed serious help.

Maybe a short fling with somebody like him was exactly what she needed to get herself back on track. She was a strong, professional female after all. She could have a brief affair, regroup, find the ass trying to shut her down, and then everything could get back to normal.

"I'll help you," he returned, his voice as low as hers. He held out his hand.

So tempting. So easy to take it. She bit her lip. "What did I tell you about that, Francesca?" He gave her a sidelong look.

She released her lip with a soft *pop*.

His nostrils flared.

Her heart hammered, and her breasts felt heavy. She'd be embarrassed if he discovered her damp panties.

Her hand trembled as she placed her sweaty palm in his, her breathing hitched in her throat and she caught herself just in time from biting down on her bottom lip again. She'd never done anything remotely like this. Sex with John had been, well, sex. Mediocre at best, she couldn't recall ever being overwhelmed by his scent, his eyes, his smile, or the tone of his voice. And she'd known him for years.

She would give this a shot. Couldn't hurt. Well, yes, it could. After all, it would be her butt wearing his mark. At the thought of that, she practiced her Kegels and stifled a groan.

"That's a good girl. Now, first we need to talk. Here." Instead of having her sit on that spanking bench, he led her over to two chairs that leaned against the wall.

She was really going to do this. She was going to let this man, a man she barely knew, spank her like a naughty child. Something that, according to Gabe, many women liked.

"Francesca, you with me?" He sat down and glanced up at her.

"Yeah." She took the chair next to him and tried again with more strength and conviction. "Yes."

He watched her carefully. "Good. Now, before any sort of play it's always a good thing to discuss expectations. What are your limits?"

"Limits?"

"Yes." Gabe the security consultant took a backseat and the owner of a sex club took his place. "Communication is one of the most important aspects of indulging in aspects of the lifestyle, regardless of how little or extreme the involvement," he explained. "If people are going to play at my club, I insist open and honest conversation occurs between all players. Those in dominant positions must be aware of what is and what is not acceptable to the person or persons they play with." He paused. "I don't insist on formal contracts of any kind as they aren't legally enforceable, but many couples have them. For some they prove useful as a visual aid and provide a level of comfort. We need to discuss what you're willing to experience and what you're not."

This was the getting in over her head part. She felt like a diver on the edge of the board ready to take the plunge. And it was a long freaking way down. She took a deep breath. "Give me an example."

"Whips," he stated.

"Fuck no."

He grinned, his eyes sparkling. "Flogger."

She hesitated. "Maybe. I'd have to see one and try it first."

"We can do that," he conceded. "Paddle."

She found it interesting how everything he suggested was not stated as a question. "Nope, would feel too much like getting a spanking from my father."

He raised his brows. "Your father paddled you?"

"No, but he used it as a threat when my sister or I misbehaved. We knew he'd never follow through, but the very idea that we'd do something horrible that he might feel the need to, scared the bejesus out of us."

"What about a spanking by my hand?" He'd relaxed and now his eyes glowed with excitement at the prospect.

This was the one he wanted to try. What would it feel like to lie across his lap? To feel the sting of his palm as it made contact with her ass. She cocked her head as she considered it. "I'll try it. Though I've got to admit, it sounds very school-girlish." She grinned naughtily. She could tell by the wicked gleam in his eyes that Gabe now pictured her in a short, pleated skirt, a white blouse, and Baby Jane shoes with knee-high white socks.

"How about hot wax?" he asked.

"Does it hurt?"

"Not as much as you're probably thinking, and if it's done properly, it's only a little hot. But it makes you hotter."

That didn't sound too bad. She nodded. "I'm game."

This time Gabe hesitated for a long moment. "Public play?" he asked quietly.

Here she truly wavered and took another significant breath. "To be perfectly honest, I don't know how I feel about that. I don't like people seeing me vulnerable. All my life I've tried to be one of the guys. I can't let my guard down at work, or they'll think I'm just a woman trying to do a man's job."

Gabe reached up and trailed two fingers down the side of her face.

She worked hard not to lean into his touch.

"First of all, nobody here will ever judge you," he assured her softly. "I'm asking you to trust me enough to let your guard down, Francesca. But nobody else needs to see that happen if you don't want them to."

Relief soared through her. "Thank you. Then my answer is not yet. I'm not ready for that."

"Fair enough." He dropped his hand to his thigh, reverting

back to Mr. Dominant. "Just to be clear, I'm not into edge play, and don't allow it at my club, so other than bondage, swings, spreader bars, dildos, and butt plugs, we've covered the main events."

Her jaw dropped open and he laughed at she assumed what must be a look of horror in her eyes. "What the hell is a spreader bar and, ah...butt plugs?"

He stopped chuckling and smiled. "Those are the only two things you're questioning?"

"Don't get me wrong, the idea of being bound, blindfolded, or strapped to something doesn't make me jump for joy, but they're things I think I can adjust to, at least once." She felt her cheeks burn. "I've never, um, had, ah, anything in my... um..." She dropped her head, avoiding his gaze with every stuttering word. Her neck and cheeks flamed.

Gabe placed a finger under her chin and tipped her face back up to eye level.

She was beginning to like when he did that.

"I know we don't know each other that well, but I'd never hurt you. I hope you at least know that?"

She nodded.

"Anything we do together that's new to you, but you're willing to try, we'll go very slow and it will be as pleasurable as I'm capable of making it. I give you my word."

She gulped.

"We also need to discuss your safe word."

"I've heard of those."

"Unless you want to use a specific word, at the club we generally use red. Think of a stop light. Green is full steam ahead. Yellow is slow down, assess the situation and proceed with caution. Red is immediate stop."

"Every time?"

"Every single time. No questions asked. Then we talk about it."

"Will you try to change my mind?"

He turned serious. "I'd want to understand what caused you to use your safe word. I'd want to put your fears to rest, ensure I didn't hurt you in some way unintentionally. But no, Francesca. I'd never force to you do something you truly didn't want to do."

That relief she felt earlier was spreading and becoming a pool for her to dive into.

Gabe removed his hand from her chin. "I want to earn your trust, Francesca. I have no intention of putting you into a position where you question that."

He waited while she considered his promise.

"I want to trust you, too," she said. "Other than that edge play stuff you mentioned, and whips, which frankly scare the crap out of me, I'm open, I think, to everything else. As least to try things once. As long as we can stop—"

"At any time, Francesca. You simply say the word."

"Rebar," she said without thought.

"Rebar?"

"Yes, rebar works for me."

"Does it have some sort of significance?" he asked, his brows pulled low in amused confusion.

She shook her head. "Nope. Just the first word that came to mind."

"Rebar it is, then."

She clapped a hand over her mouth to suppress the giggle that wanted to escape.

"Are you OK?"

She nodded. Nervous. Scared shitless. And apparently, giddy.

He gave her an odd look. "For tonight we will keep it simple." He settled his body comfortably in his chair, no longer angled to face her. "Stand up, Francesca, turn and face me."

She hesitated.

"Generally, a Dom will not tolerate insubordination."

She glared at him and he just snorted in laughter.

"I'm giving you a free pass tonight. But my patience is not unlimited. For every time you don't do as I say, I'll add one additional spank to the ten I plan to give you." He paused, she assumed to allow the warning to sink in. "Now. Stand up, turn and face me."

She did as he asked.

"Remove your dress."

She looked up at him. "But—"

"Remove your dress, Francesca, but keep everything else on."

She took a step backward and reached behind her neck, fumbling for a moment before she located the tab of the zipper. "Will anybody—"

"Nobody is here."

Nerves congealed in the pit of her stomach. "Gabe, maybe this wasn't—"

"Do you want to stop? All you need to do is say the safe word, Francesca. Say the word and we stop and I'll take you home. No harm, no foul. No bad feelings." He sat there waiting for her to make her decision.

She nodded her head once, and continued, bringing her arms back to the front of her body and tugging the shoulders of the dress down far enough to allow gravity to take over. Other than a brief pause when she needed to get it past her breasts, the black sheath slid down her body and puddled on the floor around her bare feet. She stepped out and stood there, hands fisted at her sides.

He sucked in a breath, the air hissing between his clenched teeth. "I've never seen a woman as beautiful as you, Francesca."

A warm glow replaced that lump of nerves. Frankie realized that was the first time somebody other than her father had called her beautiful. She could do this.

She stood before him in only a wet, lacy black thong and matching bra, thankful now for her sister's gift. It pushed her breasts up and together. The way his eyes zeroed in on her chest area, she gathered he approved. She trembled under the heat of his gaze.

"Come here."

With barely a second's hesitation, she stepped forward. Was she supposed to just turn around and present her ass to him? Lean on her elbows on the opposite chair? Get down on all fours?

He raised one hand. She took it and he tugged, urging her closer. "Lay down over my lap."

Her nose scrunched up. "This feels very strange, Gabe. I'm not sure—"

"Francesca, trust me."

The question was, would her dive be flawless, or a belly flop?

# CHAPTER THIRTEEN

With a sigh of pure determination, she settled herself over his lap.

And felt like an idiot. God this was embarrassing.

He'd aroused her at the restaurant, and again upstairs in the ballroom. So much so, that she had decided to throw caution to the wind and be spontaneous and adventurous. Sophie would be proud.

Judging by the erection pressing against her belly, he'd been just as affected. He had to be uncomfortable as hell in his pants. At least he wasn't wearing denim.

Gabe's breathing sounded heavy in her ear.

The whole situation made her fingers and toes tingle. Though that could be from the position she was in. She wiggled her bottom and he groaned. She smiled. Hmm, maybe she could have some fun with this. No reason she should be the only one uncomfortable.

Gabe laid his hand on the lower half of her leg.

She jumped.

He stroked up the back of her leg.

She jerked as though electrocuted.

"Take it easy, Francesca. Relax."

Easy for him to say. He wasn't the one with his ass bared and on display for a thankfully empty club to witness.

He smoothed his palm over the cheek of her ass, his fingers scraping over the lace of her thong bisecting each globe.

She wiggled. Did he just moan?

He ran his hand up her spine, feeling each vertebrae, each dimple in her skin.

Yes, that was a definite moan. The only question now however, did it come from him or from her?

He lifted his hand away.

She held her breath.

Then he brought it down with a slap on the cheek closest to him.

She jumped, but it was more from surprise than anything. He'd put no effort into it. Is that all this was? Light taps that startled more than stung? When she didn't receive another, she settled more comfortably on his lap.

Then he slapped her again on the opposite side, but not any harder.

She jerked again, but managed to calm a little quicker.

Gabe rubbed the two spots before placing the next set of taps slightly lower and marginally sharper.

This time, with each impact she gasped. He paused, but she didn't ask him to stop. Why didn't she ask him to stop?

The sounds of his hand hitting her backside echoed throughout the basement. She'd almost forgotten they were alone. Thankfully she didn't have to worry about other club members discovering them.

"That's four, Francesca." His voice sounded hoarse.

Gabe rubbed his hand over her rear end, apparently enjoying the feeling of her skin under his. Frankie certainly enjoyed his hands on her. With each touch, the sensations running rampant through her intensified. And her arousal grew.

The next set of strikes were harder but still not painful.

She shifted on her belly, trying to find a more comfortable position.

"Six. Your ass is becoming a stunning shade of red. I can already see the mark of my hand. You heat up so beautifully." The next two landed on her upper thigh just beneath the curve of her cheek.

"Ah." She groaned. When he'd said ten, she'd expected them

to be in succession and take about two minutes. Instead, Gabe took his time. Between sets, he touched her everywhere. Her legs, her back, her neck, even the lobes of her ears. He danced his fingertips up and down her spine. He tickled the divot behind one knee.

He smacked her again and then rubbed her behind, removing the sting. She started to feel warm.

But he had yet to touch the one place she wanted him to.

Gabe smoothed his hand over the same spot again and again. When his fingers roamed lower, she tensed. He grazed the edge of her thong, so close to her center. Her hot, wet center. He stilled.

She closed her eyes and held her breath, hoping, hoping…

Suddenly his fingers were sliding into the crevice between her thighs.

Frankie opened her eyes, scared to move an inch lest he stop. God she needed him to touch her.

He slipped two fingers beneath the fabric of her thong and traced the length of her sex.

Oh God. Frankie swallowed. She heard him do the same.

With tantalizing slowness, he rubbed up and down until she began to squirm, then he pushed one finger deep, thrusting in and out at a speed a turtle could challenge. When she started to pant, he added a second finger, pumping, fucking her with a steady rhythm. He never touched her clit. She wanted him to touch her clit.

"Gabe…"

"Not yet, Francesca. Hold on."

"I can't."

She grabbed fistfuls of his pants and hung on. She bowed her back as much as she could, pushing her ass higher. She shuddered with each penetration.

His own breathing grew labored as he inched her closer to orgasm. "Yes. You can."

He slowed his thrusts, grew almost lazy.

She whimpered. She couldn't hold out much longer. Her body felt tight, like an elastic stretched past its capacity. She slumped over his knees, each breath she drew sawing in and out of her lungs. She had one hand planted flat on the floor, and the other gripped his lower leg, probably leaving marks where she dug in with what nails she had. Her toes barely skimmed the floor.

Gabe dragged his fingers out and pushed them in a few more times, but still avoided her clit. Then he increased the speed in gradual increments until he was driving deep.

She gulped in air between moans. "Please," she cried out.

"Now, Francesca. You can come now."

"But..."

Gabe pumped two fingers hard into her pussy. Then, finally, his thumb passed over her clit.

She jerked.

He did it again.

"Oh, God." Suddenly she exploded. She screamed out loud, her cry echoing throughout the empty room, her body rigid as she rode the wave of her climax, shaking on his lap, sweat dripping down her face. She sucked in great gulps of air. What the fuck just happened?

Gabe gently smoothed one hand down her back, along the length of her spine, and then cupped her between the legs.

Her flesh throbbed against the palm of his hand. Damn.

Finally, her breathing slowed as it returned to near normal. With a deeply drawn and shuddering sigh, she drooped and then went stiff again.

His erection still pressed into her stomach.

She lay still for a few moments while he stroked her hair. When she began to get uncomfortable, she shifted. "Can I get up now?"

"Of course." He helped her to stand, holding one of her

hands when she stumbled on rubbery legs. "Easy."

She turned, looking to the floor. She couldn't look at him. "Um, my dress. I need to...ah...get dressed. And my shoes are upstairs."

"I'll help, and we'll get them on the way out."

He rose, but she yanked her hand free and back stepped. "No. I'm fine. Thanks." Embarrassment filled her. She'd been so wet for him. So embarrassingly turned-on by the idea of him spanking her. And then she'd come so fast and so hard. How could that be? Good girls didn't do that. But she'd never been a girl. Did that make it all right?

Frankie spun in a circle, almost tripped in her haste, but managed to right herself before he needed to catch her. She spotted her dress on the floor and bent to snag it. Keeping some distance from him, she quickly stepped into it, pulling the material into place and managing to zip it up after about the fifth attempt. Her hands shook like an addict.

"Francesca."

"I think it's time for me to go home. I can grab a cab."

"I'll take you home."

"That's not—"

"It *is* necessary."

She smashed her lips together and nodded her head once, the movement short and jerky. Her gaze roamed the room, looking everywhere and nowhere and certainly not at him. She still couldn't look at him. It wasn't his fault. He'd told her what to expect. He'd given her an out. More than one actually. But curiosity had gotten the best of her.

He watched her. He knew.

She was mortified. And she didn't want to make him angry. She needed time to calm down, get her emotions in check, and reflect on what happened.

Gabe motioned for her to lead the way and then he followed as she practically ran from the room.

She huddled in the corner of the elevator. He maintained a safe distance. He didn't say a word, but she felt the weight of his gaze, the strength of his concern.

She hurried out as soon as the doors opened. She'd forgotten the direction and turned toward security before she realized her mistake and spun on a heel, beelining to the front door.

"Frankie," he called after her. "Please, calm down. I need to grab your shoes first and then we'll talk."

Ignoring him, she yanked open the door and lunged outside, desperate for fresh air. She hurried as quickly as she could in her bare feet down the few stairs and over to the car. That's where he caught up to her. But he didn't rush. He remained calm where she felt like a deer trapped by a pack of wolves.

Gabe handed her the shoes and took a step away from her. After simply staring at her for a long moment, one that felt like forever, he opened the car door for her, waiting patiently until she climbed in.

Trapped inside after he joined her, he reclined on his side of the car. But he didn't starting the Porsche. "Francesca, there's nothing to be ashamed about."

"I've never done that before."

"Have an orgasm?"

She closed her eyes and huffed. He wanted her to say it. Fine. "Let somebody spank me."

"I know that. That's what tonight was about. And you didn't let just *any* man spank you, Francesca. You let *me* spank you. I'm very proud of you."

She raised her head. Thank God there was no exterior lighting illuminating the interior of the car. "Proud? Gabe, how can you be proud? I just laid across your lap like a naughty child arching my ass into each slap and I came all over your pants." She ended the rehash with a whimper, but not before her gaze darted to his lap and imagined the stain in the dark interior.

"Yes, you did. And I loved it. Thank you."

She closed her eyes and turned her head toward the window. "I'm not sure how I feel about it."

"Let me ask you this. Did you enjoy it?"

She hesitated but nodded. Embarrassing as it was, it was the truth.

"Then there's no shame in it. We are two consenting adults. We talked about it first. You had complete control, Francesca."

Had she? She'd never felt so out of control. She forced herself to recline into the leather seat. "I'd like to go home now, please."

Gabe stared at her for a long moment. A good ten seconds.

She concentrated on the hem of her dress.

"Of course." Gabe started the car and drove her home.

They didn't say a word the entire trip. For each of the forty-five minutes it took them to reach her farm, she rehashed the evening in her head, remembered the excitement that had coursed through her during dinner and again when he'd given her the tour of the club. And she realized she'd made a huge mistake. Not in going out with him or even for going to The Vault and allowing him to do what he did.

No. Her mistake was in her reaction afterward. She was no longer embarrassed over her reaction to the spanking. She was, however, ashamed that she'd run the way she had and probably left him thinking he'd done something wrong. Or worse, that she'd hated it.

But the truth was, she'd enjoyed every touch, every emotion his hands on her body evoked. She'd never experienced an orgasm like that before, and they hadn't even had sex.

When he pulled up to the curb, he didn't immediately exit the car, though he killed the engine. They sat in the dark for five solid minutes, neither saying a word nor making a move to leave the vehicle.

"I'm sorry, Francesca."

She closed her eyes and dropped her chin. Not for the first time tonight, she felt like an idiot. "There's nothing to be sorry for, Gabe. I should be apologizing to you for my freak-out moment."

He kept his gaze forward. "Would you be interested in seeing the club on a regular night?"

She jerked her head around to look at him. Did he expect her to have sex in front of other people? She didn't think she could go that far, but she might be willing to go back there with him. If for no other reason than to show him she wasn't a complete lunatic. "You want to do…what we did tonight? With other people around?"

"No."

A wave of relief washed over her. And oddly enough, a sense of disappointment. What the hell?

He shifted in his seat until he faced her. "I just thought you might like to see it in action. That's all."

That she could do. It was something she'd never done before and probably wouldn't again. Since she'd be with Gabe, it would be fine, and she could chalk it up to another experience her sister would be jealous of. And she'd never have another opportunity once his job with her was completed.

"OK."

The shock in his eyes indicated his surprise at her response. After the way she'd freaked out and run, she couldn't blame him.

"Good. I'll pick you up a week from Friday evening. It won't be quite as busy as Saturday."

She shook her head. This time she wanted to have a bit more control. "I'd rather meet you there. What time should I arrive and what should I wear?"

He gave her a stern look. "I'd prefer to pick you up."

"I'd like to drive myself."

He narrowed his eyes but ultimately nodded. "If you plan to

arrive for nine, I'll be waiting for you. Dress for a night out, dancing. Look as beautiful and as sexy as you'd like."

"Comfort?" she asked, and metaphorically crossed her fingers that jeans and boots were considered comfortable attire.

He chuckled. "No work books. And we don't allow jeans or runners."

"So I *have* to wear heels?"

Gabe caressed her legs with his gaze. "You rock a pair of heels, Francesca."

She glanced down at her shoes. "Time to come clean." She raised one delicate foot. "These aren't mine." She pointed to her dress. "Neither is this."

She dropped both hands into her lap and looked down. "I've only worn one dress, Gabe, and it was for my dad's funeral." She'd never felt so vulnerable before. "Actually, make that two. I'm sure I wore one to my mom's funeral."

Gabe reached for her hand. He held her fingers, rubbing his thumb over her knuckles. "You never mentioned what happened to her."

Frankie shrugged. She didn't feel anything about it anymore. Not like she did about her dad. "She had a tumor on her brain nobody knew about. It ruptured while she gave birth to Sophie. If it hadn't have happened then, it would have happened at some other time. Maybe while she was driving a car or cooking dinner."

He squeezed her hand. "I'm sorry."

"It was long time ago."

He tipped his head, trying to look her in the eye, but she continued to evade him. He reached out, rubbed one finger against her chin, and turned her face toward him. "You look stunning in your sister's dress and shoes. Check out what else she had in her closet and pick something for Friday."

"Are you sure you want to take me back there?" she asked,

surprised he wasn't already racing away from her as fast as his high-performance car could go.

"Positive." The word almost jumped from his mouth before she finished her question.

"OK. I'll be there next Friday at nine."

Gabe climbed out of the car and hurried around to open her door.

She could get used to this.

He helped her step out of the Porsche and then managed to keep hold of her hand as he walked her up to the front porch of the old farmhouse.

She liked that he wanted to touch her.

At the door he stopped. "About your issue at work. We'll get the cameras installed tomorrow. We'll make them discreet and only my guys and you will know where they're located. Don't tell anybody, not even your sister. We'll see if we can catch whoever is behind this the next time they decide to pay you a visit."

She nodded her head. "That sounds like a good idea."

"Great. I'll call you tomorrow and let you know when you can expect the team to arrive. Arrange to be here when they do the installation so they can show you how everything works." Gabe stepped closer and gripped her elbows. He leaned down, keeping eye contact with her. He paused at the last second, obviously to give her any opportunity she needed to escape.

She appreciated the offer, but didn't take it.

Gabe pressed his lips to hers.

She opened her mouth and let him in.

Wrapping his arms around her waist, he pulled her close as he dipped his tongue inside and rubbed it along hers.

She groaned into his mouth and melted against his chest.

He deepened the kiss for too brief a moment, and then he was gone, leaving her cold and missing him already.

"Good night, Francesca."

"Night."

He didn't say anything more, but he waited for her to unlock her door and go inside. He waited while she locked the door. Only then did he return to his car.

She knew because she didn't move from the door until she heard his close and him drive away. Frankie flipped out the porch light, locked the door, and turned. Bracing her back to the door, she slid down until she landed with a not so ladylike thump on the floor.

She didn't need a distraction like Gabe McBride in her life. She had a company to run, a sister to look out for, and an asshole to find.

But she realized she wanted a distraction like Gabe McBride in her life. Men like him didn't normally go for women like her. Men like him, men physically bigger than her, usually thought she needed protection from all the evil in the world.

Surrounded by men all day every day, listening to them fight, joke—the cruder the better—use profanity as an adjective, fart, mock her intelligence, height, or the fact she had boobs—admittedly, wore thin after a while.

Since she was a little girl, there'd been times she just wanted to be treated like a female. But to do her job, to be taken seriously, she had to be Frankie, not Francesca.

Gabe made her feel feminine. He called her beautiful.

Would it really be so bad to let somebody like him be the boss every now and again?

## CHAPTER FOURTEEN

"SOMEBODY GOT IN LATE LAST NIGHT."

Frankie ignored her sister's singsong declaration of the obvious and instead swallowed another gulp of strong-smelling coffee, burning the roof of her mouth in the process. She winced, coughed, and spun around to the sink, her eyes watering, the inside of her mouth probably blistering.

"Must have been a good date," Sophie fished, but Frankie wasn't about to be reeled in. "Or, maybe considering you came home at all means it *didn't* go well."

"Listen, I need to get to one of the job sites. You have a good day, OK." Frankie tried to brush past her sister. But the imp was too fast and blocked her path out of the kitchen. God, she hated that her baby sister was taller than her.

"You didn't answer me. Good or bad?" Sophie quirked her perfectly arched eyebrows, cocked one hip out, and crossed her arms over her chest. "Simple question."

"You're behaving like a child."

"And you're avoiding."

"It was…fine." Frankie hoped that satisfied her nosy sister and tried to step around her for a second time.

Sophie shifted, blocking again. "Just fine?"

Actually, it was pretty fucking amazing, but she wasn't ready to admit that just yet. She still couldn't believe he'd aroused her with just a few words at the restaurant. Lord knows she wouldn't have objected if he'd spread her across the table and finished the promises his eyes had dished out.

And those rooms at the club. She wanted to visit those

again. Yeah, for all the freaking out she did last night, once she'd had some alone time to think, which she spent hours doing, she couldn't deny the fact the whole thing teased her senses. She'd had so many questions, but not the courage to ask them. At the time, she'd been too fearful he'd offer live demos. Maybe she was more scared he wouldn't.

As he'd explained the use of some of the equipment, for the first time in her life, a whole set of possibilities flashed through her mind. She'd shocked herself. She never knew she had a potential kinky side.

Her father would have been horrified. Her sister would probably be intrigued and encourage her endlessly. Hell, Sophie would demand to tag along and insist they go on a shopping spree first. Frankie most feared her colleagues finding out or worse, the guys working for her. They harassed her enough as it was, even once offering to buy her a pink hard hat and high-heeled work boots.

Frankie faced her sister. She needed to tell her something, otherwise she wouldn't let it go, but she couldn't look her in the eye. "It was good. We had a nice dinner and then he showed me around the club him and his brothers own."

Of course the mention of a club perked Sophie up. "He owns a club? Cool. What club?"

Damn. Frankie rolled her eyes. Sophie would nag until she got an answer that satisfied her. Might as well bite the bullet sooner rather than later. "The Vault."

Sophie's jaw dropped open, and her arms fell to hang at her side.

Frankie had never seen her speechless before.

"Are you kidding me? Please tell me that's a joke." Sophie threw up a hand. "No, wait. Don't tell me it's a joke." She leaned forward, hands tucked between her jean-covered knees, eyes gleaming, and stage-whispered. "Do you know what kind of club that is?"

"Yes," she responded in kind. Frankie straightened, taking an authoritative stance with her younger sister. "Actually, I think I'm more concerned with the fact that *you* seem to know what kind of club it is." Frankie placed one hand on her hip and angled her head, peering at Sophie from the corner of her eye. "How do you know about The Vault?" She jerked upright. "Wait. Have you been there?" Frankie didn't know whether to choke, cry, or laugh. Wouldn't that be the freakin' icing on the cake? Her baby sister at a place like The Vault and being more attuned to men like Gabe McBride than she was.

"Don't give me the 'mom' look. I'm old enough to be very aware of what clubs are in town."

Really? Frankie couldn't name a single one off the top of her head *other* than The Vault. What did that say about her?

"Frankie, I don't know much, honest," Sophie continued after a moment. "But I do know that The Vault is not a generic dance club. It's not a bar. And people can't just walk in off the street. Word on the street is that you must have a membership and to get one, people are typically invited by the owners." She clapped her hands. "And now you're telling me your security guy is one of the owners."

She giggled, sounding like the sweet little girl who used to beg Frankie to play dolls with her. But Frankie only ever knew how to play with trucks.

"How cool is that!"

Frankie couldn't argue. But that was beside the point.

Sophie's eyes lit up like lasers and she leaned even closer. "So tell me, what's it like? Are the rumors true? Is there really a dungeon? Tell me *everything*."

Relief flooded Frankie. Sophie didn't know as much as she'd let on. This she could manage. She'd signed a non-disclosure agreement. Frankie understood contracts and respected their intent. She couldn't, wouldn't give out any details.

"Sorry, Soph. I have to get to work."

"Oh, come on," she whined. "At least tell me where it is. People speak of it, but they never say where the place is."

"I have to go. I need to make sure the crew at the restaurant is back on schedule." Frankie scooted past Sophie and ran up the stairs to her bedroom. She ignored her sister's grumbling, something she had years of practice doing.

Frankie finished getting ready for work and then headed over to the construction trailer. As she passed the barn, she slowed her steps. She hoped Gabe's plan to install new cameras worked. She'd already put in a call to change the locks and she'd talk with Randy today about not giving out the key.

She needed to find out who wanted her out of business so bad they'd resort to damaging her property. She never hurt anybody. She played fair in the bidding process. She never undercut a job just to win. She made money and lost money on jobs just like any other contractor. She only bid on work that was within her capacity to deliver. She wasn't going for the big projects.

So who had she pissed off?

* * *

Gabe sat with his brothers in the conference room of their security office. They'd spent the morning going through some of the old cameras to see if anything was useable. No luck there. They were now viewing recordings from the newly installed cameras to ensure everything was working as it should.

They'd placed two new devices in the trailer and four in the barn. Since they were only just installed, so far all they'd managed to capture were men from her crew coming and going, picking up material or vehicles, and then returning them at the end of day. The most frequent visitor was her foreman, which made sense, especially since the locks had been changed and fewer people had immediate access.

During the week they'd been monitoring the place, Sophie never once stepped foot within the barn or the trailer, but Francesca had told him her sister had no interest in the business her father had built. Each time Frankie passed by one of the cameras, Gabe's cock twitched at the sight of her ass swishing back and forth in those snug jeans.

They'd only had the one evening together, and he'd gone home hard as nails. Since that night, they'd only had a couple encounters, and both had been strictly business. He ached to get some alone time with her and couldn't wait until their scheduled visit to the club tonight. All week long she'd been on his mind, something few women could lay claim too. He'd been so distracted during Sunday dinner at his mother's house that she'd finally kicked him out, thinking work occupied his brain.

Gabe checked the time on his watch. He'd be heading home soon, and it would only be a few hours until Francesca arrived at the club.

"Wait, stop there," Kyle said. "No, back up a few screens."

Gabe jerked to attention at Kyle's instructions.

Kade hit reverse and they watched a blond guy walk up to the barn and look around before slipping inside.

Kyle turned to him. "Do you recognize him?"

"That's John Darwin. He's one of the men who works for Francesca." Gabe remembered his name and picture from the employee list Frankie sent over on that first day. He'd already been through the list multiple times and had memorized all of them. Especially her ex-boyfriend's.

"Whatever he's doing, he doesn't want to be noticed." Kade reversed the video and replayed it again.

"What's the date stamp?" Gabe asked.

Kyle checked. "Monday."

"Francesca never mentioned anything happening earlier this week, so I assume it's nothing."

"Maybe he's just the nervous type, but it's probably worth checking out anyway." Kyle made a note on the pad in front of him.

Gabe pulled his phone from his pocket and keyed in Frankie's number. When she didn't answer, he left a message for her to return his call. "Rewind it, Kade." They looked at the footage a second time.

"He's not carrying anything going in or out. And he wasn't in there very long," Kade observed.

"No, but it's obvious he doesn't want anybody to see him going in or out of that barn." Until they ruled the guy out, as far as Gabe was concerned, he was a suspect. "Put surveillance on him. Let's see what his habits are. I'd rather not worry Francesca until we have something solid."

"We can at least have a chat with the dude and find out what he was up to that made him look so suspicious," Kyle said.

Gabe agreed, giving a tight nod. "Do that. And send a copy of the picture to my phone."

Gabe thought they were done, but now his brothers swiveled around in their chairs to face him. Or rather, gang up on him. It reminded him of when they were younger and they'd join forces, thinking the twin approach would be enough to overtake their older brother.

They'd been wrong then. They were wrong now.

Gabe settled back in his chair, propped his right boot up on his left knee, crossed his arms, and waited for the inquisition to begin.

"How is Ms. Stevens, Gabe?" Kyle started.

His expression was innocent enough, and the question most certainly was. But the objective behind it was anything but. They'd both been anxious to meet her. They'd get their chance tonight. Gabe shrugged. "Last I spoke with her, she was fine. Why?" He knew damn well why.

"Just wondering, big brother," Kyle continued. "You've been

so involved in this particular case, we sort of thought you'd have a day-by-day account of her well-being by now."

Gabe raised one eyebrow.

"Have you seen her much this week?" Kade asked.

"Nope."

"Have you talked to her?" Kyle inquired.

"Yep." Every day he found an excuse or three to listen to her sexy voice on the phone.

"Have you seen her today?" Kade continued.

"Nope." Not yet anyway.

"Are we going to get more than one-word answers out of you?" Kade asked this time, his face split into a knowing grin.

"Depends."

They both laughed. "On what?" Kyle asked.

"On whether I think you need to know more."

They both sighed in identical huffs of annoyance.

Gabe grinned.

"I drove by the club one night last week and saw your car there," Kyle pointed out.

"I live there."

"Yes, but I also saw a few lights on in the main house. Your home was dark by the way, and your car was *not* parked in front of it."

"Ah, so you didn't just drive by. You actually drove up to the house." At least his brother had the good sense to not come looking for him.

"Was Francesca with you?" Kade asked, the suspicious gleam in his eyes piercing.

His brothers wanted answers. And he couldn't really blame them. It had been a long time since he'd gone on a date of any kind. Or even shown this level of interest in a woman. Most of his "dates" over the past few years had been more of the one-night-stand variety, and rarely did they end on a sexual note. He'd done more dinner and movie outings as an adult than he ever did as a teenager. "And if I were to say yes?"

They leaned forward. Individually, his baby brothers could be intimidating. As a pair, they overwhelmed some people. "We're only concerned for you, Gabe," Kade said. "But if you're interested in her, I say good for you. It's about time."

"Are you going to bring her to the club?" Kyle asked.

Gabe nodded. "Tonight."

"Good. If she's going to be part of your life, she needs to be able to accept that part of you," Kyle stated.

Although Kyle was jumping the gun a bit, Gabe felt reasonably certain Frankie wouldn't have a problem with the club. Although her flight instinct had kicked in there at the end, she'd seemed curious by what he'd shown her, and her body's response certainly indicated she'd enjoyed what they'd done that night. Maybe she was concerned about her reputation and any negative exposure. Gabe would do everything possible to ensure that didn't happen.

"I have to say, bro, I'm a little surprised. She's not really your type." Kyle tossed that one across the table, raising Gabe's ire.

That was the crux of it. She was the complete opposite of the women he typically dated. But he couldn't keep away from her. He'd done his best to avoid seeing her this past week, afraid he'd have too hard a time keeping his hands off her. Two in-person visits and daily phone calls were the best he could manage. In between those, he'd forcibly stopped himself from jumping in his car and heading to one of her job sites every day. Something about her drew him like a magnet.

Maybe it was the feisty owner of the construction company.

Maybe it was the pretty lady in the hard hat who liked to be in control.

Gabe suspected it was the beauty hiding beneath the hard hat, ready to throw away the hammer, desperate to rip off the tool belt and kick aside the work boots.

Gabe wanted to tap into that side of Frankie and show her how wonderful being a woman could be.

Especially with a man like him.

## CHAPTER FIFTEEN

FRANKIE HIT THE BRAKES A LITTLE TOO HARD AND TURNED right off the street at the last second to drive between the tall ornate gates. She continued toward the house, following the instructions Gabe had left in his phone message about going around to the side entrance.

While her right foot pressed the gas, her left leg jiggled at a frantic pace. She slammed her free hand down on her thigh to put it to rest. Which didn't help, because she just resorted to chewing on her bottom lip. Reminder: double check lipstick before leaving the car.

All week long she'd flip-flopped between joining him at the club and cancelling. She'd even put off dress shopping, certain she'd come to her senses and cancel. This was so not her. She called the shots. Even with John, she'd called the shots. He might have been the initiator to get them into the bedroom, but she'd taken over once they hit the bed. Left in his hands, the whole experience would have lasted less than ten minutes, with her being left unfulfilled. Near the end, they'd simply stopped having sex altogether.

In contrast, one night with Gabe, the way he'd spoken to her at dinner, the way he'd touched her at the club, the way he'd had her screaming... She'd never screamed before.

Frankie slowed the car and pulled into one of the few available parking spots. Didn't Gabe say Fridays were generally quieter than Saturdays? Judging by the number of cars, everyone decided tonight was the night to get their sexy on.

She turned the key, quieting the engine. Well, she was here.

She drummed her fingers on the leather-covered steering wheel. She was really going to do this.

She'd waited until Sophie left for the evening before raiding her sister's closet since she never did get out to buy a new dress. Shopping wasn't her thing, and no way in hell was she about to enlist her sister's help again.

Before tonight—before Gabe—she wouldn't have made the effort. She didn't wear make-up or heels. Or fix her hair in anything other than a classic ponytail. Asking for Sophie's assistance would have raised all sorts of questions she wasn't prepared to answer. Hell, she didn't *know* the answers.

But that meant Frankie had to manage her own hair and makeup. She flipped down the visor, fixed her lipstick, and gave her reflection one final appraisal. She couldn't copy the smoky eye Sophie created, nor the fancy hairstyle, so she'd gone with mascara and a little blush and left her hair down.

A hard rap on the window scared the crap out of her.

Frankie jumped in her seat. Thankfully she wasn't a screamer. Oh, wait, she was.

Gabe stared back at her, his head cocked at a charming angle, a cute quirk to his lips.

She waved at him, sucked in a lungful of courage, and opened the door. In the process of stepping out of the truck, closing the door and locking it, she found her equilibrium in her borrowed shoes, and with a fortifying breath and a prayer that she didn't make of fool of herself this time, she turned to greet him.

"Hi."

"Hi." His genuine smile reached all the way up to his eyes, which in the dark looked black rather than blue. "You look gorgeous, Francesca."

"Thank you," she said.

She'd decided to go with a deep crimson number she'd seen Sophie wear a few times and always secretly coveted. Hanging in the closet, it had looked innocuous enough, and on Sophie it looked stunning. However, second doubts plagued her. It was too short. At some point during the drive here, it had molded to her butt. Had it been this low cut when she first put it on?

At least it had straps and did up in the back like a bra, so she'd been able to go without. Though the deep dip left her back mostly bare. She wore the same shoes she'd borrowed on their first date. Figured she had experience walking in those now, so why test the waters in something new?

She looked up at the building and imagined what she'd see once she stepped inside. This whole evening was one massive test. Her choice of footwear was the least of her problems.

Gabe, on the other hand, looked very tall and handsome in black pants and a black shirt that melded to his body like a glove. But in his case, it enhanced his physique. It made her mouth water and her body tingle.

"Are you going to come in?" he asked.

Headlights sliced through the darkness and tires whispered on pavement, breaking the silence and the moment, if that's what they were having. "Yes. I am."

"Then let's, go. I'm looking forward to dancing with you."

"Just dancing?"

He gave her a sidelong glance, his stare penetrating and hot. "If that's all you're comfortable with, yes."

And she knew right then, he meant it. If she could only manage to walk through the building and be a voyeur for the evening, that's all they'd do.

Gabe guided her through the side door and down the hallway. Of course it didn't look much different than it had the other night, except she could hear the murmur of voices and almost feel the beat of the music swell the floor beneath her feet. The walls must provide good soundproofing though, because she definitely couldn't sing along with whatever song played.

They reached the main foyer, and Frankie stumbled a bit, not sure whether to proceed or not. Gabe addressed that for her by taking her elbow and gently urging her forward.

A stunning woman wearing a long, red dress chatted with a couple near the round table in the center of the room. The bouquet of flowers had been switched to blood-red roses, their fragrance strong but not overpowering.

Movement on the second level caught her attention and Frankie glanced up to see people moving around, their soft laughter reaching her ears. Was that a woman's cry? People were up there having sex. Could she watch them? Could she allow herself to become one of them?

"Would you like to go upstairs, or stay down here and dance?"

His breath fluttered over her shoulder; the heat of his body warmed her back. Far too easily, she could simply close her eyes and lean back, instinctively knowing he'd catch her and hold her.

"I'm not that great of a dancer." She could count on one finger the number of school dances she'd attended, and only going that one time because her father insisted she spend time with kids her own age. Like every other attempt she'd made to do the normal things high school girls did, it had been a complete and utter disaster. After spending over half the evening standing in a corner, not having said a word to a soul, she'd finally made her way to the exit and escaped into the night. She'd walked home and then killed another hour in the barn organizing the nails and screws.

"Then how about we start with upstairs?"

She wanted to dash back out to her car. She nodded.

As they moved in that direction, the woman in the red dress acknowledged Gabe just as she wished the other couple a good night. She strolled over, her dress flowing around her.

"Hi, Wendy. We have a pretty full house tonight."

Wendy smiled. "It's the best Friday night I've seen for a while. Will your brothers be stopping in tonight?"

Gabe shrugged, and though she smiled politely, Wendy's gaze zeroed in on the arm he had slipped around Frankie's waist and his thumb tracing circles on her side.

"Kyle may. Not sure about Kade and Brienna though." Gabe squeezed Frankie's side, including her in the exchange. "Wendy is our hostess slash office manager," he explained. "Wendy, this is Francesca."

Wendy held out her hand. "It's nice to meet you, Francesca. Welcome to The Vault."

Frankie accepted the welcome and returned it. "Thank you. And please, call me Frankie."

"I know you're in good hands with the boss here, so I'll let the two of you begin your evening." She turned back to Gabe. "I'll only look for you if there's anything major needing your attention. Deacon or Josh can help with everything else that may come up."

"Thanks, Wendy. I'd appreciate that." Gabe removed his arm and ushered Frankie over to the round table and the guest book. He handed her a pen. "We all sign in. It's our way of ensuring we know who's in the building in case of an emergency."

Frankie signed her name. Gabe did the same and then took her hand. He led her to the stairs.

The other night everything was so quiet and relatively dark until Gabe lit the way. Frankie had been so focused on him and how he'd made her feel at the restaurant that she hadn't paid too much attention to the tiny details. Like the classic erotic photos hanging along the curved wall up the stairs. Or the beautifully carved balusters in the railing. Or the exquisite crown molding at the ceilings. She could spend hours scouring the building and discovering all the special touches that added to its character.

She stepped onto the second floor landing. There was a love seat, some plants, and a couple of people making out on the love seat. The show was starting.

"Friday and Saturday nights are open to all members. Thursday's are for Platinum members only," Gabe said. "And the first Wednesday of every month we open the ballroom for dancing only."

She pulled her gaze from the couple and back to her escort. "I remember you mentioned that. Why would you do that?"

"Because it's an opportunity to test out potential members without putting my regulars at risk. And they can get an impression of the club without feeling obligated in any way. Many are not sure on their first visit. I'd rather they test the waters before they pay for a full membership. We also have an elevator just outside the guest entrance that takes you to the second level as well as the basement for anyone unable to take the stairs."

"Wow, you've thought of everything. I like that you've taken the accommodation of people with disabilities into consideration." Not enough builders included those with special needs into their design. And in older, pre-existing buildings it could be very difficult and costly to implement the necessary upgrades. Her respect for Gabe and his brothers grew.

He led her down the hallway.

She could see people moving from room to room. A small group congregated in front of one of them. Her apprehension escalated as they drew nearer to the group. She slowed her steps and tried to think of ways to stall. "Um, so I don't think you told me anything about…" She searched her mind. "Um, rules. What about the rules?" Frankie understood rules.

"Well, they're simple really. I have three key ones. No

means no. Condoms always except for your spouse, and I don't supply toys."

"Toys?" Did he mean—?

"Vibrators, dildos, butt plugs, nipple clamps, whatever. I won't supply them or have my staff clean them. People can bring them, but they can take them home or toss them into the trash before they leave. I supply lube and towels. And condoms of course. Those three items you'll find all over the place. Along with baskets to discard trash and used towels."

Convenient. He'd thought of everything. Of course she'd tried a vibrator a few times. They performed the job, but in her opinion didn't really add any excitement or any sort of wow factor. But to each their own. She'd never tried the other things he mentioned. Frankly, some just scared her. Nipple clamps? Ouch.

Gabe paused and moved close to her, entering her space a bit at a time. She stepped back until she hit the wall. He didn't crowd her. Instead he slowly leaned in, his eyes locked on hers, and lowered his voice. "Tonight is really about introducing you to this part of my life, Francesca. If you're interested in testing it out, or coming to the club on a more frequent basis, I can arrange that. You'd need to complete the formal contract and provide a medical certificate with a clean bill of health."

She must have had an incredulous look in her face, because he continued in a bit of rush as though apologizing. "Every single member must do the same before I allow them entrance to the club."

"But you let me in."

Was that a hint of a blush on his cheeks or just the lack of lighting in the hallway?

In the room nearest them, the one where the group had assembled around the open door frame, the sound of flesh being slapped startled her, followed by a long, low moan and a gasp.

“You’re right.” Gabe placed the flat of his palm against the wall above her head and bent his head. His lips grazed her cheek as he tucked in close to her ear.

She closed her eyes, inhaling the scent of soap and a very light but very nice cologne.

“But I have no intention of letting you out of my sight tonight. Nor do I plan on letting anybody else touch you.”

A shiver raced along her skin.

“I’ve already taken the liberty of drafting a membership contract based on the limitations we discussed last week. I’m hoping after tonight you’ll be prepared to revise or accept them.”

“But the cost—”

“Don’t worry about that,” he said.

“I don’t want a free pass, Gabe. I pay my own way.” Since when had she decided she’d become a member?

“Frankie, it’s the same for my brothers.” He swallowed. “Anybody we personally bring gets a free pass. There has to be a perk for being an owner,” he teased.

She felt his mouth curve into a grin. “Fair enough. And then?” she asked, her voice lower and raspier than she’d ever recalled hearing it.

He shifted just a touch and pressed his lips against her cheek. He rubbed his nose along the soft spot in front of her ear.

She shivered. Again. This was becoming a habit.

“And then I’ll be one very happy man. And I’m hoping you’ll be one very happy woman.”

## CHAPTER SIXTEEN

GABE LIFTED HIS HEAD, DROPPED HIS ARM TO HIS SIDE, and backed away to see the expression on Frankie's face. He watched a tremor work its way through her body as her pupils dilated, obliterating the green that a reminded him of a lush garden.

"I think I'm willing to agree to that," she said, the top edge of her cheeks stained an enticing shade of pink.

He dropped his gaze. Her breasts rose and fell in a tempting dance, her nipples prominent beneath the fabric of her dress. He raised his eyes so he could look at her straight on. There could be no miscommunication. "You must be certain, Francesca. We can have a temporary arrangement. There's nothing wrong with that. I'm not asking you to sign your life over to me." Though strangely enough, the prospect wasn't unappealing in the least. "Our agreement can be for tonight only if you wish. But even temporarily, we need to be on the same page. I need to know your limitations, and you need to give me permission to proceed based on those. You still have the ability, at any time, to stop anything you're not comfortable with simply by saying your safe word."

"Rebar."

He chuckled. "Yes, rebar."

"That, I can agree to."

He smiled. "Good."

"But I thought tonight was all about dancing and watching."

"Tonight is whatever you want it to be, sweetheart."

All around them people flowed from one room to the other. The sounds of couples in the middle of play or reaching their completion echoed throughout the floor, but he tuned all of it out.

"Would you like to watch some of the action?" he asked his lovely date.

She nodded.

Gabe took her hand and turned. He realized he reached for her hand often. He couldn't remember doing that with other women he dated. With Frankie, the need to touch her surpassed almost all other temptation. Almost.

They continued down the hall, pausing often so she could take a few moments to assess the surroundings, the people and the images he suspected were crowding her brain, vying for attention. He knew it could be overwhelming for some. Especially those who'd never been to such a place. People-watching at its finest. Fully dressed bodies. Nearly naked bodies. Naked bodies. People of all ages, shapes, sizes, and religions.

Lynette, one of only two Dommes in the club, strutted toward them in her leather boy shorts, corset, and knee-high stiletto boots. She offered her famous warm smile with a slight nod of acknowledgement to him, and a light chuckle at Francesca's openmouthed expression.

Lynette stood about five-foot nothing in bare feet. But her five-inch heels and shoulders-back, don't-mess-with-me posture intimidated even some of the men. She always wore her hair in a tight bun on the top her head and dark purple, almost black lipstick. Frankly, some days she scared the crap out of him.

Out of uniform, however, the woman was a peach. She loved to bake, was always bringing treats for the staff, and never had an unkind word to say. However, when the leathers were on and the whip was in her hand, as it was now, the tail swishing behind her like a pet snake, she commanded attention and respect.

She stopped before them. "Master Gabriel. How are you this evening?"

"I'm good, Mistress Lynette. No pet tonight?" Lynette had yet to find a permanent partner. Many nights she simply wandered the floors, providing extra security where needed. Gabe hoped she'd find the right man soon, because she was a lovely person and deserved to meet the man of her dreams.

"Actually, I just finished a scene with a young man. I filled in for Mistress Laura who had to leave. She was ill."

"Is she OK?" Concerned for one of his members filled him.

"The flu I think. I sent her home in a cab."

"Good. I'll give her a call and check on her." Gabe made a mental note to check in on Laura. She lived alone and had no family in the area. Maybe he'd have Wendy go see her tomorrow. "How did it go with her client?"

"Fine. He's tried to capture my attention a few times in the past, so I guess tonight he got his wish," she said. "But I'm finished for the evening. I think I'm going to head home." Lynette cast a glance to his side where Frankie stood patiently.

Of course she didn't know she should be showing respect to the Domme in her presence, but considering he hadn't discussed roles and expectations with her, he couldn't fault her for that. Lynette would understand.

"I'm sorry. Please forgive my rudeness. Mistress Lynette, this is my date for the evening, Francesca Stevens."

Lynette blinked like an owl. "Date?" She narrowed her eyes and gave Frankie a curious assessment.

He'd better get used to it. He suspected other members and staff would have a similar reaction.

"It's very nice to meet you," Lynette said.

"Likewise."

He didn't know if Frankie was simply being polite or if Lynette frightened her. But her smile seemed genuine and it reached her eyes. Gabe relaxed as relief flowed over him.

"This man will take very good care of you, Francesca. He's one of the best people I know."

Lynette's words humbled him. He ducked his chin and tried not to be embarrassed by the praise.

Francesca gazed up at him. "That's good know, Mistress. Thank you for telling me that." The lines around her eyes relaxed and she smiled at him.

He cleared his throat.

Lynette wished them a pleasant evening and continued on her way.

They paused to watch a threesome just beginning to play in front of a small crowd. Francesca watched them for a few moments, but Gabe kept his focus trained on her. He wanted to know what turned her on and what turned her off. Clearly, nothing about the scene in front of her affected her in either way.

He pulled her away from that room and led her to the next one where a couple were providing a flogger demonstration. Scott and Tammy were longtime members, and Gabe enjoyed watching them. When Francesca showed more interest, Gabe nudged her into the room and over to the corner on the right, away from other spectators.

He said silent hellos and gave nods of acknowledgement to members as he passed, but he didn't engage in any conversation. When a couple or a group were demonstrating or in the middle of a scene, the audience was to refrain from disturbing them in any way.

Gabe pressed his back to the wall and arranged Francesca in front of him, the curve of her ass snug to his groin, the top of her head below his chin.

At the front of the room, Scott had stripped Tammy of all of her clothes except for her red thong and matching demi-bra. Her hands were raised above her head and cuffed to a suspension bar hanging from the ceiling. Another spreader bar at her ankles kept her legs about two feet wide. A blindfold covered her eyes, and a ball gag filled her mouth. That was new for Tammy. Public play was typical for the couple, but this was the first time he'd seen them engage in any form of bondage games, and he'd never seen Tammy with a ball gag.

Scott circled her slowly. He dragged the flogger over her shoulder, down over her breast to her stomach. He trailed the tassels across her middle, around to her back, and over to the other side. Then he repeated the action from the opposite direction on the other side of her body. Her nipples stood erect. He paused to whisper something in her ear, and her nostrils flared. Gabe heard a whimper escape past the gag, and she rose to her toes.

Scott pulled his hand back and brought the flogger down across the top of her left breast, then the right. He laid it over her left thigh and then the right. The sound of the leather slapping against the cheek of her ass caused Frankie to jump in his arms. But she didn't bolt or demand he put a stop to the display, both encouraging signs.

While Francesca watched the interplay between Scott and his wife, Gabe cast his gaze around the room. Other members had crowded into the room to watch. They kept a respectful distance and remained quiet. In most cases one person softly stroked the other, the tactile combined with the visual enhanced the experience for everybody. He hadn't come across many who didn't either enjoy being watched or watching. The degrees of voyeurism or participation varied, but most people were honest enough to admit curiosity won out.

He rubbed his hands up and down Francesca's arms, feeling her tremble the slightest bit beneath his touch. He lowered his head slightly so his breath would warm her neck and shoulders, but not so close that he'd be a distraction. Not yet anyway.

In the scene being enacted before them, Tammy cried out after a particularly stinging blow.

Gabe wasn't concerned in the least. He trusted that Scott knew what his wife liked and what she could handle. A little pain often heightened the experience, and from the sounds of it, she had just about reached the point of her endurance.

Tammy's chest rose and fell with each labored breath she took.

Scott leaned forward and wrapped his lips around one taught nipple.

She dropped her head back. Moans mumbled from behind the ball gag.

After paying homage to each breast, he flipped the flogger to run the handle down the middle of her stomach, pausing to caress her between her legs with the hard leather covered shaft. Not penetrating her, but teasing her with the contact.

She jerked in her constraints.

"What do you think, sweetheart? Should I let you come here, or shall we wait until we get home?" Scott asked the question just loud enough for most people in the room to hear.

Francesca stilled in Gabe's arms. Her own breathing had deepened.

If he were to risk a touch, would she be wet between her own legs? Without knowing for sure she would be receptive to the idea of any public display of intimacy, he restrained himself from testing his theory. Though it pained him not to. His only course of action was to press his erection tight to her backside.

She gasped quietly.

He swiveled his hips, and she pushed back against him. Automatic reaction? He held his breath, waiting. When she ventured to do it again, a sense of victory coursed through him.

Back at the front of the room, Tammy nodded her head in response to Scott's question.

He chuckled. "Well, that doesn't really give me a clear answer, dear. Come now…" He paused, as she frantically nodded her head. "Or at home?"

At the end of his question, she shook her head hard, screaming behind the gag her opinion about the second option.

"I don't know…" Scott taunted.

Tammy whimpered. Her chest heaved. Her hair, damp with sweat, swung like whips with each movement of her head.

Finally her husband took pity, and after a few more love taps with the flogger, he used his tongue on her breasts and his fingers in her pussy to bring her to a high-pitched orgasm.

Replete, her whole body slumped. Scott quickly uncuffed his wife, gathered her into his arms, and strode over to the love seat in the front corner of the room where he dropped down and settled her across his lap.

One of the other members brought him a blanket to wrap around Tammy.

She snuggled against his chest as her husband removed the blindfold and gag.

Scott wrapped his arms protectively around his wife and reclined against the back of love seat, speaking softly to her.

Gabe kept his arms circled around Frankie's waist while the room emptied. "What did you think?" he asked, keeping his voice low so as not to disturb Tammy's after care. He'd never been so anxious over somebody's opinion before.

"Well. It was different. I can honestly say I haven't watched anything like that before. Talk about live theater."

He chuckled, kissed the top of her head, and then led her out of the room where they made their way further down the hall.

They checked out some of the other action, but nothing really seemed to draw her attention. Damn. What now? She hadn't seemed too interested in dancing. Did she want to go to The Vault? He wasn't sure she was ready to see that in full swing.

"You know what I'd like to do?"

He jumped at the chance to find out. "What?"

"I'd like to see where you live." She peered up at him, almost shy. Biting her bottom lip and fidgeting in her sister's shoes.

No date had ever asked to see his home before. Most, or rather all, of the women he'd been with over the last number of years only saw the inside of this building. The few he'd played with were only interested in relinquishing control to him. They had no desire to know him. And to be fair, he'd felt the same. Until Francesca.

Gabe reached up and placed his thumb on her lip, preventing her from biting it. All the people around them disappeared in the woodwork. All sound drifted away. His voice dropped low. "You would?"

"I would like that very much. You don't strike me as a man who shares his private life with many people, Gabe."

He shared it with nobody but his immediate family. "You'd be right about that."

# CHAPTER SEVENTEEN

PLACING HER HAND IN HIS, FEELING SOMETHING WARM and comforting flow through her as his fingers wrapped around hers, Frankie followed him down the stairs to the main entrance where he took a few moments to speak with Wendy. Then she was trailing behind him out the front door and across the courtyard.

He moved like a man on a mission. You'd think he'd never had guests in his home before. He didn't say a word. He walked and she did her best to keep up in heels she had no business wearing.

They took a quaint flagstone path that wound its way to the front porch of a decent-sized cottage that architecturally resembled the larger home. Gabe unlocked the door and ushered her into the dark interior, engaging the locks behind them.

She remained near the door while he strode forward and flipped on a table lamp that brightened the room only enough to create an intimate yellow glow. Dark shadows still filled the corners.

He swept his arm wide, a tentative grin on his face. "This is the living room slash kitchen slash dining room."

Total open concept. Before her, spread out over about twelve hundred square feet, was a family space centered around a large, stone fireplace on the right that she bet would be stunning all decorated during the holidays. A large window, similar to the one in his office in the other building, probably looked out onto the same yard space. Dark chocolate leather furniture you could sink into, off-white lamps, and colorful throw rugs over dark, hardwood flooring created a comfortable, cozy, yet masculine room.

A long center island with a pot rack hanging overhead separated the kitchen from the great room. A rack like that would look awesome in her kitchen. Bar stool seating circled three sides of the counter. Stainless steel appliances and light colored granite counter tops on dark wood cupboards provided a stunning contrast. A formal dining table large enough to accommodate eight stood off to the side in an area the limited lighting didn't extend to.

There was no giant flat screen television. No towers of empty beer cans. No video game controllers. No piles of magazines or dirty dishes. The kitchen was spotless. The counters shone. Frankie bet if she ran her finger along one of the bookshelves against the wall, she'd find not a speck of dust. And she'd be the books were in alphabetical order.

"Do you have a cleaning lady come in regularly?"

He gave her an odd look. "No. Why?"

She hadn't moved from her spot just inside the door. "Your home is very neat and tidy."

His mouth twitched as though he fought a smile. "My mom instilled both a good work ethic and the knowledge of how to keep a clean home." He waved her forward. "You're welcome to come inside."

He might be grinning at her, but for the first time since she'd met him, it didn't quite reach his eyes. He wasn't as comfortable as he wanted her to believe. He'd jammed his hands into his pockets and rocked back slightly on his heels. His eyes darted around the living space, a clear indication of his unease. He was nervous.

"You have a lovely home, Gabe."

"Thank you." He removed his hands from his pockets and walked toward the kitchen, calling back over his shoulder. "Can I get you something to drink?"

She joined him, placed her handbag on the island, and climbed up onto one of the tall bar stools. "Sure. A beer would be great if you have one."

"Another thing we have in common."

"Excuse me?"

Gabe shook his head. "Never mind." He grabbed two cold beers from the refrigerator and two glasses from a cupboard.

Frankie waited silently while he poured their drinks, using the time to look around and decide what her intentions for coming here were.

The Vault had been…interesting. But it really wasn't her thing. She understood the purpose of such a place. The environment and activities intrigued her. She could even admit she found it arousing. Although she couldn't see herself publicly displaying herself for other people's enjoyment or curiosity, she didn't begrudge others their desire to do so. But she didn't want to be their foreplay.

She had no plans to return the favor to that couple she watched tonight. She'd never been totally at ease in the sex department. The other night with Gabe had pushed a boundary for her. She'd allowed him to do it. And she'd enjoyed it. But it had been just the two of them. Frankie preferred her intimate moments to be just that. A private moment between her and the man she wanted to be with.

And right now, that was Gabe McBride. In his own personal space. A big step for her, putting herself out there like this and risking rejection. Gabe enjoyed a certain lifestyle. Would he be willing to spend time with her without an audience?

"What are you thinking about?" He slipped onto the stool next to her, their knees touching.

"Can I ask you a question?" Would he be straight with her?

"Of course." He took a drink of his beer, placed the glass on the counter, and gave her his full attention.

She looked deep into his eyes. In the room, with the light

behind him, they appeared almost black. He patiently waited for her to get to the point. She feared his answer and that saddened her because she realized she really liked this man and truly did want to spend more time with him.

"Do you need to be at The Vault to be with a woman?"

He tilted his head, his brow line furrowing in a frown. "No."

"Do you prefer to be over there when you have sex?"

His facial features softened, and he picked up one of her hands, his thumb sweeping side to side in a gentle caress. "No, Francesca. I will admit that over the last few years, any time I've spent with a woman has taken place at the club. But it's not a requirement." He cocked his head to the right and studied her for a moment. "Why the questions? You seemed fine there last week. At least until you ran out shoeless," he pointed out with a kind smile and laughter in his eyes. "What happened tonight that turned you off?"

"Nothing."

"I don't understand then."

"It's not that it didn't excite or fascinate me. People-watching at your place of employment must be a blast."

He laughed. "I suppose."

She swallowed. What she was about to say would probably bring an end to whatever this thing was between them. She hadn't wanted the distraction, but she couldn't seem to avoid it either. It was like slowing to see the collision on the side of the road. Her curiosity had gotten the better of her, and the end result, right or wrong, quick or not, was that she wanted to know Gabe McBride. She wanted to experience what he was offering.

But she couldn't do it at The Vault. "Gabe, I'm not the kind of person who can do that in front of other people."

"Did I ask you to?" he said quietly.

His expression didn't provide any insight into his thoughts.

Was he disappointed? "No. But it's your club. You live on the premises. I assume you must be interested in all of it."

"Of course I am interested. It's my livelihood, and I enjoy elements of the lifestyle. But running the business and liking dominance or a little kink doesn't mean I want or need to have sex in front of other people all of the time."

"What about some of the time?" she asked.

He drew in a deep breath and let it out. "Have I? Yes. Is it a regular occurrence for me? Far from it. I can probably count on one hand the number of times I've played publicly. Just as you obviously do, I like my privacy."

"That woman called you Master Gabriel."

"As a sign of respect. All the Doms at the club are called Master."

"But that must mean—"

"It means I have standing at the club. It means I prefer to be the dominant in the relationship. It doesn't mean I want all women kneeling at my feet all the time. It doesn't mean I want a full time submissive or a slave or that I have a desire to put on a show in front of other people. Don't get me wrong, Francesca. For some in the lifestyle that's exactly what it means. It comes down to what each person wants out of the relationship."

She bit down on her bottom lip.

"Stop that."

She instantly released her lip.

Gabe stared at her for a moment and then stood. He held out his hand. "Come with me."

Placing her palm in his, she rose and followed him down a short hall to a closed door.

He opened the door and stood aside. "Go on in." He flicked on the lights as she crossed the threshold.

She came to a stop and blinked. "Is this your bedroom?" It had a bed, so it was a justified question. But unlike other bedrooms, it also had a few additional decorative items and pieces of furniture she'd never seen in somebody's bedroom before. She did recognize some of it though, because she'd seen similar pieces at The Vault.

He came up behind her and placed his hands on her shoulders. "No. My bedroom is down the hall. This is my playroom."

"Your playroom."

"Yes. I prefer to keep my private life out of the public eye as well."

"So you bring your girlfriends here?"

"I haven't had a girlfriend in a very long time."

He removed his hands and she missed the comforting strength they'd provided.

"You're the first woman to ever see this room."

She turned and looked up at him. "The first?"

He nodded. "Yup. I've only played with women at the club. This is my home. I've never brought those women here."

Which meant he'd never played with anybody in this room. She was stumped. "Then why bring me here? Why are you showing me this room?"

"Because you asked." He cupped her cheek. "And because you're not like them."

"Oh." Frankie really didn't know what more to say to that. A warm, tingly feeling settled in the pit of her stomach though. Sort of made her feel queasy.

"Francesca, do you want to be here with me tonight? I'm not forcing you. I'll never force you. Say no, and I'll take you home. Say no, and we'll have some coffee, talk, and then I'll take you home. You're the one in control here. You're the boss."

This was it. This was her intention all along. She'd wanted to be with him tonight and now here she was, about to indulge in something she'd only had a brief taste of the last time she'd been with him. She'd been the sole beneficiary that night. Tonight, she'd make sure Gabe was on the receiving end as well.

She gazed up and him and nodded slowly.

"Say it."

"I want to be here, Gabe."

He closed his eyes, leaned forward, and kissed her on the forehead. Shocked, she realized they hadn't even kissed yet. She had no clue what he tasted like.

"I have something for you. Wait here." Gabe left the room.

While he was gone, she took in her surroundings but didn't move from where she stood.

Similar to The Vault, it was rather dark. The walls were painted a dark gray, and the bedding was black and white. A king-size bed took up most of the space, as the room wasn't that large. But it was big enough for the bed and a strange-looking curvy chair of some sort. There was also a harness hanging from the ceiling and a massage table against one wall. There were two windows, but the closed blinds afforded no view. The lamp on the bedside table provided the only lighting, but there were sconces on the wall in various spots that could provide more.

Gabe returned carrying a bag in one hand, holding it out to her as he approached.

"I bought something for you." He shrugged one shoulder. "On the off chance I'd get to give it to you."

She glanced down, but didn't take the bag. "What it is?"

"It won't bite. I'd like you to put it on."

She raised her eyes to his. "You bought me clothes."

"Well, not jeans or anything. It was a spur of the moment thing." He grinned sheepishly. "I bought you lingerie. I'd very much like it if you'd wear it for me."

"How did you know my size?"

"I'm a good guesser."

She had no response. Taking the bag, she opened it to see sheer black—and not much of it. "Where should I change?"

He nodded to a spot behind her. She turned.

"There's a washroom right in there. You change and I'll be waiting out here for you."

He said nothing more, just watched her, those eyes of his assessing but not judging her in any way.

Frankie walked into the bathroom and closed the door behind her. She turned on the light and gazed at her reflection in the mirror. She was certain the décor in here was as nice and as clean as it was in the other areas of the house she'd seen, but she didn't notice.

Her hair was slightly mussed, and her cheeks were flushed. The eyes staring back at her in the mirror resembled those of a startled deer caught in the headlights of an oncoming car. How fitting.

She pulled the ensemble from the bag. Wow. Um. She'd never owned, never mind wore, anything like this before. It was so…dainty. Pretty. See-through. Girly. Very sheer.

Frankie quickly removed her dress and exchanged it for the lingerie. Should she keep her shoes on? No. She didn't want to ruin the moment by tripping and embarrassing herself by breaking an arm or something. Slipping her heels off, she carefully folded the dress and set it on the counter. After checking her makeup, her breath, and her armpits, she opened the door and stepped back into the room.

Gabe stood by the end of the bed. He'd removed his shirt and his shoes and exchanged his dress pants for a pair a comfortable-looking jeans, the button left undone. She never realized how sexy a barefoot man could be. She only did now because she knew if she focused on his chest, her gaze would be superglued there. The man defined six-pack. Broad shoulders, muscled chest, and narrow waist. Totally drool-worthy. She started to cross her arms to hide the hard points of her nipples, but the slow shake of his head stopped her.

"Are you ready for this, Francesca?"

She honestly didn't know.

She nodded.

"Same limits as we discussed last week?"

"Yes." She could barely get the word off her tongue.

"Good. To start, I'd prefer if you only speak when asked a direct question."

She nodded again.

Gabe crooked his finger at her. "Come here, Francesca. I'd like you to please sit on this bench."

Frankie swallowed. Granted, he had the sexiest voice and the hottest look in his eyes when he ordered her to do something. And he never really *ordered* her. He simply and politely stated his expectations.

But, still, some tiny nugget in her brain argued against this. Against all of it. She didn't need a man to tell her what to wear, what to say, and what to do. A strong, determined, professional female such as herself should stand up strong and proud and face off with a man like Gabriel McBride. Hell, she'd made it in a man's world. She was one of the guys.

Yet here she stood, wearing nothing but a black lace teddy and a matching thong, because he'd presented it to her as a gift and requested she wear it just for him tonight. It hadn't been a question or a command. Just something he'd like to see her in.

She pinched her lips tight together because Gabe had suggested she not speak unless he specifically asked her a question. She glanced down to see if her feet would propel her forward.

"Look at me, please."

She jerked her head up, but other than a very slight pause she hoped he hadn't noticed, she crossed the room, stopping where he stood next to a black leather, curved bench.

She didn't remember a single word of the small talk they'd exchanged since they walked through the front door. She had, however, memorized every crease in his pants, noticed each frayed thread decorating the ripped material near his right knee since she stepped out of the bathroom. She'd stored images of how the soft denim hugged certain areas and flexed or relaxed in others inside her memory for later use. She could describe how his thighs tightened with each stride and how his biceps bulged when he bent his arm to run his fingers through his short hair. Was he nervous too?

She pictured him hefting a reciprocating saw, his hair damp with sweat beneath a hard hat, his safety classes protecting those beautiful eyes from the fine dust flinging back as the blade ripped through a piece of fresh lumber.

Needing a moment to collect herself, she pulled her gaze away from him to sweep the room. Hanging on the wall farthest from her, were two whips and a few objects that reminded her of a horse's tail. She hadn't noticed those before. A short dresser had an I-pod docking station and two candles on it, their flames flickering, a spicy scent just now wafting over to her. Cinnamon? The hardwood floor was cold beneath her feet.

"Francesca."

She blinked out of her thoughts, took a hefty breath, and returned her attention back to him, where it should be anyway.

"You look beautiful."

She opened her mouth but didn't say anything. Was she allowed to speak? He inclined his head a tiny bit.

"Thank you," she said, though the words came out on a breath. She hated the way she sounded, like she was some simpering female. So she cleared her throat and tried again. "Thank you, Gabe." Much better. Louder, stronger, more conviction. Although inside she quivered like a scared rabbit.

He raised one hand and ran a finger lightly down the side of her of face, pausing to tuck her hair behind her ear. "You have nothing to be frightened of, Francesca. I would never, ever, hurt you."

"I know." That was the one thing she was absolutely certain of. Although they'd only met a few short weeks ago, instinct told her Gabe would never intentionally cause her pain or suffering. But based on her last experience with him, she had a strong feeling his version of pleasure might sometimes be associated with a sting of pain. And she was beginning to suspect that he could break her heart if she let herself become too attached to him. Or maybe it was too late.

"Do you remember your safe word?"

"Rebar."

His low chuckle sent swirls of delicious yearning through her. "Good. Now, if at any time you feel like you cannot continue, or you truly do not like something, simply say your safe word. We will stop immediately and reassess."

"OK."

He studied her for a moment. When he finally seemed to accept that she was ready, he turned away and walked over to the dresser and tinkered with the I-pod. Sexy jazz chords invaded the room through hidden speakers, startling her.

Spinning to face her again, he prowled forward. He truly was one of the most gorgeous men she'd ever seen. He was the kind of man people noticed when he walked into a room. His height, the piercing eyes, the broad chest, and the confident swagger made people pause. His employees respected him, some men probably envied him, and women wanted him.

But tonight he was hers.

Frankie licked her lips as he drew near. Inside her chest, her heart beat faster. Just watching him move created a tingle of anticipation between her legs. Her nipples hardened beneath the fabric of her lingerie, and she knew if she touched herself, she'd find moisture dampening the tiny thong.

He stopped directly in front of her, his warm breath bathing her face. He placed a finger under her chin and tilted her head up and back to almost an awkward position. But he never took his eyes from hers.

Everything around them melted away. The music dimmed. She concentrated on Gabe, staring at the specs of color in the irises of his eyes. She was fascinated by the different shades of blue and gray that converged to create that unique shade that was all his.

He lowered his head, bringing his lips closer to her hers. When barely an inch separated them, he stopped, his gaze darting to her mouth for a split second before jumping back up. "I'm going to kiss you, Francesca. First here." His other hand appeared out of nowhere and he laid his finger to her closed lips. "Then here." He trailed that finger down to her right breast and circled her tight nipple.

She sucked in a breath as the lace grazed her tender flesh and white-hot desire raced through her bloodstream.

"And here." He continued a path down her belly to between her thighs where he pressed his finger against her clit.

She let her eyes fall closed so she could concentrate on keeping her knees locked.

Even through the material of her thong, she knew he'd realize how wet she already was. She wanted to squirm and rub against him, but instinct and a boatload of nervousness held her still.

Then his touch disappeared and she found her face cupped within the palms of his hands. And at last, after what seemed to take forever…*finally*, he kissed her.

Gabe's lips pressed smoothly against hers. He licked the seam between her lips, encouraging her to open.

Invitation accepted, she eagerly granted him entry.

And then his tongue was inside her mouth, softly, slowly stroking the side of hers, teasing the inside of her cheeks, the roof of her mouth. Even her teeth. He groaned and deepened the kiss. Wrapping his arms around her waist, he dragged her up tight to his body, his erection huge and hot as it smashed against her belly.

He tasted like coffee. He smelled like heaven. A very sexy heaven.

Suddenly Gabe released her mouth and pulled back. "Francesca," he growled, his voice hoarse with desire. "You make me forget who I am."

She opened her eyes, not even remembering when she'd let them drift closed again. She saw what looked like happiness in his before he smiled.

"On your knees, sugar. I know I said I didn't need all women on their knees before me, but I've changed my mind. I think I want to experience that sweet mouth of yours. Let's just say it's been one of my fantasies."

Lust seeped through her pores as she melted to the floor, barely noticing any discomfort when her shins hit the hardwood. Sitting back on her heels, she peered up. She had never envisioned herself in this position. Never believed she'd willingly drop down, eager to suck a man's cock. Hell. She could count on a couple of fingers how many times she'd actually performed the act. What if she fucked it up? What if she couldn't arouse him? What if he hated her mouth on him?

Fingers shaking, Frankie raised both hands to the button on his jeans. She glanced up. Gabe's eyes were now a dark navy blue and full of something hot, hungry, and just a little bit scary. Something that caused a shiver to roll over her body but no desire to run.

He fisted his hands at his sides, and his hard stomach expanded and deflated with quick shallow breaths.

Since he'd already helped her out by leaving his pants

unbuttoned, she only had to drag the zipper down, tine by tine.

Holy fuck. Saliva filled her mouth. The man went commando.

"Let me help." Gabe shoved his jeans over his hips and partway down his legs until his cock sprang free to bob in front of her eyes.

She couldn't look away. Eight solid inches and too thick for her fingers to fully wrap around, the head a dark plum color that looked velvet soft. A pearl of creamy liquid seeped from the tiny slit. She licked her lips.

Reaching up with her left hand, she ran the tip of one finger around the top and down his length, amazed at the silky texture over hard muscle. She curled the rest of her hand around him. Frankie tipped forward on her knees and flicked her tongue out to taste him. She closed her eyes as his flavor burst inside her mouth and danced over her taste buds.

# CHAPTER EIGHTEEN

GABE TIPPED HIS HEAD BACK AND STIFLED THE GROAN that crawled up the back of this throat. He'd had to clench his hands to hide the tremor when she dropped to the floor and reached for him. He'd been so excited at the thought of watching her give him a blowjob, that when she'd taken control he'd been stunned. He'd planned on directing the action himself. He'd intended to instruct her through each step from removing his cock from his pants, to how to grip him, and finally how to use her mouth.

When he'd felt the whisper soft touch of her tongue across the very tip of his cock, lapping in delicate little swipes, almost hesitantly, he'd locked his knees in position. But then she'd sighed and wrapped her soft lips around him, enveloping him in her wet, warm mouth. The urge to drive his fingers into her hair, to cup her head in his hands, and slowly fuck her mouth overwhelmed him to the point he'd nearly begged.

Generally, he was a patient man. Even in his role as a Dom, he avoided aggressive behavior. Some Doms liked to bark out orders, took joy in being in total control. Not him. He'd found over the years women responded better to softly worded commands.

However, with Francesca he felt his control slip every day. In total opposition to his true nature, he longed to be more primitive with her. He wanted to make love to her, to treasure her, but he also wanted to fuck her. He wanted it hot and dirty. But, considering this was really their first time together, and he still had some common sense whirling around in his brain, he didn't want to scare her off. At least not before he'd had the opportunity to taste other parts of her body. Their shared kiss only whet his appetite for so much more. He wanted to devour her. He wanted to own and intimately know every part of her, which scared the crap out of him.

So Gabe forced himself to remain still and let her do her thing. It was no hardship, really. She had the mouth of someone far more experienced than he guessed her to be.

When she applied wet suction to the sensitive area just beneath the rim, he rocked forward on his toes, unable to stop himself from thrusting his hips, pushing more of his length along the stretch of her tongue.

Not surprisingly, she had a tiny mouth. Her teeth raked his skin each time she traveled up and down, which only ratcheted up his arousal on every single pass as jolts of sensation shot through him. It was as though somebody had plugged him in.

"Christ, Francesca. You're killing me here." Gabe couldn't resist touching her any longer. When he'd seen her hair cascading down her back as she'd stepped from her car earlier, he'd immediately envisioned wrapping it around his fists. He speared his fingers through the long, silky strands and grasped the sides of her head. She stilled, but only long enough to allow him to guide her into a slow, steady pace.

Finally, he had control again.

One song ended, and in the small span of time between the end of that one and the beginning of the next tune, he listened to the music of her going down on him. Each sweet slurp, each wet suck, each inhalation through her nose, became his new favorite lyrics.

Distracted by the sound of her savoring him, he almost missed the softness of her hair sifting through his fingers and the floral scent of her shampoo rising up to tease his senses. Gabe inhaled as he shifted his hips forward, urging her to take him deeper, just kissing the back of her throat each time.

His orgasm broiled. His spine tingled. He couldn't decide if he wanted to come in her mouth or wait until he could bury himself between the softness of her legs.

Her lashes fluttered against the crest of her cheeks as her mouth stretched around him. She used her tongue to tease the underside of his cock.

Suddenly she opened her eyes and stared up at him.

The sight of those big round eyes and her mouth jammed full of his cock had his balls drawing up tight.

"Stop."

She paused and blinked those beautiful eyes. Resting inside her warm mouth became pure torture. She released him slowly, leaving him bereft and cold and ready to demand she take him again. "Did I do something wrong?" Her question sounded so small. Her voice shook. Her eyes welled with tears.

Gabe bent forward, cupped her cheeks, and stared into her eyes. "Not at all, sweetheart. I just don't want to finish too early with you. I want to enjoy you too."

"Oh." She blushed.

He was astounded at how sweet and innocent she looked. So different from the boss who'd torn a strip off one of her workers.

"How about you do as I initially asked?" He nodded toward the sex chair. "Sit on there, Francesca."

Gabe helped her stand and then instructed her how to lie on the uniquely curved bench. It cupped her body and gave him easy access to her pussy. He knelt before her. "Let's take this off." He reached under her teddy and gripped the band of her thong. Placing a hand at each hip, he stripped the tiny garment off. "Put your arms above your head and grip the back." Gabe wrapped his fingers around her ankles and gently pulled her legs apart, placing one foot on the floor on each side of the chair. With her spread wide, he could see her arousal. She glistened with desire. Saliva filled his mouth.

Sliding his hands under the cheeks of her ass, he pulled her closer. He'd wasted enough time. He bent down and swiped his tongue up through her wet folds, gathering proof that she wanted him as much as he wanted her. He moaned with delight at the flavor spilling onto his tongue. A little spice, a little salt. He could make a meal of her. He'd never sampled anything so delicious before. There hadn't been scores of women in his life, but with a hand over his heart, he could honestly say he'd never been with one as beautiful as Francesca, nor one that he desired as much.

Gabe nibbled at her labia, sucking the plump flesh into his mouth, satisfaction shooting through him when she wiggled and moaned her pleasure. He licked over her opening then dipped the tip of his tongue inside in short stabs. She quivered as he lapped at her and moved up the center toward her clit again, where he teased it with rapid flicks. Moisture pooled at her opening and trickled down to coat his chin. Her earthy scent filled his nose. Her salty taste flowed over his taste buds.

She rocked her hips against his face.

He buried his tongue between her legs.

Gabe paused to kiss the soft skin on her inner thigh. Then he ate her some more before deciding it was time to test his ability to make her scream again. He raised his head and looked up the length of her belly, still covered in the sexy, lace teddy. He'd just happened to pass a small shop on his way to meet with his brothers the other day and seen it on a mannequin in the window and knew it would be perfect for her.

Frankie watched him, her eyes wide and dark, her cheeks rosy, and her chest heaving up and down with each long breath she pulled in through her mouth and exhaled through her nose. He could stare at her all night.

"Do you like that?" he asked.

She nodded.

"You taste as sweet as I imagined."

Her eyes widened at his words.

"Would you like to come?"

She nodded a second time.

Gabe thrust one finger inside her, then another, grinning when she jumped. She quickly latched onto the tempo and worked with him, her body moving in such a way that she was fucking his fingers as eagerly as he was enjoying how her body grabbed and sucked him in.

He lowered his mouth to her clit, sucking on that engorged bundle of sensitive nerves, driving his fingers deep, pumping into her until her back arched, her elbows locked, and she tossed back her head with a thump on the leather.

She let out a scream as she climaxed, soaking his hand, her pussy convulsing around his fingers.

Gabe slowly eased her down, reluctantly removing his hand, but he couldn't not touch her. He sat back on his heels, his thigh cramping after kneeling in an uncomfortable position, though he hadn't noticed at the time. He trailed his fingers down her leg, testing how ticklish she was behind her knee, and further down to the arch of her foot.

She twitched when he hovered over her ankle.

Francesca, her face flushed a very becoming shade of scarlet, swung her feet around and pulled herself to a sitting position.

She licked her lips, drawing his gaze to that spot, and making him remember the feel of her lips on his cock. He wished he'd taken the opportunity to experience the full effect from her.

"Um, Gabe?"

He raised his head, his gaze catching hers.

She stared at him, blinking in an awkward way, her eyelids drooping, and her eyes hazy with satiation.

He sensed a shyness surrounding her now. "Yes?"

"You didn't…um…well…"

He chuckled. For somebody who had no trouble telling the men who worked for her what to do, she certainly seemed to have trouble finding words with him. It made him feel special.

"You, ah, didn't…" She cocked her head and looked pointedly as his crotch, where his very hard cock strained and poked out through the top in the gap between his open zipper.

"I'm fine." He really wasn't.

"You look like a guy on edge and ready to…blow." She giggled.

He loved the sound.

She slid off the bench and knelt before him. Her hard nipples poked at the lace, tempting him.

His fingers itched to caress them. "I promise, I'm fine, Francesca. I can wait."

Confusion showed on her face. "Wait for what? Don't you want to have sex with me?"

He felt like a heel for his casualness. "More than you know. We are far from finished, Francesca."

* * *

Didn't he want her to make him feel as good as he'd made her feel?

He bent forward to kiss her, and at the same time his thumbs brushed over her nipples. They sprang to attention. Not that they'd relaxed, thinking the party was over. She arched and moaned into his mouth, opening so he could slip his tongue inside. She tasted herself on him and wavered for a moment, not sure if she found the taste pleasant or not. Maybe it was an acquired taste.

He waited for her to decide, not forcing her to accept his kiss. In fact, he backed off, hovering just out of reach.

To hell with it. This was all about trying something new. She melted into him, swaying close so he could encircle her in his arms, a place she suddenly realized she *really* liked to be.

She'd expected him to spend the night ordering her around. Telling her everything he wanted her to do to him to make him feel good. But he hadn't done that at all. She'd willingly sucked his cock and wouldn't hesitate to do it again.

Oral sex wasn't something she'd enjoyed doing with John. Her ex had requested it frequently, although he'd rarely gone down on her. The few times he'd attempted it, he'd always made her feel like he was simply returning a favor.

Gabe kissed her like he needed her to breathe life into him. He played with her breasts, molding them in his hands, plucking at her nipples in a way that sent tiny sparks of painful pleasure arcing between the tips.

"Francesca, I need to be inside you."

Yes, please. She was onboard for that.

Bending at the knees, he placed his right arm behind her and scooped her up into the cradle of his arms, catching her by surprise. He strode to the bed and laid her out, stretching over her, bracing himself with one hand on each side of her body as he climbed up to join her.

He straddled her body and gazed down at her. Lowering his head, he kissed her again. Not a deep diving French kiss, but rather a sweet, innocent one, a slow one—his lips to hers— a peck that was packed with a lot of heat.

Then he crawled backward until he hovered over her chest. He lowered again, this time to capture one of her nipples in his mouth, lace and all. He sucked her in, filling his mouth with her breast, and flicked his tongue back and forth over the tip. He moved to the other side, leaving the first bereft, cold, wet, hard, and aching for more.

Gabe reared back. "Sit up."

She did, and he pulled the teddy over her head, then growled his appreciation. "Much better." Cupping her breasts, one in each hand, he squeezed. "First, I want to feel my cock trapped between these. Then I'm going to fuck you, Francesca."

He looked her square in the eye.

Waiting for a refusal? He'd be waiting a long time. Never in her life had a man treated her the way Gabriel McBride treated her. This might be a short-lived romance, probably a mistake, but she had no intention of backing away now. At least when he left, she'd have some pretty awesome nights to remember while she sat at home doing paperwork and her sister was out on one of her many dates.

Gabe pushed gently on her shoulders until she lay back on the bed, the pillows firm and cool beneath her head. Then he jumped off, stripped out of his jeans, and opened the drawer on the bedside table. From there, he retrieved a condom and a tube of lube.

Holy fuck the man's body rocked. Thick, solid-muscled thighs supported that upper body she'd drooled over earlier. Seeing him completely naked for the first time brought a hiccup to her throat. He was beautiful. Filled out in all the right places, a sprinkling of body hair, the man could model underwear. He had a tiny, reddish brown blemish on his left thigh that she'd have to remember to investigate later.

Straddling her waist and bringing her back to the moment, Gabe took the lube and opened it. "Have you ever had somebody fuck your tits before, Francesca?"

Was this a good moment to giggle, because she really wanted to giggle. He looked so big and serious, and she was so turned on that it wouldn't take much effort for her to come again. Most men looked at her boobs before they looked at her face. It's not that they were large, but she was small so they looked big on her. She'd never been asked for that particular act though. Maybe that's what they were all thinking. "Can't say that I have."

A smug smile curved his lips. "Good. I like that I'll be your first."

She waited while he squeezed a generous amount of the clear non-scented substance into the palm of his hand and coated his cock liberally. Shimming up closer, he tucked his knees almost into her armpits. He grabbed both breasts in his strong hands and pushed them together. Then he slid his hard cock in between them.

What a weirdly thrilling feeling. Frankie cast her eyes down to watch as the head of his penis popped free and then disappeared only to reappear a second later. Maybe she could reach it with her tongue.

Gabe groaned as he slid in and out of the tunnel he'd created.

The sensation of his hard length slipping back and forth had her breasts tingling. Her nipples became rigid points. Even though she'd come not long ago, she could feel her arousal building again.

He applied more pressure, creating a smaller space to force himself through. Frankie watched his eyes roll back in his head.

She didn't know what to do with her own hands, but she felt silly with them simply resting on the bed beside her, leaving him to do all the work. So she started to caress his thighs, but that didn't seem to be enough. She wanted to touch him in a more intimate way.

Gabe rocked above her, apparently not in any hurry, though he looked as though he were going through hell. His body was tense. His eyes were closed, his head tossed back. Bright red spots stained the upper ridges of his cheeks.

He bit his bottom lip and Frankie had the insane urge to tell him to stop.

She raised her hands to his torso, running them up the wall of his chest, delighting in the way his muscles quivered beneath her palms until she reached his nipples. Tiny brown discs with a little pebble that, oh, when she grazed them with the pad of her fingertips, made him gasp and jerk.

His eyes flew open. His hungry gaze zeroed in like a laser, captured and held hers in its grip.

Feeling bold, Frankie rubbed each one of his nipples, pausing to pinch them lightly, pleased when his eyes widened and he sucked in a harsh breath.

He increased his movement, driving his cock in and out, the lube and his own excitement easing the way. He tightened his hold, pushing her tits tight together. "Frankie. I'm not sure I can stop. Fuck, I don't want to stop."

"Then don't," she whispered.

Preparing for when the head of his cock breached the top of her breasts the next time, she raised her head. As it made its appearance, she kissed the tip. On the next she swiped it with her tongue. On the next she tasted him.

His rolling hip thrusts bordered on frantic, each one shoving his cock through the barely there opening.

She tried to work with him, giving him more of what he needed to get him to where she wanted him to go.

And then he was gone.

"What…?" She opened her eyes.

"I need to be inside you." Gabe was tearing open the condom wrapper and rolling the latex down his length. His arms shook, his glazed eyes looked wild. "God, I hope you're ready for me," he mumbled.

"I am."

Even in a state of desperation, he reached out to touch her between the legs, running two fingers through her moisture, taking the time to test by pumping them in and out a few times.

"I told you." She couldn't resist teasing him. She'd never wanted to tease before while having sex.

He growled at her. "You did. But I needed to make sure. I refuse to cause you any sort of pain."

She sobered. "You won't." As least he wouldn't hurt her body. She was beginning to think her heart might be an entirely different matter. She was so far from the type of woman he'd told her he was looking for. She might scratch an itch, but she was hardly lifetime commitment material for him.

Positioning himself between her legs, he placed his cock at her opening and began to push inside. He paused and came down over her, resting on his forearms. "Ready?"

She could only nod. But he surprised her again. How the man had the patience to give it to her slow she'd never understand. If she'd been him, she'd have thrust hard and fast.

But soon enough that's exactly what he was doing. Rolling his hips, driving inside her. Each deep plunge had her reaching for the stars. Then he grabbed one of her legs and brought it up, bending it to her chest, changing his angle, stimulating an entirely new set of nerves.

Frankie gasped. "Gabe. I'm gonna come again."

"Of course you are, sweetheart. I wouldn't have it any other way." He grunted and increased the momentum.

The spiral was quick and hard, shoving her straight over the edge into sensual oblivion.

Gabe only slowed long enough to allow her to catch her breath, but he never actually stopped.

As soon as her chest stopped heaving and she could see without spots dancing in front of her eyes, he reared back and pulled out of her. He flipped her over to her stomach and tapped her on the right hip. "Up on your knees, Francesca."

She rose to all fours, her stance shaky at best.

Gabe wasted no time, seating himself back inside her, his hands gripping her waist, probably leaving marks she'd treasure as he plunged deep. Faster and faster his groin slapped against her behind. His thrusts shoved her forward on the bed, but she somehow managed to stabilize her position and rock her body back to slam against him. She couldn't believe it, but she felt her body rising to the occasion one more time.

He dug his fingers into her flesh. He filled her so completely.

She felt stuffed in the most erotic way. And it felt good.

"That's it. Come on, Francesca. You can do it. This time we're going to do it together."

Then, with one of his fingers, he found her clit. And it was all over.

Frankie cried out as she exploded around him.

Gabe fucked her with a few more hard strokes and then drove into her one final time.

She felt a shudder work its way through his big body as he uttered a harsh sound, his muscles straining, his hold on her hips bruising.

Had she said she didn't need a distraction? Boy was she wrong. So wrong.

# CHAPTER NINETEEN

After she'd collapsed on the bed with Gabe's weight warming her back last night, she'd fallen asleep, too exhausted to move a muscle. She barely remembered him leaving the bed that first time and coming back with a warm washcloth to clean her. She should have been mortified, would have been if she'd had her wits about her, but she'd been as spent as a wet noodle.

Then he'd carried her to his bedroom and tucked her into his big cozy bed. Wrapping his large body around her, he pulled her back into his chest, settled a heavy arm over her hip, and splayed his fingers over her belly in a possessive fashion, keeping her close.

She paused in her steps, a smile curving her mouth. She couldn't ever remember feeling like this—almost giddy. But then guilt assailed her for the way she sneaked out of Gabe's place early this morning. She'd never spent the night with a man before. At the time she'd been too spent, and too caught up in watching him sleep, that she couldn't bring herself to leave.

No doubt he had rocked her world, more than once, during the night. He'd given her about an hour's reprieve before waking her to the sensation of his talented tongue. They'd only stopped to hydrate themselves and swallow slices of pineapple and chunks of cheese in the early morning hours before one final round of some of the best sex she'd probably ever have.

When she'd closed her eyes, her lids far too heavy to remain open any longer after he kissed her behind the ear, he'd mumbled something that sounded very much like "you can be the boss of me any day Francesca Stevens."

She must have heard wrong.

She'd woken, the sun already attempting to work its way through his bedroom blinds. And by that time, unfortunately, doubt filed in like a marching band as soon as she'd opened her eyes. And like a thief, she'd sneaked out from beneath the warmth of the sheets and his Adonis-like body, leaving him snoring quietly on the opposite side of the bed. She had gathered her clothes from where she'd piled them in the bathroom, snapped her purse and shoes up from where she'd dumped them on the floor just inside the door, and then she'd made her getaway in a cab.

Frankie juggled a set of drawings under one arm, while she gripped the rim of her half-empty coffee cup between her teeth and turned the key to unlock the trailer door.

After a quick shower back in her own home, she was ready to face the day—and a busy one at that. But at least she could honestly say she'd gotten well laid last night so her body was relaxed and she didn't think anything could knock her off such a glorious high.

Just as she was about to turn the key, her cell phone rang. Damn it. Setting the drawings and her coffee down, she pulled her phone from her pocket, noticed the caller ID, and answered.

"Hi, Lawrence. It's kind of early for you to be calling, isn't it?"

"Hello, Frankie."

"Look, I'm just about to start work."

"I'm sorry."

"Sorry for what?" She responded the same way each time, because this wasn't the first time Lawrence had apologized.

"I'm s…s….sorry about your d…d…dad."

"I know." Since the day her dad died, Lawrence had been

looking out for her. His best friend's death had been hard on him and he'd been drinking more than usual over the last few months. Where the passage of time generally helped in the healing process, for Lawrence, it only made him sadder. "Are you OK, Lawrence?"

One of her drawings rolled away from the pile, and she hopped over the others to stop it from getting too far.

"You don't deserve," he mumbled something she couldn't make out. "It was supposed to be me…mine."

"What was?" She heard a thump followed by a muffled yelp. "Lawrence, is everything all right?"

"No. No…your…fault. All of it. I…You'll…" He coughed, the sound brutal and sad at the same time. "Pay… Will…will be though. Soon. I promise."

His words were slurred and confused. She couldn't make out what he was trying to say. Her heart went out to this man who had been there her entire life. "Lawrence, try to—"

The line went dead.

She sighed and stuck her phone back in her pocket before she bent down to pick up the drawings, making a mental note to check on her godfather later in the day. Sticking her paper coffee cup back between her teeth, she jiggled the key in the lock.

In this weather, the trailer door typically would stick so she gave it a good, solid shove, startled when it flew wide in an easy arc and crashed against the wall with a resounding bang that reverberated throughout the structure, shaking it on its moorings.

She stepped inside and stumbled to a stop. Not that she could go much further. Her feet were glued to the spot. Her drawings fell from her tenuous grip. Her coffee cup fell from her mouth and splattered all over the floor. Again, not that it mattered.

Tears of frustration and rage welled, but she pushed them

back, determined to keep it together. But holy crap was it hard. Who the hell hated her so much that they would do this? Damn it.

Frankie moved only her eyes. Swinging from left to right she captured the scene as though through a camera. She really should be backing out, going up to the house and getting one. That would be the smart thing to do. This time she couldn't just sweep up the mess. A little cleaning product, elbow grease, and trash bags wouldn't put it in quick order.

This wouldn't be a cruel memory in thirty minutes.

She squeezed her eyes closed. Maybe it was a dream. Maybe she was still in Gabe's warm bed, curled up in his arms, the scent of sex heavy in the air.

She opened her eyes and sobbed. Fuck.

The entire inside of her workspace was destroyed. Whoever had the balls and intent to do this much damage went for maximum effect. They'd left the outside of the trailer intact so she wouldn't know until she walked through the door. Why bother?

"What the fuck!" someone said behind her.

Frankie screamed at the harsh expletive and spun around. Gabe stood behind her, his eyes flashing, his nostrils flaring, and his chest rising and falling like a bull about to rush the red cape.

Her very first instinct was throw herself into his arms, but she shook off the feeling, disappointed and pissed that after only a few short weeks with the man and she was ready to toss away her independence and let the big strong male take care of her.

But was that really so bad? Because today, she could really use it.

"Don't touch anything." His quietly controlled words didn't match the expression on his face, one that reminded her of a volcano about to erupt.

"I just got here."

Two quick steps and he was right next to her, his arm out and blocking her from going any further into the trailer. "Go outside, Frankie. Let me check to make sure they're gone."

She hadn't even thought of that and now cursed her stupidity for standing there like an idiot while the perpetrator could very well be hiding in the bathroom or her office.

Clearly her foolishness showed on her face because Gabe rested his palm against her cheek and dialed it down a bit. "Stay here while I take a quick look."

He picked his way carefully through the trailer, avoiding strewn pieces of drawings and documents, spilled coffee grounds, broken pencils, and shredded furniture.

While he searched and she wondered about the state of her office, Frankie cringed over the permanent marker designs on the walls, the dangling window blinds, the dented filing cabinets, and the splintered chairs. Not only would she have to paint, she would also need to purchase new furniture and window coverings. Everything was ruined.

"There's nobody in there."

She turned toward him. "My office?"

"Same as here. Worse, probably."

She closed her eyes. "How bad?" At least she didn't keep anything truly personal in the trailer. These things could all be fixed or replaced.

"They emptied your cabinets and tipped them over; spray painted the walls and gouged your desk pretty good. Smashed your pictures." He stopped directly in front of her, toe-to-toe.

The scent of his cologne drifted to her, oddly comforting as he placed one hand on each of her shoulders, his fingers curling into a gentle grip. "I'm sorry, Frankie."

She frowned. That was the second time in as many minutes that he'd called her Frankie instead of Francesca. She didn't like it. It meant he felt sorry for her. She didn't want him feeling sorry for her. She wanted him to help her find the bastard who did this and then step aside while she kicked his fucking ass.

Frankie backed out of Gabe's hold when he tried to take her in his arms.

"I'm fine, Gabe. I'm pissed. Like royally ready-to-rip-somebody-a-new-one pissed off. But I'll be fine." She was always fine. Other people counted on her. She had to be.

He stuck his hands in his pockets. "I'll call my brothers. There may be something they can glean from the security equipment."

They both looked up to where a camera had been mounted in the corner of the trailer. It was one of the new ones installed by the security firm Gabe's brothers hired. Red paint covered the lens and it dangled from its mount.

"It's across the room, Francesca. At the very least it captured an image of the intruders as they entered the trailer. And they don't have the tape. We do."

He was right. They'd be able to tell who did it. At last, she'd have some answers. "Call your brothers. I want to know right now who's doing this and why." And then she'd kick some fucking ass.

Gabe retrieved his phone from his pocket and stepped outside to make the call.

While he talked, she walked through the trailer, careful not to disturb anything this time. Each step she took, her irritation grew. She searched her mind, like she had so many times already, looking for anything she might have done that deserved this type of retaliation. Was it somebody she didn't hire? A client who didn't like her work? A job she won instead of another company? She couldn't think of a single person she may have crossed that would be this upset. In her business, contactors won and lost bids. It happened to everyone, her included. She didn't win the biggest, brightest, coolest projects. In the big scheme of things, she was small potatoes.

It just didn't make sense.

"Thanks, Kyle. Yeah. Have them send a copy of the tape as soon as they can. I'll meet you at the office by end of day and we'll take a look ourselves before we turn it over to the police."

Gabe had stepped back inside, but Frankie waited until she heard him end the call before she turned around.

"Do they have the tape?" she asked.

"Kyle called the security company while I was on the phone with him. And yes, they have the tapes from the last twenty-four hours and they took a quick look at the interior ones while I waited. The camera did catch somebody."

Excitement bubbled within her regardless of the caution she heard in his voice.

"Unfortunately he was wearing a hoodie and avoided looking at the camera."

Her excitement deflated like a popped balloon.

"We have the exterior cameras, too. The security company only glanced at the interior one, but they'll send all of them."

"Good." She didn't want to get her hopes up.

"I've also put in a call to the police. They should be here any minute."

She'd forgotten about them. It should have been the first thing she'd done after discovering the break-in. She nodded. "Thank you. If you're heading over to see your brother..." As she looked around the room, Frankie couldn't disguise the disappointment in her voice. She didn't even try. She just hoped he attributed it to the damage surrounding them. "I'll just stay here and clean up this mess."

He moved closer and placed two fingers under her chin, lifting until they met eye to eye.

He had a habit of doing that. Or did she just have a habit of not looking him in the eye?

"I'm not going anywhere at the moment, Francesca."

"But–"

"No buts," he said. "I'm not leaving until after the police have finished their initial investigation, taken your statement, and we've locked up the trailer for the night." He paused, and when she dropped her gaze, he bent lower, dipped his head, and captured her line of sight again. "Then you and I are going to head to my brothers' office and take a look at the video together. Maybe you'll see something or recognize something about the guy that we wouldn't catch. We *will* find out who's behind this. I promise."

She closed her eyes and licked her lips, doing a slow count backward from five before she looked at him again. "I know. And I appreciate everything you're doing, Gabe. I really do. I just can't figure out what I've done to cause such destructive anger in somebody. What did I do to cause somebody to hate me so much? This is beyond simple vandalism. It's not just a bunch of kids screwing around. This is hate, Gabe. Somebody hates me so much they're doing their best to put me out of business."

This time when he pulled her into the safe haven of his arms, she went without hesitation. Frankie burrowed into his strong chest and took a deep breath. She shuddered as she let fear battle with her rage. She couldn't say which emotion was winning.

Gabe tightened his hold.

This was where she felt safe. She knew without a doubt that no harm would come to her as long as Gabe McBride was around.

# CHAPTER TWENTY

THROUGHOUT THE ENTIRE PROCESS OF THE POLICE ARRIVing, scoping out the scene and taking Frankie's statement, then waiting for her to confirm if anything appeared to be missing, Gabe stood nearby and let her take control of the situation.

At the moment, Gabe knew she needed to feel empowered. Having somebody enter your space uninvited and then destroy something you'd worked hard to build would leave anybody feeling violated. Although he wanted nothing more than to tuck her away in a safe corner where nobody could cause her any additional grief, including the cops who were only doing their job, Gabe respected the fact that Frankie had to do this on her own.

But he refused to leave. If she needed him, he was only a few steps away.

When he stepped outside to call his brothers with an update, a few of the guys from her work crew drove up in one of the pick-ups, sliding to a dusty halt when they saw the police cruiser parked near the trailer.

Two men jumped from the cab of the truck and rushed over. Her foreman, Randy, was one of them. The other man was closer to Francesca's age. Blond, built, and good-looking, judging by the additional bulk he carried, construction labor wasn't his only form of exercise. Gabe recognized his face from the picture he'd seen and the video he'd seen him on. This was John, her old boyfriend.

Instant jealousy flared. An unfamiliar sensation, but recognizable for what it was.

Gabe stepped forward, blocking John's path to the trailer stairs. Nothing had turned up on the guy when his brothers checked into him, but Gabe still didn't trust him.

The younger man hesitated and glared. "What the hell do you think you're doing? Move out of my way, asshole."

Gabe shook his head. "Sorry. You can't go in there right now."

Randy's eyes widened. John paused, his mouth hanging open in astonishment. "What?" He tried to push past Gabe again. "Get the hell out of my way. This is Frankie's place, and if she's in there and needs help, I need to get to her."

"Sorry. Not going to happen."

Randy moved to intercept. He hitched a thumb in Gabe's direction, but spoke to John. "This is the security guy Frankie hired."

"That's right, sir. I am," Gabe didn't extend his hand yet for a formal introduction. "I'm Gabriel McBride, one of the owners of McBride Security." He turned to stare straight into John's frigid glare.

Behind them, the door opened and Francesca preceded Officer Peters and his partner out. Gabe moved out of their way.

"Frankie, honey. Are you OK?" Given the opportunity to get to her, the chump sprung forward and tried to put his arm around her shoulder.

Gabe barely managed to conceal his growl of protectiveness, but he couldn't prevent his fists from clenching at his sides or his back molars from grinding together.

Only when Francesca cringed and wiggled her way out of the man's embrace did Gabe relax his stance, though only slightly.

He worked his way between her and John and took a position at her side. He was startled by an overwhelming sense of comfort. And when she leaned against him, a surge of male satisfaction filled him.

"John, I'm fine. Give me a few minutes to finish up with the police."

John pinned Gabe with a nasty stare and then returned his attention to Frankie. "What happened? Why are the police here?"

Frankie glanced up at him, her stance stiff against his side.

Gabe sensed her unease and could see the questions in her eyes. She wondered how much she could or should divulge. He shook his head the slightest bit so as not to raise the curiosity of the other two men more than it already was.

"It looks like somebody broke into the trailer during the night," she said. "That's all."

"What? That's all? Did they take anything, do any damage?" Randy asked the obvious questions while John continued to glower at Gabe.

Gabe couldn't help it; he puffed up his chest a little and widened his stance. It took everything in him not to snake an arm around Frankie and watch the jerk explode.

Even though she pressed against him for support, Frankie faced the men without hesitation. "No, it doesn't look like they took anything, but I'll need to do a thorough check after the police are finished. They're trying to lift fingerprints. That's why we need to wait out here."

She impressed Gabe with her smooth-as-silk answers. But the slight tremor running her through body indicated she was more rattled than she let on. They still needed to discuss her disappearing act this morning. He thought they'd made headway. After a fabulous night together, one that he'd be thinking about for a long time to come, he'd actually indulged in some daydreaming. Gabe easily envisioned waking up with her and making love to her before their morning coffee and then again in the shower. For many mornings to come.

She'd taken flight on him twice now.

When he'd woken alone this morning, he'd hoped she'd just

decided to get up and find his coffeemaker. Had that been the case, he would have been here when she opened the trailer this morning. He would have been with her instead of waking up in a bed gone cold and a sense of emptiness in his home he'd never experienced before.

What would have happened if the intruder were still on site? She could have been hurt. The thought of her being hurt, or worse, created a cold lump in the pit of his gut and a bad sense of foreboding he couldn't shake.

"Look, Frankie," John said, with a sideways sneer in Gabe's direction before he poured on the syrup. "Maybe you should come and stay with me for a while. Where it's safe. Where I can take care of you, baby."

Gabe tensed. Like hell that would happen. And he suspected Frankie hated being called baby.

"John, I'm fine. Besides, I can't leave Sophie here on her own."

"Then I'll come here. I'll just run home and pack a bag." John turned.

Gabe grabbed his arm and hauled him around before he managed more than a step.

Frankie's ex struggled and looked like he might take a swing.

Gabe almost, *almost* wished he would. It had been years since he and his brothers had resorted to using their fists to solve their problems. Insane jealousy raged through him as he pictured Francesca in bed with this asshole, and he clenched his right hand into a tight fist.

"What the fuck?" John said.

Gabe resisted the urge to use a show of strength and called on the control he closely guarded, even though right now it appeared to be bursting at the seams to be set free. "I don't think that will be necessary. But I'm sure Francesca appreciates the offer."

"Frankie, who the hell does this guy think he is? Haven't you told him who I am?" He shrugged, yanking his arm free from Gabe's tight grasp. "Get your hands off me, asshole."

"John, you're an employee."

Shock showed on his face. "Employee? Babe, I'm a lot more than an employee to you, and you know it."

Gabe's attention snapped to John's face at the confirmation of his relationship with her. Was Frankie still seeing this guy? She'd told him about their relationship, but had said it was in the past. The details his brothers had uncovered in their background search confirmed the two had dated, but that it had ended well over a year ago. Had she been hiding whatever she had going on with him?

They had him on camera once already, though it didn't provide any damning evidence. And now he shows up just after the vandalism. Maybe he was smarter than he looked and he was the one behind the break-ins and the destruction. Was it as simple as a jealous lover?

Suddenly, Gabe was very interested in wrapping things up so they could get to the office and take a look at the video. If they found John on tape entering the trailer, they had their man.

"John?" Gabe feigned ignorance. "Where were you last night?"

The guy looked perplexed at the question. "Last night?"

"That's what I said."

Frankie was giving him a strange look.

John shrugged. "Home, watching TV. Why?"

"Just wondering. Can anybody confirm that for you?"

"No."

"Well then, I guess we'll just have the police check into your alibi."

"Wait. What? Alibi? What the fuck are you talking about?" He spun to Frankie. "What the fuck is he talking about?"

"I don't know." Frankie looked at him, obviously wondering the same thing.

The police saved him from providing an immediate answer, but he wasn't going to let John get too far away.

Officer Peters stopped next to them, while his partner continued on to the patrol car.

"Ms. Stevens, we've got everything we need for now. I suggest you take the time to go through the trailer and see if anything has been stolen. I'm sure your insurance will cover the damage. If you can think of anyone who might have done it, please give us a call. Do you still have my business card?"

"I do."

He turned to Gabe. "You'll need to turn those tapes from the cameras over to the police."

"We will." Gabe had told Peters earlier that the surveillance tapes were being sent to his office. He simply hadn't indicated that he and his brothers would be looking at them first. Gabe pointed to John. "I think you might want to question this gentleman though."

"What!"

"Excuse me?" John's offended outburst coincided with Frankie's exclamation.

Voices rose, but Officer Peters settled everyone down. "Mr. McBride, why do you suggest that? Do you know something?"

"We have this man on tape sneaking in and out of the barn a few days after the flooring was damaged."

"I didn't do anything," John shouted and then spun to Frankie. "Frankie, I don't know what he's talking about, but I didn't do anything. You know I wouldn't do anything to hurt you. You know how I feel about you."

"John, shut up for a minute. Gabe, what are you talking about?"

"When we checked the tapes the other day we saw John here sneaking into the barn. He looked suspicious. Did you know many perpetrators show up at the scene of their crime? They like to see the reactions of people."

Poor Francesca. He hated the look of betrayal on her face. She glared at John.

Peters gave Gabe a pointed glance. "I'll take that tape as well, Mr. McBride." He looked at John. "Sir, would you mind coming down to the station and answering a few questions?"

"Fucking right, I mind," he stated. "I wasn't doing anything wrong. I was only planning on borrowing a tool that I'd borrowed once before."

"Borrow?" Gabe didn't believe him. "Your hands were empty."

John rolled his eyes. "Yes, borrow. Frankie doesn't like when we use work tools for personal purposes. I broke my drill at home and needed to borrow one. But I couldn't find the bits I wanted, so I left it."

Gabe still didn't believe him. "Officer, I'll call my security office and have a copy of the tape in question sent to your station within the hour," Gabe offered.

Frankie straightened her spine and pursed her lips.

John refused to budge.

All this time, Francesca's foreman had stood by watching the whole scene unfurl. Now, he glanced toward Frankie, then looked at John. "I'll drive you to the station," he said.

John glared at all of them, but stomped over to the truck, climbed into the passenger side, and slammed the door shut.

Frankie faced Randy. "When you're done with John, go check on the jobs for me. I've got work to do here."

"Sure thing, Frankie. If you need any help cleaning up, give me a call. I can send a few of the guys over to get it done for you."

"Thanks, Randy. But I'll take care of it. I need to go through it anyway and make sure nothing is missing." She patted him on the arm. "Thanks anyway."

While the police finished with Frankie, Gabe called the office and arranged to have a copy of the tape from last week sent to the police station.

As soon as Frankie joined him again, he ended the call and pulled her into his arms, unable to wait a moment longer, his gut wrenched by the look of utter defeat on her face.

"Come on, sweetheart. I'll help you clean up and take notes and then we'll head down to see my brothers."

"Gabe, I need to find out who's doing this."

"We will." And it was a vow he intended to keep.

# CHAPTER TWENTY-ONE

Hours later, Gabe walked into his brothers' office with Frankie. After the police had left, she'd entered the construction trailer with a determined expression on her face, but she hadn't uttered a word. Other than responding to his requests about missing items or questions about what she wanted him to do with certain things, she'd been silent during the time it had taken them to clean up the trailer.

At no time did her sister come to help. When he'd asked why, Frankie simply stated that her sister did not set foot inside the trailer or the barn for that matter. Something about mice. Although he thought it a silly excuse, he didn't mind that they'd spent the time alone. They didn't speak, but he enjoyed having her near him. Where he could watch over her.

Every now and then, the sound of her soft sobs had reached his ears. He'd pause in whatever he was doing, but not wanting to embarrass her, he had remained where he was, finishing the tasks she needed him to focus on.

He'd worked in the main area while she worked in the back office. On the surface, nothing seemed to be missing. Which meant whoever had slipped in during the night and tore the place apart had solely been intent on hurting her. A crime of passion. But passion came in many forms, and in this case, he didn't think it was a jealous rage.

As the afternoon had worn on, he'd come to the conclusion John wasn't their guy. The damage was too random. Generally people in fits of jealous rage focused on their target's personal items, things that meant the world to them, and did their utmost to destroy them. The vandalism in the trailer was more like a child having a major tantrum lashing out from spite. No specific area or item received more attention than any other.

When the broken furniture was gone, the floors and windows cleaned, and the binders and drawers returned as best they could, they'd taken stock of what needed to be replaced. The walls needed new paint. A couple of the windows in the back needed new glass. Frankie made notes of drawings she'd need to replace, as well as basic kitchen items.

They'd left the trailer, turning out the lights and locking up after Gabe reinstalled the camera, though this time he hid it temporarily behind a plant. He'd arrange for a different style of camera later, one that could easily be hidden. Then he'd waited on the front porch while she'd gone inside to take a shower. When she'd reappeared in clean clothes and sporting red eyes, he'd hustled her into his car for the drive to McBride Security.

"Hey, stranger." Melissa jumped up from behind the reception desk and ran to him, throwing her arms around him. He caught her up and hugged her. He'd loved this woman like a baby sister since the day Kyle had found her beaten to a pulp in the alley behind their office.

"Hey, Mel. How are you? More importantly, how are Jamie and Daniel? Keeping you occupied and in-line I'm sure."

For months, they'd tried to find out who the bastard was that had hurt her, eager to dish out some of the same treatment. But she'd been tight-lipped until Jamie Stewart and Daniel Oliver entered her life with the intent of making her happy. When her ex made an appearance at The Vault deciding to cause a scene, they'd finally been able to hold him accountable for his actions.

"They are. But I'm not sure you really want to know the details of my sex life, now do you?"

"Don't go there, bro," Kyle said as he walked into the reception area and over to Melissa's desk to drop a file folder into her in-basket. "Because she is so fucking happy she will tell you all the gory details. I see enough of them at the club, thank you very much. I don't need to hear her non-edited version of it as well."

Kyle tweaked her nose.

She slapped his hand away.

Since he was the one who had actually found her, the two had a very special relationship.

"I wouldn't tell him everything, Kyle."

"No, I'm sure you'd stick to things like how special the guys make you feel and how perfect your life is with the two of them." He mimed sticking his finger down his throat.

"Actually, I was going to tell Gabe about the puppy they brought home." She winked at Kyle and then turned and faced him. "The guys went to work last week and found a box with an abandoned puppy waiting for them."

Jamie and Daniel were Doms at The Vault who had captured Melissa's heart a while back. Actually, she'd dated Jamie when they were teenagers, and he'd had no idea she was even in town. When she'd accidently run into him, she'd decided to track him down. She'd met his partner in the veterinary clinic during the process. The three had become a happy and satisfied threesome and apparently the owners of a new puppy.

Behind him, Frankie cleared her throat.

"Oh damn. I'm sorry. Kyle, Melissa, this is Francesca Stevens—Frankie. She's the woman we've been working for." Gabe stepped aside so Frankie could come forward.

Kyle stuck out his hand. "It's nice to finally meet you, Frankie."

"Likewise."

"Hi, Frankie." Melissa motioned between him and Kyle. "If these two give you any trouble, just let me know."

Frankie smiled at Mel's attempt to lighten the mood, but

Gabe could see the tightness in her jaw, the dark emotion in her eyes. She just wanted to get some answers.

He turned to Kyle. "Any luck on the tape?"

"It's set up in the conference room. Come on back."

Gabe and Frankie followed Kyle to the conference room while Melissa promised to follow with bottles of water for everyone.

Kyle headed straight to the DVD player and flicked it on while Gabe pulled out a chair for Frankie, taking the one right next to her. Melissa joined them two minutes later.

"Only one person entered the trailer. Time stamp of two a.m." Kyle swiveled in his chair. "Unfortunately, he's wearing a dark hoodie and gloves. We don't get a view of his face. We do know he's Caucasian though. He kept his head down most of the time, but he raised it slightly when he reached for the camera, so we got a flash of skin on his neck."

The image of the inside of the trailer appeared on the television screen. Frankie leaned forward to study the image.

"Judging by the size and build of the person, I'm guessing it's a man," Kyle continued.

They watched as the door opened and a person dressed in black plants and wearing a dark hoodie and gloves entered the trailer.

"He looks around, spots the camera, and then sprays and disables it for good measure."

As Kyle gave the play-by-play, Gabe watched each movement of the guy, trying to see something.

"It could be anybody." Frankie's whispered statement echoed his own, only hers contained deep disappointment.

Gabe reached for her hand, twining his fingers with hers and squeezing, wanting to reassure her. "We do know one thing." When he looked up, his brother was paying close attention. Too close. When the grin appeared on his face,

Gabe didn't know if he should snarl or thump his chest. "He knew about the camera."

Kyle got serious. "Yup."

Frankie looked first at Kyle then at him. "What does that mean?"

Gabe shifted closer to her. "It means it's somebody who probably knows you. He's certainly been in the trailer before." He hated the pained look on her face.

"Hey there, what did I miss?" Kade strode in behind them, his wife Brienna on his arm.

Kyle jumped up and slapped him on the back as he passed and took a seat on the opposite side.

Gabe rose to give his sister-in-law a welcoming hug and a kiss on the cheek.

"I was just showing them the video from the trailer," Kyle clarified.

Kade pulled out a chair for his wife and leaned down to kiss her on the cheek. Then he stood and looked straight at Francesca. "Frankie Stevens, I presume." He reached across the table to shake her hand. "It's a pleasure to meet you."

"Yes. Hi."

"I'm Kade, and this is my wife Brienna."

Brienna gave a little hand wave and mouthed hello.

Kade took a seat. "Sorry I'm late. I decided to double check the information we've pulled together from the employee list you gave us. Other than Lawrence Diamond having a bit of a drinking problem, everyone is fairly clean I'm afraid."

"That's a bad thing?" Frankie asked.

"No. Of course not. Not from your perspective anyway. It would have made our job a whole lot easier if one of them had a record."

"I make a point of hiring people I can trust."

Gabe hated how small her voice sounded. Usually she was a force to be reckoned with. Right now she simply looked beaten.

"How do you know about Lawrence's problem?" she asked.

Kyle leaned forward and put his elbows on the table. "We did a little bit of digging. He's spent quite a bit of money at various liquor stores around town. Unfortunately, it's starting to affect his business."

Frankie straightened in her chair. "What do you mean?"

"He hasn't had any new jobs for about two months now. He's had to let most of his crew go. He's only got a couple of guys working, finishing up a few projects."

Frankie's frown deepened. "He hasn't said anything to me."

"I take it there's nothing on the video you recognize?" Kade asked.

Gabe watched Frankie shake her head. He could tell she'd disengaged. "Nothing," he said. "He, and we're assuming it's a he, damaged the camera. And he was wearing gloves when he entered the trailer."

"What about the camera from the office?"

Kade shook his head. "Nothing. Wires ripped and the camera smashed before it recorded anything."

Francesca rose to her feet. "Thank you for all you're doing. I think I'd better get home now. I'd like to check on my sister."

Gabe jumped up. "I'll take you."

A look of relief crossed her face.

He reached for her hand again and moved to head toward the door. Did she really think he'd just stick her in a taxi and send her on her way?

"Hey, before you go, Brienna and I have some news," Kade called out.

Gabe stopped in his tracks.

Kyle gave his twin his full attention.

Gabe could tell by the light in Kyle's eyes, he knew about the announcement. Had to be the twin thing. It had driven him nuts as a child. Those two seemed to communicate without words sometimes. But this time, Gabe could guess, and joy began to build in his chest.

Kade looked at his wife and beamed. "We're having a baby."

Melissa squealed as only a female can and ran to Brienna.

Gabe couldn't be more pleased for the two of them. He rounded the table to hug and congratulate both of them. After they'd exchanged a few more words, he remembered Frankie and spun around, but she was gone. Again. He'd have to deal with this habit she had of running out on him.

"I'll catch you guys later," he said. "Congrats again." He kissed Brienna on the cheek and hurried from the room. He expected to find Francesca hailing a cab out front. But he found her in the reception area staring out the window. And not a cab in sight.

He slowed his steps and came up behind her. "Hey."

"Hey."

"You OK?"

"I'm thinking about something I found the first time somebody broke into my trailer."

"What did you find, Francesca?"

"I found a picture of my family ripped to shreds."

Gabe could only stare at her, shocked. "And why is this the first time I'm hearing about this?"

She shrugged. "I chalked it up to vandals screwing with me. Now I'm not so sure."

"Did you tell the police?" he asked. He shoved his anger aside, his worry for her safety taking precedence.

"Nope."

Gabe gently turned her around. "You need to tell the police, honey. This is serious."

"I realize that now, Gabe. Then it was simply something else that was tipped over or ripped. It didn't stand out before." She sighed, her exhaustion showing. "I'll call them on the way to my place. I need to get home, now. I'm not comfortable leaving Sophie there all by herself."

"Let's go. Give her a call too, and let her know we're on our way."

## CHAPTER TWENTY-TWO

"SO HOW'S THINGS WITH GABE?" HER SISTER ASKED. "Please tell me you guys have been having wild monkey sex behind closed doors."

After Gabe had arranged for additional security and dropped her off with a promise to call if she heard anything or thought there might be any sort of danger, Frankie had changed into her favorite pajamas and joined her sister in the kitchen.

She didn't want to frighten Sophie, but she needed to tell her about what had happened and make sure she understood the potential danger. Of course, her sister brushed off the whole conversation, more interested in Frankie's sex life than the fact that somebody had come onto their property and damaged their things.

"Sophie. Please. I need you to take this seriously."

"I am. But is there anything I can do about it right at this instant?" she asked.

"No."

"And you're here with me, so I don't have to worry about you out there on your own, now do I?"

"No."

"Beauty is sleeping by the door. If anybody comes to the house, she'll let us know."

Frankie rolled her eyes. The dog would probably fart, roll over, and go back to sleep. "Sophie, this is serious. Somebody is targeting me for some reason. Now Gabe is arranging for additional security to keep watch on the property. We'll meet whoever he hires so we have no unnecessary surprises. In the meantime, the police will check in during their rounds so don't be alarmed if you see them roaming around."

"Fine, fine. I get it. Bad guy. Extra security—hopefully they're as hot as your guy." Sophie sat on a chair at the kitchen table, one leg bent and curled under her while she peeled an orange, dropping the rind on a paper towel and popping slice after slice into her mouth. "Now, back to my original question."

When he'd dropped her off, Gabe had insisted on coming in and checking all corners of the house, the barn, and the trailer to ensure all locks were locked and nobody lurked in the shadows.

Sophie had watched from her perch as he'd moved throughout the house.

Frankie envied her sister's laidback view of life, her carefree attitude in everything she did. She'd been like that since she was a little girl. She never worried about things. She'd never known their mom, so didn't really miss her. The severed link Frankie had experienced with their mother's death, Sophie couldn't relate to.

While Frankie and her father had spent years making sure Sophie had everything she needed growing up, Sophie felt none of the pressures of running a family business. She made it clear she planned to find a job she loved. She didn't want one handed to her that she felt obligated to take. She didn't understand or want the responsibility of having to ensure payroll would be completed on time. Instead, she'd had her friends and school dances and parties.

Not that Frankie couldn't have had all those things too. If she'd really wanted them, her father would have done his best to ensure she'd had the opportunity to experience them. But after her mother died giving birth to Sophie, Frankie had felt a sense of obligation, even at a young age, to be the surrogate mother her sister needed. She'd done everything her tiny five-year-old brain could think of to help her daddy with the new baby.

Those self-directed duties continued throughout the years. And though tools interested her far more than Barbies, she'd made an effort to play with dolls for Sophie's sake, and still put extra time in with her father, learning everything she could about the construction industry.

"I'm not going to discuss my sex life with you." Frankie poured herself a cup of decaffeinated coffee and leaned against the counter to flip through the newspaper she hadn't had time for this morning. Was it only this morning she'd sneaked way from Gabe's bed? It felt like years ago.

"Oh, please. I'm no longer little. And frankly, I probably have more sex than you do." She rolled her eyes. "Which is sad for you."

"I don't want to hear about your sex life either." Frankie lifted the mug to her mouth and took a sip of the hot brew. After spilling hers this morning, she'd never replaced it. Come to think of it, she'd never eaten either. Not that she had an appetite at the moment.

"You've got access to this freakin' hot guy and you're telling me you're not taking advantage of that?" Sophie didn't look convinced.

"I said I wasn't going to talk about it."

Her sister slapped her palm against the table. "So you *are* tapping that hunk." She pointed a finger. "I knew it."

"Tapping that hunk," Frankie echoed slowly. "Did you seriously just say that?"

"Yes, I did. That's what the 'kids' say these days. God, Frankie. Sometimes you're so old." Sophie stood and walked over to toss her pile of orange peelings into the garbage. She spun around and leaned against the opposite counter, her expression somber, her tone genuine for a change. "Seriously, sis. Gabe seems nice and you deserve to have somebody nice in your life. Mind you, it doesn't hurt that he's sexy as sin." She grinned and waggled her eyebrows before turning solemn again. "You've taken care of me since the day I was born. And you were just a little girl. You should have been playing with dolls, not with a live baby. Having tea parties, not preparing formula for your little sister."

"I don't regret a moment, Sophie."

"I know you don't."

"Mom would have wanted me to take care of you."

"Mom would have wanted to you be a child. I cannot believe she would have wanted anything different."

"Dad needed the help," Frankie insisted.

"Dad hired help, Frankie. But you didn't let them do their job," Sophie scolded gently. She pushed away and crossed the room, stopping a few feet away. "I appreciate everything you did for me. I still do. But it's past time you started living your own life. I'm old enough to take care of myself."

Frankie dropped her gaze, staring into the cup of now cold coffee. "The business…"

"Is yours. It was always yours. I have no interest in construction. I told Dad that a long time ago. That's why he left it to you."

"But what about what you want?" Frankie asked.

"Dad left me enough money to give me a few options."

"And do you have any idea?"

"Of course I do. You may think I have no real life plan, big sis, but I'm not as carefree and non-decisive as you've assumed. I've simply not given away my secrets."

"But maybe I can help."

Sophie pointed a finger at her. "And that's exactly why I've kept my mouth shut." She sighed. "Look, I've been taking those business classes at night. I want to have my own business."

This news stunned Frankie, and judging by her sister's roar

of laughter, it showed on her face. After picking up her jaw, she swallowed the instinctual desire to ferret out the information and decide on the best path forward for her little sister, including developing a plan for how to help her financially.

"Wow. I never knew," Frankie said.

"You never asked."

Touché. Frankie never once asked her sister about her goals or her plans. Instead she assumed and offered suggestions. And to be perfectly honest, she'd always hoped that one day Sophie would take an interest in the family business so they could work together.

It was past time to start over with her sister. It was time she treated her sister as a sister and a friend, not a child she needed to raise. "What kind of business are you thinking of?"

Sophie blushed a deep red that colored her cheeks. One of the few times she'd witnessed the vulnerable side of her little sister. "Promise you won't laugh."

"I'd never laugh about your future, Sophie," she replied in absolute truth. Regardless of her sister's plans, she'd support her one hundred and ten percent.

"A bakery. I want to make cupcakes and cookies." Sophie's shy smile told Frankie her sister still expected some sort of negative response.

"I think that's a wonderful idea."

"You do?"

"You make the best cupcakes, and your cookies are melt-in-your-mouth delicious. How far have you thought this through?"

Excitement shined in Sophie's eyes. She bounced on her toes. "I've already picked out the location, prepared a business plan, and talked to potential suppliers and the bank."

"How have I not known about this? You've been planning this for some time, haven't you?"

There was that blush again. This time she dropped her

gaze to the floor. "A while, yes. You've been busy with your projects and making a name for yourself. I didn't want to intrude."

"Yeah, but—"

"Frankie, you've been working hard for a long time. And now having to deal with whoever is causing you trouble, adding my plans to the mix didn't seem fair. And I wanted to do it myself. This is *my* baby."

Shame filled her. Shame that she'd been ignoring her sister. "I'm so proud of you." Frankie smiled through the tears burning in her eyes. Her baby sister was all grown up.

"There is something I need your help with," her sister said. "Or at least, I will."

Frankie wiped at the tears. "Of course, anything."

"I want you to do the renovation of the store."

Frankie gulped and blinked. "I'd be honored."

Sophie's face lit up. "Good. Now." That serious expression was back. "Can we please get back to my original question?"

"What was that?" A lightness entered Frankie's chest, in a spot she didn't realize she'd been carrying a weight.

"Gabe. Are you guys an item or what?"

Frankie laughed. For the first time in their relationship, she felt as though she were bonding with her best friend. And it was long past time for a good old-fashioned heart-to-heart confession. "Yes. At least I think we are, or at least we could be." She didn't think she'd object to it at any rate.

Sophie giggled. "Wow, and I thought I was the indecisive one."

"We've been spending time together and I really like him."

"Hmm. Would you love to lick him all over, or like him all over?"

"Yes, exactly."

Sophie grinned, pulled out a chair, and plopped her ass down. "Give me the details. Is he good? He looks like he'd be good. And does he have any brothers? Cousins? Anybody who looks like him?"

"Well, I can't tell you everything."

"Sure you can. I'm your sister."

"I will tell you that, yes, he's good. Yes, he has brothers. I don't know about cousins, and his brothers look a lot like him." When she'd first seen Kyle, she'd experienced a "holy hell that guy is hot" moment. When his twin had joined the party, she mentally gave thanks to their mother for adding such gorgeous specimens to the male side of the population. She figured the woman deserved a trophy for making it through their teenage years.

Sophie's eyes sparkled with evil intent, and she actually started to rub her hands together.

"His younger brothers are twins," Frankie added.

"Oooh..."

"Take it easy and wipe the drool off your lip. One of them is married."

"Hey, that still leaves one as a possibility. I'm open to possibilities."

Frankie shook her head, but she couldn't wipe the smile off her lips.

"Are you in love?" Sophie asked.

Frankie stopped short. "I—"

"Frankie, since the moment you met Gabe McBride you've had a semi-smile on your face. I don't hear you swear as much. You seem happier. And you haven't had sex since, well I don't know when. Every day, night, hour you've been spending with Gabe has put a spring in your step. Admit it, he makes you feel good. He makes you feel happy."

"I—"

"When he drove away, you watched until his taillights disappeared."

"I—"

"And you stood at the window for an extra ten minutes after that."

"Um."

"Face it. You're in love. And I'm *so* happy for you." Sophie sprang up from the chair and drew Frankie into a warm, vivacious hug. "You deserve this," she whispered in her ear.

"I don't know if I love him, Sophie. I don't know him *that* well. But I do really, really like him." Even if she wasn't the type of woman he wanted for a wife. Wife? Where had that come from?

"You know everything you need to know." Sophie pulled back but kept her hands on Frankie's arms. "You deserve to be happy like mom and dad were before mom died. You deserve to have a partner that can support you. You deserve to one day have babies that actually belong to you."

"I don't know what I'd do without you, Sophie Stevens." This time Frankie couldn't stop the tears from spilling.

"Well then, I guess it's a good thing I don't plan on going anywhere soon."

## CHAPTER TWENTY-THREE

Gabe drove up to the front of Frankie's house and stood on the brakes, spraying gravel as his car fishtailed before coming to an abrupt stop. Frankie jerked violently toward the dash, the seat belt preventing her from sustaining serious injury.

"Francesca, we can't go rushing in there. We don't know what we're dealing with. Let's wait for the police. They'll be here any minute."

Seriously? Would he wait around patiently if one of his brothers was in danger? "I'm not waiting." He barely had the car in park before she was fumbling with her seat belt and hopping out.

"Damn it, Frankie, at least let me go in first."

She ran to the porch, bounded up the steps, and tried to open the door, but found it locked.

Gabe was right behind her, "Frankie, wait!"

"Fuck." She yanked open her purse, spilling half the contents at her feet in her rush. She dropped to her knees and dug around through all the crap, searching for her keys. Locating them at last, she jumped up, shoved the correct one into the lock, and twisted the handle. She pushed the door open and ran inside.

"Sophie," she screamed. "Sophie where are you?"

Two weeks had passed since the trailer incident, and they weren't any closer to finding the culprit. As each day had passed and nothing came to light, Frankie's anxiety had only risen. Somewhere this person was building to some sort of endgame. She could sense it. They just needed to figure out who, what, and most importantly, why.

In the meantime, she'd become much closer to Gabe. He'd become her crutch and admittedly, that worried her. Normally a self-reliant, get-the-job-done type of person, she wasn't sure who this new individual was when she looked into the mirror. This new *woman* liked to look pretty for her date. She liked being told she was beautiful. And she liked how she felt in his arms.

He made her feel safe. With Gabe, nobody could touch her.

In an attempt to take her mind off the situation for one night, Gabe had taken her to the club for some dancing. As she'd swayed in his arms, listening to the sultry music and watching other couples around her in various stages of dirty dancing, she'd realized she had begun to fall in love with him. And it scared her, because she was nothing like the woman he'd told her about. She wasn't housewife material. She was house-building material.

Then they'd received a call from the security firm who'd been asked to keep watch on the video feed from her place. An alarm had been tripped. An alarm that, at this time of night, had no reason to be tripped other than if somebody were on her property. Not long after that, she'd received a text message from her sister. An odd one that had been cut off. All it had said was "I think somebody's" …and then nothing. Sophie hadn't responded to the hundred or so times Frankie tried calling either.

Gabe appeared at her side. He gave her a hard look.

Well, he could be pissed at her later.

"She's not here."

He didn't need to tell her that. She'd known as soon as she walked through the door. "I haven't looked upstairs yet."

"Then let's go look for her."

"I'll check upstairs and you look down here." She placed one foot on the bottom step, but Gabe stopped her by placing one strong hand on her arm.

"We'll go together." Judging by the expression on his face, there was no room for argument.

Frankie nodded. She bent down to fling off the ridiculous heels she'd worn.

Taking the stairs two at time, she directed Gabe straight to her sister's room. Empty. She followed on Gabe's heels as he checked each room, including the bathrooms. All of them empty. Even though she expected it, pain sliced through her. *Sophie, where the hell are you?*

Dejected, she stumbled on the way back down the stairs, but Gabe caught her before she fell flat on her face on the floor.

"Are you hurt?"

She waved him off, ignoring the sharp stab of pain slicing across her right knee. "She's got to be here."

Frightened, Frankie punched her thigh in frustration. "Let's check the barn. She's never gone in there as far as I know, but I can't think of any other place she'd go. She told me specifically that she had no plans tonight and promised to stay put."

Hiking her dress up higher, Frankie hustled out the front door. She knew she should let Gabe take the lead, but if Sophie needed her, nobody, Gabe included, would keep her from her sister.

Frankie flew down the stairs, running across the lawn as fast as she could. She took only a second to acknowledge the relief and comfort she felt hearing the pounding of Gabe's shoes just behind.

Even from this distance, she could see the barn door gaping open. As she drew near, she heard a vehicle running. That was odd. It was too late for the guys to be here, and she'd told them never to put the vehicles into the barn.

Frankie's steps slowed as intuition took hold and settled deep and cold in the pit of her stomach. She swallowed. "Sophie," she whispered.

Shooting forward, she darted inside, stuttering to a stop when she saw one of the work pick-ups. It had been backed into the aisle. The running lights were on, and the engine was running. The windows were closed. The inside of the cab looked like it was filled with fog but she could make out the shape of a person in the driver's side. A person with long hair.

Then reality slammed into her as the seriousness of the situation kicked in and the truth of what was happening in front of her became a film she had no desire to see.

"Oh, God, Sophie." Frankie dashed to the driver's side of the truck, grabbed hold of the handle and yanked. She tried again. It wouldn't budge. "No!" She pounded on the glass. "Sophie," she yelled, pounding some more, stopping to pull again, ineffectively, at the handle.

"Let me." Gabe nudged her aside. "Do you have spare keys?"

"Yes, but they're in the trailer. We don't have time." Desperation fueled her whimpered words.

"Find me a hammer, Frankie."

He didn't yell at her. He didn't look at her or waste time banging on the window. He calmly instructed her while he jumped into the bed of the truck and jerked the hose from where somebody had lodged it in the small back window, the gap covered in duct tape.

She hadn't even noticed it.

He tried to slide it open further, but it was wedged. He kicked the window with his foot, shattering the glass and letting fresh air inside the truck. Gabe jumped back to the ground and rushed around to try the other door.

It felt like each minute dragged by, but only seconds passed. Still, each second was one too long for her sister to be locked in the truck filled with carbon monoxide.

Shaking away her fears, Frankie ran over to the industrial-sized black toolboxes and yanked open the middle drawer where she kept the hammers. Grabbing the first one to fill her fist, she returned to the truck and handed it to Gabe.

He wielded the hammer with a heavy but accurate swing and smashed the glass, sending a spider web of cracks splintering through it. It took a few attempts until he was able to break through and create enough of an opening to reach his arm through. Unlocking the door, he swung it open, reached in and turned off the truck.

Frankie stood nearby, eyes squeezed shut. *Please be OK. Please be OK.* The very thought of losing her sister sent a sharp wave of nausea barreling through her and she nearly vomited.

"I've got her," Gabe called.

He sounded so far way, like they stood at opposite ends of a tunnel.

"She's alive."

Relief swamped her, buckling her at the knees. She grabbed the edge of the truck to steady her shaking legs and took a couple of deep breaths while Gabe pulled Sophie from where she slumped in the driver's seat and backed his way out into the clear.

"Call an ambulance," he yelled.

Sophie hung limp in his arms, her head flung back, exposing her neck and her arms dangling like broken limbs. Her hair hid her face. Frankie couldn't see Sophie's face.

Frankie swallowed hard. He'd said she was alive.

Gabe laid Sophie out on the ground, gently straightening her legs and laying her arms at her sides. Then he stood, stripped off his jacket, folded it, and tucked it under her head.

"Francesca," he snapped.

She dragged her gaze from her sister and up to look at him.

"Call 9-1-1." He tossed her his phone. "The police should be here any minute, but make sure an ambulance is on the way too."

Nodding as though on autopilot, Frankie snatched his

phone from the air and dialed. She desperately wanted to drop to her knees, pull her baby sister into her lap, and rock her until she opened her eyes and gave her hell. But instead, her feet seemed rooted to the spot. She couldn't breathe from fear of Sophie never opening her eyes. She didn't know what to do.

She needed somebody to tell her what to do.

When the dispatcher answered, Frankie confirmed the policy were already on the way and gave the details asked for regarding the need for medical aid. When the lady assured her help was on the way, Frankie dropped the phone.

Gabe checked the pulse in Sophie's throat. "Damn it." He dropped to the ground next to her, shoved his coat aside, cleared her airway, checking her breathing, and started CPR.

It took a couple of sequences for the knowledge of what he was doing to sink into Frankie's brain, and when it did, she gasped. The glue holding her to the dirt released her, spiting her forward, sending her to the ground. She knelt there on the dirt floor, tears streaming down her face, helpless as Gabe worked to save her sister.

The wail of a sirens filled the night. Two police cruisers came screaming down the long driveway, an ambulance hot on their trail.

Time slowed down.

Two paramedics rushed in.

Gabe spoke with them. She saw their lips moving, but couldn't hear a word.

Then Gabe jumped out of the way and the paramedics took over. Finally, they were strapping her sister onto a gurney and running toward the open doors at the back of the ambulance.

She was so cold.

Everything appeared to be happening around her while she remained in a fog.

Gabe appeared beside her and draped his jacket over her

shoulders. He pulled her up from the dirt. He held her while she watched them load Sophie into the ambulance. Gabe patted her on the shoulder before he stepped over to the police officers, presumably to tell them what happened and to find out what she needed to do now.

Sound started to intrude. But everyone talked in Peanuts-speak—they sounded like a flock of geese. She just stood there, Gabe's coat around her shoulders.

She couldn't get warm.

* * *

Frankie sat on the edge of the chair as she stared at the video, watching with horror as a man she'd trusted, a man she'd considered family, crept up behind Sophie and hit her from behind, knocking her out cold.

He didn't face the cameras in the barn either. But this time he hadn't been wearing a hoodie. And even with the grainy footage and the poorly lit interior of the barn, she'd recognized him instantly when he'd stumbled out of one of the stalls and spotted Sophie. How he managed to keep from looking in the direction of the cameras while obviously intoxicated astounded her. But it didn't matter. His shirt gave him away.

Then she watched as he dragged Sophie's limp body over to the truck he'd backed into the barn. He carefully—and this is what killed her—he *carefully* settled Sophie into the cab of the truck, even going so far as sweeping the strands of hair off her face and tucking it behind her ear. *Like he gave a flying fuck!*

Then he methodically attached a hose to the exhaust, stuck it through the back window, and taped up the gaps.

Frankie gripped the edge of the chair as he jumped down from the truck's bed and walked back to the driver's side. He leaned in, started the engine, and closed the door. The lights blinked as he used the fob to lock the doors before he left the barn.

"I can't believe it." First, disbelief overwhelmed her. Then rage, unlike she'd ever known, shoved that emotion away and took its place.

"Frankie, do you recognize him?"

Gabe's voice, laced with concern reached the edge of her awareness. But it didn't yet break through the ringing in her ears. She felt his hand on her arm, knew his fingers wrapped around her wrist. She gathered no warmth from his touch though. Ice flowed through her veins.

A collage of images skipped through her mind. Some fast, others slow. All of them happy times. But now as each appeared, pain sliced through her like a sharpened knife. If only she'd bleed, then maybe it would make sense.

Family dinners, holidays, field trips to his job site with her father. Birthday presents, Christmas presents. He'd taught her how to ride her bike because her father had been busy with a new project. He'd shot hoops with her while her dad cooked dinner. He'd been there when she'd won her first contract after her father died. He'd bought her a bottle of Champagne when she finished her first construction job, because her father couldn't.

He'd stood by her and Sophie, his arms around their shoulders, giving them comfort as they buried their father on a sad and dismal rainy day. For a while he'd been there for them after her father was gone. But he'd been scarce over the last few months. She had chalked it up to grief.

"Yes. I know him."

Gabe leaned down to look her in the eyes. "Who is he?" he asked softly.

"Lawrence Diamond." She gulped, still unable to believe that she'd just watched a man she loved like a second father try to murder her sister. "He was my dad's best friend. He's my Godfather."

"Are you sure? You can't see his face that clearly. He's

managed to do everything without once looking toward the cameras."

"It's him," she said through teeth she'd clenched tight together for fear they'd chatter. She'd given him that shirt last Christmas. The one that said "Best Godfather Ever" on the front.

Gabe stood and scooped her right out of the chair. He sat down, settled her on his lap, and wrapped his strong arms around her, hugging her close to his chest.

He was always doing that. She liked that about Gabe. He liked to hold her. And funny thing, she'd discovered she liked to be held.

Frankie knew he tried to warm her, to comfort her, but she couldn't return the embrace. All she felt was cold emptiness. No, no that wasn't true. She did feel something. She felt like she'd been kicked in the teeth. Again. People in her life either left or betrayed her.

People who were supposed to be there as pillars to support her, to guide her, and to love her continued to let her down. Her mother when she died giving birth to her sister. Her father when he'd had his first stroke and left her to figure things out on her own, while simultaneously caring for him and her sister. And then again when he died, leaving her and Sophie all alone in the world. John when he cheated on her.

And now Uncle Lawrence. The worst of all of them. Her parents couldn't help what happened to them. Lawrence had planned this. He'd purposely set out to cause her pain.

He was a man who had known her since birth. He'd helped to raise her. He'd stepped in when her father died. He'd coached her through that first construction project and was the first to congratulate her when she'd completed the job.

Lawrence Diamond held a place of honor in her family. He held of place of honor in her heart.

Or at least he had.

"I'm so sorry, sweetheart." Gabe kissed the top of her head. He stroked her back in a gentle caress.

She was scheduled to meet with the police so they could show her the video. Thankfully Gabe had managed to get a copy of the tape as well and he'd shown it to her in private. Neither the police nor his brothers would witness her shame at how she'd allowed herself to be duped by a man she once considered family.

"We need to go see the police, Frankie."

"I need to go to the hospital and check on Sophie first. I want to be there when she wakes up. Then I'll go to the station." Frankie mumbled the words against Gabe's chest. She inhaled the soft scent of his cologne. She'd much rather dig herself a nice little niche in his arms, let him shelter and protect her. Let him take care of her problems.

But that's not who she was.

Frankie closed her eyes, sucked in a deep breath, and shielded her heart for the confrontation she'd be facing. First she'd see how her sister was doing. And then she'd find Lawrence and demand answers. If that man thought he'd be able to screw her over, he didn't really know her after all. *She* was in charge. *She* was the boss. And she would show him exactly what he was up against.

"I'll take you. Let me just grab my keys."

"No. Thanks anyway, Gabe. But I can handle this." She pushed away from him and stood. She yanked her sweater down and ran a hand through her messy hair.

He rose and narrowed his gaze as he gave her a sympathetic but hard look. "Francesca, I'm not going to let you face this on your own." He pointed to the stilled screen on the camera and the frozen image of Sophie inside the cab of the truck as it began to fill with noxious gas. "He tried to kill your sister. I won't let him do the same to you."

Although she didn't need to look at the screen, she glanced in that direction. "He won't."

"Damn right he won't. As soon as you confirm his identify for the police, they'll bring him in and I plan to be there when they do."

"Thank you, Gabe, for doing this for me. You've completed the job I hired you for. We know who's behind everything now. I can take it from here."

He flinched as though she'd slapped him.

She regretted her harsh words, but it was too late to pull them back.

"I'm just a hired hand? It was just a job?" He shook his head slowly, his eyes sad. "I don't believe that, Francesca. But regardless, I still want to see this through to the end. That man attempted to murder your sister. I won't risk your life."

She crossed her arms around her middle. She suddenly felt so alone. "I need to see him, Gabe. I need answers before the police lock him away." Gabe wouldn't be happy with her. If he knew what she planned to do, he'd probably handcuff her to a chair and give her a spanking—and not an erotic one.

"What answers, Sophie? All we need to know is that he wants to hurt you."

Maybe, but she wasn't yet convinced he'd meant physical harm. She remembered the tender way he'd touched Sophie's hair. He could have locked the barn door and delayed her finding Sophie. There was more going on here and if she went to him backed by Gabe or surrounded by the police, she wouldn't find out the truth. She had to talk to him first.

When she thought back to her encounters with Lawrence over the last number of months, she realized each time he'd avoided looking her in the eye. And the few times she'd managed to catch his attention, his expression had been troubled, but another, indefinable emotion had lurked deep in his eyes.

She needed the truth. She needed to understand why.

"I'm coming with you, Francesca. We'll call the police from the car. Then we'll swing by the hospital. I'll drop you there to stay with your sister. The police will bring him in and if you insist on talking to Lawrence, then you can do it at the police station where he'll be secured and you'll be protected."

He pointed his finger at her. "Wait here. I'll be right back." Gabe turned and strode down the hall to his office.

As soon as he disappeared from sight, Frankie snatched up her purse and hurried out the door. Thank God she'd insisted on picking up her own truck after they'd left the hospital. Once Sophie was out of danger, Gabe had tried to convince her to go home with him. But she'd refused. Instead she'd sat for hours in the chair next to Sophie's hospital bed, watching every breath her sister took while Gabe wandered the hall and checked in on her every thirty minutes or so.

She jumped into the cab of her truck, shoved the key in the ignition, and cranked the engine. Throwing the vehicle into gear, she checked her side mirror and then peeled away from the curb.

First, she needed to stop at the hospital and see Sophie.

Then a man she'd loved since she was a little girl had a hell of a lot of explaining to do before she'd let the police take him away.

# CHAPTER TWENTY-FOUR

Twenty minutes later, she pulled into the underground parking at the hospital. Through sheer luck she somehow managed to avoid a speeding ticket.

Stupid wasn't her middle name, though. As soon as Gabe realized what she'd done, he'd call the police and he'd be hot on her heels while the police tracked down Lawrence. She didn't have much time, but she hoped she could talk with Sophie quickly and then find Lawrence before they did. She had the advantage of knowing his typical daytime behavior.

Frankie rode the elevator to the fourth floor and headed straight to her sister's room, the heels of her shoes squeaking with each hurried step. Upon entering, she slowed her pace. Sophie was all she had in the world. The thought of how close she'd coming to losing her made her sick to her stomach.

At the bedside, she reached out and took Sophie's hand in hers, wincing at the almost cold feel to her skin. White gauze wrapped around her head and held a bandage in place. Thankfully the blow had been glancing. Enough to knock her out, but not enough to cause any severe or lasting damage.

Her pale face struck a chord though, and a lump of pure emotion lodged in Frankie's throat. She squeezed her eyes shut and cringed as her mind replayed the video she'd watched. Seeing Lawrence swing that chunk of wood. Her stomach turned viciously at the memory and she groaned.

"Hey."

Frankie snapped her eyes open to see Sophie gazing at her. Though clouded with drugs for the pain, at least there was recognition in her expression. Frankie's knees buckled for a second time in twenty-four hours and fresh tears, these ones of gratitude, sprung free to flow down her cheeks unchecked.

"Oh, Sophie, I'm so, so sorry."

"Frankie? Don't cry. Please."

Her words were weak, but Frankie was so happy to hear them, she just let the tears fall.

"The doctor said I'm going to be fine. I have a concussion and I'll have a hell of a headache apparently for the next few days, but I'm good, sis."

"I know. He told me that. And I can't even begin to tell you how happy I am to hear it's not worse. I was so worried." Frankie leaned over and kissed her sister's forehead. "I love you, Soph."

"I know." She swallowed harshly, and licked her dry lips.

Frankie grabbed the glass of water on the stand and held the straw to Sophie's mouth so she could take a sip.

"Thanks." She flopped back against the pillow after a couple of small mouthfuls, her eyelids drifting closed. "Now tell me what happened. I step into the barn for the first time in I don't know how long and look at what happens. Who's the bastard that took a swing at me and why? I don't remember anything."

Frankie stalled. She didn't want to upset her sister. But she didn't see how she could keep the truth from her either. The police would have questions. And Sophie deserved to know.

"Frankie?"

"It was Lawrence."

Her sister's eyes popped open and widened in disbelief. "What? Why would he do that?"

"I don't know why." Yet. "I'm sure as hell going to find out though. But I suspect it's because of me." Guilt. She was feeling that a lot lately. Lawrence had some unknown beef with her and he'd taken it out on Sophie. And for that, Frankie would never forgive herself. She only hoped her sister could one day forgive her.

"You? Why would he want to hurt me because of you?" Then clarity must have struck because understanding replaced the incredulity in her expression. "You think Uncle Lawrence is the one behind what's been happening? I don't understand." Pain pervaded her sister's words. It tightened her features. Soreness from the injury and anguish at the knowledge that a person she'd known and looked up to all her life had caused it.

Frankie wished she could take it away. At least she could find the answers they both deserved. "Listen. I need to go and find out. You'll be fine here, just rest. I'll be back as soon as I can."

Sophie gripped Frankie's fingers, her hold strong and urgent. "Frankie, you can't go there. Please. Stay here. Let the police take care of it."

"I'll be fine," she assured her sister. Though she couldn't say the same for Lawrence.

"You can't know that," she argued.

Frankie disentangled her fingers from Sophie's and patted her sister's hand. "Don't worry about me. I'll be careful. I'm not walking in there blind. I think you surprised him, Sophie. I don't think he really wanted to hurt you. I think he was desperate."

"Desperate people do desperate things, Frankie."

"I know. But I need answers. I need to speak to him face-to-face and find out why he's let us down this way. Why he let Dad down."

Sophie closed her eyes. A few tears slipped free and rolled down her cheeks.

Frankie reached over and wiped them away. "Do me a favor?"

Sophie opened her eyes and looked up. "What?"

"If Gabe shows up here, don't tell him we spoke. Stall him if you can."

"Why? If you won't let the police handle this, at least take Gabe with you."

"He wants to take control of the situation and protect me."

"Frankie—"

"I need to do this on my own." She implored her sister to understand.

"I don't like it."

"Thanks, sis." Frankie leaned over and placed another kiss on her sister's bandaged head. "Get some more rest. I love you. I'll be back later."

"Be careful, Frankie. Please."

"I will."

She gave her sister a smile she dug up from somewhere deep inside and then turned on a heel and left the room. She walked to the elevator, pushed the button, then decided to take the stairs. She ran down them, exiting into the garage. Hopping into her truck, she geared herself up for the face-off with her godfather. Then she'd happily turn the key of his jail cell.

She slid a glance to the glove box. Like she'd told Sophie, she didn't need to worry. People needed to accept that she might be tiny, but she packed a punch.

* * *

Goddamn that woman. He'd left her alone for five minutes. He'd gone to get his keys and then stopped to update his brothers, telling them who the perpetrator was and his connection to Frankie. Regardless of her brushing off his support, he had no intention of simply walking away.

Gabe had planned to take Frankie to the hospital and leave her with Sophie. He'd asked Kyle to locate Lawrence's address while Kade contacted the police and filled them in. Then Gabe would join the police as they looked for Lawrence Diamond. He wanted to be there when the man was brought in. He hoped their contact in the police department could get him access to the interrogation so he could hear what could possibly drive a man to hurt people he supposedly cared about.

He was such a fool. He should have known that Frankie would not just sit around and wait for him. Now, he hoped to catch her at the hospital and convince her to stay with her sister while they located Diamond and had him arrested.

He very nearly ran down an elderly couple in his sprint from the elevator. Apologizing profusely, he made sure they were settled safely in the elevator and on their way to visit their granddaughter, who apparently had just had a baby named Bill, after his granddad of course.

When he'd located Sophie's room and barreled in through the door, he'd found her asleep, looking pale, weak and exhausted. He was just about to retrace his steps when her eyes fluttered open. She gasped and jerked before she realized it was him.

"I'm sorry, Sophie. I didn't mean to startle you." Gabe moved up to the bed. "How are you feeling?" She looked like hell warmed over.

"Tired. Mother of a headache. And a bitch of a bump. But I'll be fine."

"Good. Your sister was very worried."

"Did you run into her on your way in here?"

"No. How long ago did she leave?" he confirmed.

"You just missed her."

"Did she tell you—?"

"That it was Lawrence? Yeah."

"I'm sorry, Sophie." Gabe hated that both women had been let down by a man they considered close family.

"She's gone to talk to Lawrence, Gabe. You need to get there. I'm worried."

"Yeah, me too. I need his home address." Kyle had texted him the business address, which they already had from their initial background check. A check that indicated absolutely nothing except for a man who'd had a well-run business until a few months ago when he seemed to simply lose interest in bidding for new projects. But he'd kept his nose clean and did decent work. He was a bit of loner, never married, and no family. But that wasn't a crime. Even though he was a business rival, they'd ruled him out as a suspect because of his closeness to the Stevens family.

Sophie gave him the information.

"Thanks, honey. You get some rest."

"Do you love her?" Sophie asked out of the blue, just as he turned away, anxious to find Frankie, worried that she was putting herself in a dangerous situation.

Gabe considered the question. The answer was easy. The hard part was rationalizing how it happened so quickly. "I do."

"Make sure she's safe, Gabe."

He leaned over and kissed Sophie on the forehead. "I will."

## CHAPTER TWENTY-FIVE

"WHY, LAWRENCE?"

She'd driven past his work office, but the lights had been out, so she'd gone to his home. As each mile passed beneath the tires on her truck, her anger and disappointment grew in equal amounts. She'd turned into his drive, killed the engine, and sat staring at his front door.

A place she'd always considered her home away from home. She faintly remembered nights in front of his television with a movie and popcorn while her parents had a date night. Or later, when he'd taken her off her father's hands for a while and used the time to teach her more about the business.

He answered the doorbell, with a drink in his hand, after three rings and then silently led her into his home office where he collapsed into his chair, placed the glass on the desk, and dropped his head into his hands. In front of him sat a bottle of whiskey, three-quarters empty. The place reeked and would take hours to clean judging by the mess she'd witnessed as they'd walked through the house to reach his office.

"I'm sorry about your sister," he slurred. "I hadn't planned that. I didn't want to hurt her."

"You didn't want to hurt her?" Frankie's words escaped as a whisper at first, but as she found her voice, it increased in volume with every charge. "You hit her over the head, put her in the truck, and stuffed a hose taped to the exhaust into the window. You almost *killed* her, Lawrence," she screamed. She wanted to reach across the desk and slap him.

He sat there like they were talking about a bid she didn't win.

She'd always looked up to this man her father had called his best friend, the man her parents had trusted her with enough to ask him to be her godfather.

"She surprised me."

Her father would be so hurt.

She vibrated with rage.

"I've loved you like an uncle my entire life," she ground out. "You've been as close to me as my own father, especially since he died," she accused. "How could you do this to me?" She couldn't stop the ache that filled her throat and choked her, or the resulting tears that spilled from her eyes. She stuck her hand in the pocked of her coat and stroked the cold barrel of the gun she'd taken from the glove compartment of her truck.

Years ago, her father had taught her how to protect herself. He'd seen the looks she received from some of the guys on job sites. He'd heard the whispered catcalls and lewd comments. She'd ignored them. He'd wanted to make sure she never found herself in a vulnerable position, especially when she started working for him in earnest and made it clear she planned to follow in his footsteps.

To make her father feel better, she'd followed his instructions and learned how to use the weapon. Then she'd tucked it away, hoping she'd never have to see it again. Since the vandalism, she'd been keeping it locked in her truck when she wasn't at home.

She didn't know if she could actually use it, but she couldn't ignore the fact it gave her a measure of comfort knowing she wasn't completely unprotected. And even though she'd run out on him again, she knew Gabe and the police wouldn't be far behind. That reassured her more than anything.

Lawrence raised his head. His eyes were rimmed in red

but flecked with simmering anger. He just stared at her for a long time.

She couldn't take it anymore. "Why!" She pounded her fist on his desk.

"Because the company was supposed to be mine," he spit out between clenched teeth.

That brought her up short. "Excuse me?"

He leaned forward, his eyes sparking. "Your father's construction company should have been turned over to me, not you."

She shook her head, not understanding in the least. "Why would you think that? You've got your own company."

He shot to a standing position.

She tightened her grip on the gun and stepped back out of reflex.

He only moved around the desk to pace.

"Since we were kids, your father and I had planned to go into business together. We did everything together, all through grade school and high school. We were inseparable," he said. "Hell, the only time we were split up was while we were in the army."

"What does that have to do with anything?"

Lawrence continued to march back and forth, his anger rising with each sharp change of direction. "While I was away serving our country, he got *married*."

The venom coating that word surprised Frankie.

"By the time I got back home he seemed to have no room for me as a partner. So I decided to go into business for myself."

Confused as to where this was going and what it had to do with her and Sophie, she could only sputter. "You were angry that my dad was working, so you decided to start up your own company. As what? Competition?"

He cast her a quick, dark look. "Initially. Then, one night over too many beers, he told me that if anything ever happened to him, the whole thing would be mine." He snorted. "At the time, I didn't need his company. I was doing very well on my own. Better than him." He seemed smug about that. "Your father could have grown his business, taken on the big projects. Made a lot more money. But he preferred the smaller, more mom-and-pop jobs."

She blinked. This was all about the company? Now *she* was getting pissed. Greed. He was just a greedy bastard who couldn't be happy and satisfied with what he had, what he had built for himself. He wanted it all.

Lawrence stopped pacing and glared at her. "*You* got his company, though. You don't need the company, Frankie. You're young. You have time to build from the ground up." He clenched his fists at his sides. "I'm not. And now I do need it."

She gaped. It took her a moment to gather her words because she couldn't believe what he was implying. "Are you telling me this is all because you're mad that my father left the company to me instead of you?" She shook her head.

"He promised it to me."

"Over a beer." This whole situation was just too bizarre. "Then why Sophie? If it's me you're angry with me, why hurt Sophie?"

"I didn't set out to hurt her. I didn't want to hurt either of you. I just wanted you to give me the company. Sophie surprising me in the barn was an opportunity. The vandalism wasn't scaring you. I hoped an accident would convince you."

"You left her there to die, Lawrence. That was *no* accident." She counted to ten. "How did you think you'd get away with any of this?" she asked.

"I was desperate. Getting my hands on your father's company would have saved mine." He tried to look sheepish. "Look, I really had hoped the break-ins would scare you enough to reconsider your future. I figured you'd rethink your plans to continue the company and let me take it off your hands."

She couldn't believe what she was hearing. She wasn't buying his crap anymore. "And you'd just step in, be my savior, and steal my company in the process."

The truth was written all over his face. But there was something else there, too. "There's more to this than just the fact that my father left his construction company to me."

"I don't know what you're talking about." He distanced himself again, rounding his desk.

"Why not just come to me? I would have helped if I could." She had the savings her father had left her; she would have helped Lawrence if he'd only asked.

He paused, glanced at a photograph of him and her father from years ago. An odd look came over his face.

She recognized the picture. It had been taken not long after Sophie's birth and her mother's death. She found it one day when she'd gone through a box of her father's things after his funeral. Her dad had been grieving, but he'd pushed most of it aside to take care of his daughters. This particular photo was one her grandmother must have taken. Her father was holding the baby. Tears were streaming down his face. But it wasn't her father's image she focused on. It was Lawrence's as he stood off to the side. He wore a pained expression on his face and he was looking at her father, not the baby.

The notes she'd found, the smashed family photo, the odd, jumbled conversation she'd overlooked as a sad and grieving man now all began to take shape.

Red stained his cheeks at first, but then he turned on her, and the anger that a few moments ago simmered, now flared white hot. So intense, she leaned back for fear of being burned.

"*I* was his best friend." He pounded on his chest with his finger and spittle flew from his mouth. "We'd been doing everything together, as partners, since we were in kindergarten. I thought I could be there for him. He needed me. But he had you and Sophie to take care of. And then when you showed an interest in what he did, he started taking you everywhere he went. He started spending more time with you. He loved you so fucking much, his eyes lit up like fireworks when you were in the vicinity."

Shocked, she glared right back at him. "You were jealous of a father's relationship with his children," she accused. "Unfuckingbelievable."

"Not of his children. Not really. But I wanted to spend time with him too. He no longer had time for me. I missed my best friend."

Anger soared through her body. She trembled from the force of it. This man who had been so involved in her childhood—hell her entire life—held his friend's love for his own child over her head. "Why didn't you have your own children then?" She stopped and glowered at him. "Huh, Uncle Lawrence? Why didn't *you* get married and have your own family so you could…" She stopped when his face blanched and cold realization washed over her as his hateful accusations replayed in her head. "Oh my god."

His face turned beet red and he spun away.

"That's why you never married."

He strode to the corner of the room, as though physically trying to distance himself from her. Maybe even hide from her.

"You loved him," she whispered.

He flinched. His body jerked like he'd taken a physical blow. His shoulders rolled in and his back curved like he was trying to curl into protective mode.

"You loved my father," she charged. "Didn't you?"

He said nothing, though his breathing stilled, his whole body was rigid.

She gazed around the room, her eyes locking in on the various pictures he displayed. Almost every single one of them contained him and her father at different points in their lives. It all made sense now.

Her rage drained away as though a plug had been pulled. Pity filled her. She'd always wondered why he never found a woman and settled down. As she thought back over the years, Frankie realized she couldn't picture a single woman in his life other than his housekeeper and office administrator. She couldn't remember him talking about dates or a special woman in his life. Ever.

Lawrence glanced at her briefly, this face devoid of emotion, then his shoulders slumped. The fight emptied out of him.

"By the time I came home, he was married to your mother." His words, muffled because he spoke with his back to her. The corner of the office captured most of the sound. "He'd dated her a few times before we'd gone to boot camp, but I didn't think it was serious."

"You never told him how you felt?"

He spun around and stomped back to his desk "It wasn't acceptable in our time."

"So, you just thought…what? That he'd realize one day he loved you back?" She sounded cruel as she hurled the words at him, but she didn't care.

"I know he loved me," he stated with conviction and a slight growl.

"Yes, he did love you, Lawrence," she said. "Like a best friend. A *trusted* friend," she emphasized.

He winced.

"Did he know?" she asked again. Certainly her father had never treated Lawrence as anything less than his best childhood friend and confidant. Her father would never have held his sexual orientation against him. She was absolutely positive of that.

"He never said one way or the other, but, yes, I think he knew."

"So all of this, everything you've done to discredit me, to put me out of business, *to hurt Sophie—*"

His anger exploded. "That company should have been mine. Not yours. Your father promised it to me. Besides, you have no business running a construction company."

Talk about spewing just the words she needed to hear to rid her of every ounce of disappointment, sadness, and guilt *she might have felt* over the situation.

"I have no business?" She took two steps closer to him. The weight of the gun pulled at her pocket, but she no longer worried for her safety with this man. He might be angry that he'd been found out, but he was broken. It was over.

She placed her hands flat on the desk and leaned down. "And why is that? Please, tell me, *Larry*," she purposely used that title because she knew only her father had ever called him that. "Why can't I run the company?" She needed to hear him say it.

He curled his lip into a snarl. "Because you're a woman. Women should be at home keeping house."

She'd half expected the "women don't belong in man's world" speech, though it still stung hearing it. She straightened. When she found her voice, she couldn't restrain the disappointment from flowing through or the sarcasm from dripping. "Wow. I have to admit, for a gay man I'm surprised you feel that way."

"I may be gay, but I still grew up in a time where women knew their place."

"And it wasn't out in the working world?"

"It wasn't doing a man's job," he clarified.

"Huh. I have to say, I'm really and truly surprised you and my father were friends after all, never mind best friends."

"Why, because I'm gay?" Contempt filled his words and his sneer only emphasized them.

Frankie huffed. "Hardly. I don't care that you're gay and I know my father wouldn't have either. But I know he didn't ascribe to the barefoot and pregnant stereotype or that working women were only meant to be secretaries or nurses. How did the two of you get along so famously if you didn't hold the same values?"

Lawrence didn't respond. He just scowled.

"I'm guessing you never told him that either. Hell, Lawrence, it seems you kept a lot from my father."

"He promised *me* the company."

"And he left it to *me* in his will," she countered. "So regardless of what he may have said over a beer, he knew I loved working there. And I know he loved that I wanted to follow in his footsteps." She took a deep stabilizing breath. "You may have been his best friend once, but I am and always will be, his daughter."

And now that she had her answers, it was time to bring in the police before she jumped across the desk separating them and strangled him with her bare hands.

Lawrence started to say something just as the doorbell chimed and then the front door crashed open, slamming against the wall.

"Frankie?" Gabe's voice sent a wave of relief rushing over her.

"Back here," she called. "Through the kitchen."

Gabe hurried in with two police officers trailing close behind him. He gave her a look, his eyebrows raised in question, ready to step in and help her if she needed him to.

She shook her head.

He smiled that sexy grin that he reserved only for her, but she saw naked relief in his eyes.

All she wanted now was to let the man she loved take care of her for a little while. Wow. She knew she was falling, but she hadn't realized she'd landed.

The police moved in, one maneuvering behind Lawrence to haul him from the chair and put him in handcuffs while the other read his Miranda rights.

As they led him past her, he paused.

Before he could say a word, she stopped him, shoving aside her anger for a moment. "He thought the world of you, Lawrence. He loved you enough to entrust the care of his children to you." She sighed at the sad reality of the entire situation. "Dad would be so heartbroken if he were here to see you now."

The officers took over and led him away. When the door closed behind them, silence filled the space.

"Are you OK?" Gabe touched her arm.

She nodded, paused, and then shook her head.

He slid his hand down her arm and took hold of her hand, twining his fingers through hers.

He tugged, and she willingly went to him, slipping her arms around his waist and laying her cheek flat against his chest, the beat of his heart comforting beneath her ear.

Gabe rubbed her back. "I'm sorry, honey."

"How can you know somebody your entire life, and not really know him?" Listening to Gabe's deep breathing helped to drain some of the fury and disappointment away. She sighed. "He was in love with my father."

Gabe didn't seem surprised by this news. "One of our contacts finally came through with more info on Lawrence, though it's a little late. Everything we dug up portrayed a well-adjusted, moderately successful, if lonely, man. He's been *very* discreet over the years, in everything. He's only had a handful of relationships. But our contact managed to find one guy who told him that all Lawrence ever spoke about was your father."

"That's what this has all been about. That and some promise he said my dad made about leaving the company to him."

"That was probably long before you were in the picture."

"I'm just glad my dad's not here now. I've missed having him around so much, but I wouldn't want him to see how his friend betrayed him so horribly."

"Do you think your father would have had a problem with him being gay?"

"Not in the least," she said. "But he would have had a major issue with him attempting to kill his daughter just to get his hands on his company so he could get himself out of debt."

Frankie snuggled closer to Gabe, inhaling the subtle scent of the soap he'd used in the shower. "I grew up knowing the company would one day belong to me and Sophie. Dad always made it crystal clear that was his intention. He worked hard to ensure we had something to be proud of, something that would support us. He never once suggested that he'd ever hand the reins over to Lawrence. Quite the opposite in fact, especially once I took an interest in construction."

She smiled. "When I was kid, he thought it was just a fad. But as I got older and he realized my intent was serious, we had some good heart-to-hearts about the future. He knew Sophie had no desire to wear work boots and he never begrudged her for it. But I'll always remember the pride in his eyes when he and I talked shop." Those would be some of her fondest memories. Frankie peered up at Gabe. "Thanks for calling the cops by the way."

"Kyle called and filled them on while I was on my way to find you. *After* you'd run out of the office," he growled in her ear. "Frankie. You scared the shit out of me. How could you put yourself in danger that way?"

Frankie realized Gabe trembled. He'd really been worried about her. He was trying to check his anger, but she felt it radiating off him. He was furious with her. Or maybe he was scared for her.

"I'm fine, Gabe. I was always fine."

His eyes sparked. "You don't know that. He tried to kill your sister."

"I have a gun with me."

"What?"

"You heard me."

"Where the fuck did you get a gun?" Now his eyes blazed.

It probably wouldn't be a good idea to laugh. Instead, she ran one hand up his chest, soothingly. "I own a gun, Gabe. I know how to use it. My father taught me a few years ago. He was a marksman in the military. He taught both me and Sophie how to use one."

"How come I didn't know this?" He looked perturbed.

She shrugged. "You didn't ask."

"I assume you have a permit for it."

"Of course."

"Would you have used it?"

"I don't know. But I also knew you would be coming after me."

"Kade and Kyle went to his construction office," he said. "The police and I took a chance that he'd be here. Apparently, Lawrence has been struggling for a while. Initially, we didn't find anything noteworthy until we started putting the pieces together. With a little more digging, we found out that he took some shortcuts on a few jobs and got caught. After that he had trouble landing jobs."

"Thank you. For everything." Frankie shuddered to think what would have happened to her sister had Gabe not been there with her. She'd stood by frozen, while Gabe calmly took control. "I need to get back to the hospital and check on Sophie," she said.

Gabe tucked an errant strand of hair behind her ear. Then he smoothed a fingertip along her brow and down the side of her face to her chin. "Do you want me to take you?"

She shook her head. "I'll be fine. I need to do this myself."

"I feel better knowing you weren't completely unprotected, but I still wish you hadn't run out on me, *again*. You put yourself into a very dangerous situation, Francesca. I should spank you for that."

So we were back to Francesca. "I had to get answers, Gabe. If you or the police had been here, he wouldn't have talked."

"Maybe not. But if he was willing to kill your sister, he wouldn't have hesitated to harm you."

She led him out of the house. The police could take over now. She had a life to move on with.

Gabe walked her to the truck and waited until she climbed in behind the wheel. "I'll follow you to the hospital," he said.

She started to argue, but he placed the pad of his finger firmly against her lips.

When he released her, she smiled. "Yes, boss."

## CHAPTER TWENTY-SIX

"Hey, boss. Great night."

"Deacon." Gabe acknowledged a key member of his security team. "Any trouble?"

Deacon shook his head. "Not a one. Even with this crowd, everyone seems to be in a good mood. There are a few demos and some public play going on tonight, so the distractions are probably keeping them occupied."

"Let me know if anything comes up."

"Will do." Deacon slapped a beefy hand down on Gabe's shoulder as he passed by, heading upstairs to do rounds.

Gabe flinched and fought the urge to rub the sore spot. The man didn't know his own strength. Gabe wandered through the ballroom. Saturday nights were typically busy, and tonight was no exception.

"Mr. McBride."

He turned, not even attempting to hide his grin at seeing his lovely Francesca strolling in his direction, looking much taller tonight. Poised and more self-assured than he'd ever seen her, she looked stunning in a short, black leather miniskirt, fire-engine-red heels that he knew she hated, and a matching low-cut top with short sleeves. He hadn't yet convinced her to wear a bustier or just a bra, but the skirt was a giant leap. The shoes he'd requested she wear for her torture and his pleasure.

When she reached him, she stopped and lowered her eyes like he'd taught her. She refused to kneel, using limits as her excuse. He chided her for it, but secretly didn't mind. He had no desire to see Frankie on her knees for anyone, himself included.

She and Sophie had spent the last couple of weeks together. Sophie had even begun to take a mild interest in the business. He'd been curious as to why she'd gone out to the barn in the first place that night when Frankie had always insisted her sister never stepped foot out there. But she'd explained she'd seen the door was opened again and this time wanted to make sure everything was OK. She never saw Lawrence come up behind her.

He'd been reluctant to intrude on their personal time, but couldn't completely stay away. So he and Frankie had dinner a few times, spent the night together a few more times, and she hadn't yet kicked him to the curb. Though she'd fired her ex. She came to discover that he'd been borrowing tools often and not returning them.

The upside was that her interest in the kinky side of him hadn't yet waned. Though she'd outright howled and told him no fucking way when he'd reminded her that others addressed him as Master Gabriel. He'd listened to her laugh for a solid twenty minutes, loving every moment of it. They'd compromised on Mr. McBride when she decided to visit The Vault with him again.

"All cleaned up?"

When they'd come in from outside, she'd had to make a detour to the ladies' room. But her face was still rosy and her eyes bright as diamonds. "Yes."

"Good. I thought we'd start the evening by dancing."

She groaned. "You know I suck at that."

"Too bad. I like to dance."

She glanced up, a wicked gleam in her eye, but she managed to keep her tone respectful. "Then I guess dancing sounds fine."

Together, they moved into the ballroom and straight into the center of the floor. Once he had her in his arms, he calmed down, not realizing how tense he'd been.

In their own little world and spinning slowly to the music, he hugged her close, relishing the moment. He'd never thought he'd end up with a woman like Frankie Stevens. But he would trade her for all the stay-at-home housewives in the world if only she would say yes.

"You know," she said conversationally. "I don't think you ever did tell me why you and your brothers started the club."

Her scent, lilacs and sawdust, drifted up to his nose. He loved that smell. "Well, I certainly didn't set out to create an adult club like this," he said. "The idea of creating The Vault was actually conceived from a nugget of an idea I had after visiting a club a few years back in Las Vegas."

She stopped and peered up at him. "You went to clubs like this in Vegas? Like BDSM places?" She gave him a funny look and then started swaying to the music again.

He'd been to Sin City on a business trip. He'd gone to that particular club as a single man, more out of curiosity than to participate in any activity. One of the guys he'd chatted with at the conference told him about the club. That loser used it as an excuse to step out on his wife, and apparently based on the level of bragging, the man made a point of locating such places in most of the cities he traveled to for work.

"A guy I knew dragged me along one night when I had nothing better to do. I'm not a gambler and wasn't in the mood to walk the strip. Let's just say it was an interesting experience. Especially when I found out why he specifically was there."

"Why was that?"

"To cheat on his wife."

She paused again and frowned. "That's horrible."

He started them moving again, but the sensual melody that the many couples grinded their bodies to barely registered. Glancing around, he realized the actual beat was much faster than the speed he and Frankie were circling their spot with. He didn't care.

"There were people lined up outside waiting to get in," he said. "Many of the couples I saw were the pretty people. Attractive. Fit. No outward flaws. I had no idea if the person they came with was who they went home to every night."

Frankie cuddled closer to his chest.

He tightened his hold.

She sighed, the sound so content it melted his heart.

He loved this woman. He wanted to hear that sound until the day he died. "I love you, Frankie," he whispered in her ear.

She sucked in a breath, pausing in their dance briefly, but she didn't say a word.

"When I got home," he continued as though he hadn't just proclaimed his love, "I did some research and found nothing of its kind here in Rosewood. Although, I'm sure there's a few small places operated privately by people in the lifestyle," he explained. "I wanted to give people a place to go that combined the general club experience with the lifestyle. And different from the one I'd been to in Vegas, I wanted to build a place for people in committed relationships."

When Gabe had approached his brothers with the idea, they'd all been in agreement that they didn't want to operate anything that could be considered or compared to a brothel or sex club, or even a dungeon for that matter. The Vault itself catered to members in the BDSM community but not of the hard-core variety. He didn't allow any of the more risky practices like blood play, knife play or breath play. After some experimentation for his own curiosity, he strongly believed pleasure could be found in pain, but that didn't mean the dominant needed to spill blood, damage skin, or risk asphyxiation to achieve it.

"You'd told me before you didn't live this lifestyle twenty-four seven. So The Vault, it really is more of a job for you?" she asked, her head back so she could look into his face as he answered.

He considered the question for a moment. But only a moment. A couple of years ago, even months ago, he would have considered it a lifestyle choice even if he didn't need it around the clock. Even though he didn't prescribe to it to that extent, he'd still wanted his wife to be at home waiting for him every day. He wanted her to look to him for protection.

Now, he knew that wasn't the case. The Vault was a business. He enjoyed certain aspects of it and what it meant, but it wasn't his life. He hoped his life was here in his arms.

This sometimes foul-mouthed, tiny individual who could swing a hammer and manage a crew of cranky, mouthy men, meant more to him than what The Vault represented. He liked being with this woman who was out of the house earlier than him in the morning rushing to one job site or another to check on progress. He liked driving her around town and having her show off the projects she was responsible for building or fixing.

"This is my business. It doesn't define me, Francesca." He hoped she would want to define him one day though. But it wasn't time yet to ask her.

They finished the dance and then he took her hand and led her out of the ballroom and up the stairs, bypassing the second level and going straight to the third.

"What are we doing up here?" she asked.

Gabe paused to unlock the door to the private apartment they maintained for personal use. He didn't normally come up here. "I know you're not interested in the public areas, but I thought you might like some privacy. Other than walking over to my place, this is a private as it gets here. Only my brothers have access to the apartment and they know I planned to bring you here tonight, so there's no chance they'll interrupt us."

Gabe flicked on a couple of reading lamps and lit the small artificial fireplace. He walked over to the stereo system and chose a light classical station, turning it low enough to be heard, but only as faint background ambiance. They settled into the butter-soft leather, sitting next to each other, Gabe stretching his arm out over the back, Frankie tucked into his side.

"Francesca, I know you don't want to play in public."

"I'd be willing to try it for you."

Humbled, he took her hand, raised it to his lips, and kissed the back of her knuckles. "Honey, I appreciate your willingness, but public displays are not something I want you to do unless you're one hundred percent comfortable with it." He leaned in to brush his lips across hers. "If one day you feel it's something you want to try, we can talk about it then. For now, I want you all to myself."

A look of relief flashed in her eyes, and he knew he'd made the right decision and said the right things. Frankie was not a woman to be forced into any situation. That had happened to her a few times already in her life. She deserved to make her own choices based on her wants and desires.

"I appreciate that, Gabe."

"I want you to be happy." He ran his hand from the top of her head down the side of her face and cupped her cheek. "Have I told you how lovely you look tonight?"

"Yes," she grinned and lifted one of her feet. "Though you didn't comment on my new shoes."

He glanced down at her footwear. "They are very nice. I knew they'd look hot on you."

"This doesn't mean I'll wear them all the time."

"Only when I ask you to," he confirmed.

"You mean when you order me to," she teased.

"Does that mean you're not finished with me yet?"

"I'm not finished with you yet." Her eyes darkened with desire. "I love you, too, Gabe."

His breath caught.

"I'm sorry I didn't say it back to you downstairs. You just caught me by surprise. I've known I loved you since the day we found out about Lawrence. I know I'm not the type of woman you see yourself with long term," she rushed to say before he could stop her. "And I'm not willing to give up my company for any man." She looked him in eye, heart and soul bared. "But I think we have something good. And I'd like to see where it might go. But no pressure. Even if it's only for a little while, you're good for me. I'd like to be naughty with you for a while, Mr. McBride."

He couldn't stop the grin that formed. His brothers had been ribbing him about how often he smiled these days. He'd never realized he didn't smile much until a few of the regulars mentioned it at the club. Even his mother commented on his good mood last weekend when he'd dropped in on her.

"You're good for me too." He swallowed around the lump in his throat. "You know what I'd like right now, Francesca?"

"I'm sure you're going to tell me, Mr. McBride."

"How about a compromise? Let's not think about the future right now. I want to be with you too. I want to explore every sexual fantasy you have from start to finish. It can be here at The Vault, in my home or in yours. I just want to be with you too," he said.

"I'd really like that," she said. "And I'm OK with staying here. I may not be ready for the playrooms downstairs. But being up here, while there's dozens of people just one floor down, is sort of naughty in itself."

"Good. Do you know what I'd like now?" he asked.

She shook her head.

"I'd like for you to remove whatever panties you're wearing and spread your legs so I can see that pretty pussy of yours."

"I'm not wearing any panties."

Surprised at this display of confidence, he beamed. "I like a woman who's proactive." Gabe slid to the floor and faced her. He grabbed her by the butt and yanked her forward until he could easily reach her, the movement actually shoving her skirt up higher on her hips. He spread her knees.

"Very nice." They'd had a make out session in the car before coming into the club. He'd fingered her until she came, gasping for breath. Then he'd taken her into the ballroom. She still looked all pink and glossy. "Mmm…very pretty." He sniffed. "Smells good too."

She wiggled her butt, still not at ease with dirty talk. Which amused the hell out of him, considering she threw curse words around so freely.

Gabe trailed the tip of one finger through her folds. "Warm. Wet." He inserted his finger into her vagina, pumping it in and out slow and gentle. He was in no rush. "I like doing this to you, Francesca."

"I wish you'd go faster."

He paused and glanced up. "I don't recall asking you a question."

Her eyes widened, but she grinned. "Sorry."

He continued. "I wonder how you taste tonight." He twisted his hand so his palm faced up and he added another finger, curling them slightly.

With his other hand, Gabe caressed her thigh, running his hand up and down her leg, sometimes centering on her inner thigh, close to her sex. Sometimes focusing on the underside of her knee, a sensitive spot he'd discovered and loved to exploit.

She fidgeted, moaned, and lifted her hips a bit.

Gabe leaned in close.

She sucked in a breath as his exhale warmed her tender flesh. She strained without trying to be obvious about it.

Gabe appreciated the attempt because he wasn't torturing only her.

"Please, Gabe."

"Ah, ah. You know the rules."

"Please, Mr. McBride."

"Please what?" Gabe increased his pace enough to enjoy the automatic thrusting of her hips now.

"I'd like to come, please."

Weeks ago, she wouldn't have spoken to him this way. Since they'd dealt with Lawrence, she'd been making an effort to learn more about what he liked. Though he'd found he actually preferred her company more than anything. And they didn't need to be at The Vault or having sex for that to happen. He truly liked *her*.

Gabe looked up to see her glazed eyes, her bottom lip caught between her teeth, which she quickly released. "Play with your nipples, Francesca. Pull them. Pinch them."

She raised her hands, covered her breasts, and squeezed. Then she directed her attention as he requested, plucking at the ripe buds for all she was worth.

Gabe watched her for a moment, loving the attention she was giving herself. Then he turned his to the treasure between her legs. With two fingers still buried inside her, he kissed her pussy. He ran his tongue along the length. He flicked the tip of his tongue over her clit. One of these days he'd surprise her with his flogger. She'd shown her curiosity about it through questions, but he'd sensed her nervousness and decided to hold off. Although, he couldn't wait to see her pale flesh striped from a gentle flick of his wrist.

Gabe lapped at her folds and captured her juices on his tongue as they spilled around his fingers. He played with her clit, taking a moment after every few licks to suck on it, adding a little pressure through gentle suction.

Frankie's hips began to buck.

He applied more force to her clit and drove his fingers a little deeper, a little harder, a litter faster.

She moaned.

Gabe removed his fingers, laid his hand on the inside of her thighs, pressing them wider and stuck his tongue in her pussy as far as he could reach. He began to eat her with vigor, loving the taste, texture, the smell of the woman he loved. He adored how she worked to grind her pelvis to his face. He used the flat of his tongue to push her toward orgasm.

When her body started to shake and soft grunts fell from her lips, Gabe pulled out and reached into his back pocket for a condom with one hand while with the other he fumbled with his zipper.

Shoving his pants down as far as he needed to free his cock, he wasted no time ripping the latex from its package and covering himself. Then he was standing, bending at the knees, and driving into Frankie, plunging as far and as fast and as hard as he could, succumbing to what she offered him. He pulled out and drove back in.

She pulled him deep into her body.

He felt like he'd found heaven.

He didn't want to leave, but he needed to experience the delicious torture of each movement in and out. Of snug and release. Of hot and then cold. And then hot again as he thrust back inside her.

Frankie cried out. Her body clamped down around him.

Gabe fucked her hard, his impending release coiled, ready to surge through his body.

She reached up, wrapped her hands around his biceps, and screamed.

He pounded into her, once, twice more, and then groaned as he felt the hot cum race from his balls and out through the end of his cock.

One day, they wouldn't have any barriers between them. One day he vowed she would be his forever. "I love you, Francesca Stevens."

"I love you, Gabriel McBride."

# EPILOGUE

She and Gabe stood in front of the building where she'd first met him, the day he had decided to cover for his brother. The day she'd fallen in love but just hadn't realized it yet because she'd been blinded by the sexy stranger leaning against his car.

"Gabe, would you do me the honor of marrying me?"

Frankie held her breath. Her heart raced inside her chest cavity. She'd practiced saying those words in front of the mirror for an hour after breakfast every day for the last week, each time envisioning how she'd screw them up, how he'd laugh at her.

How he'd say no.

She'd taken special care in dressing today too. She'd chosen a sleeveless, pale pink knee-length dress with a tapered waist and a flared skirt. Sophie had preened over her makeup and hair, helping to make everything perfect. Her sister had given her sultry eyes, pouty lips, and created some fancy braid thingy leaving a few tendrils of hair cascading along each side of her cheek. Then Sophie had stepped back and claimed Frankie looked beautiful.

She felt like an idiot.

This wasn't her. Is this what Gabe wanted though? He'd said he'd always envisioned a girly girl on his arm. A woman he needed to care for and protect. A stay-at-home wife and mother.

Frankie could whip up a set of stairs, but she couldn't whip a pot of potatoes. She could frame a house, but she couldn't fix her hair in fancy ways. She could talk you through curing concrete, but she couldn't tell you the shade of pink she wore on her toes.

Gabe wanted a woman. Frankie was a tomboy with a weird fetish for pink nail polish and sexy underwear. He wanted control in the relationship. She could only give him that in the bedroom. Would it be enough?

Would he be angry with her for stealing his thunder and asking him first?

He'd told her he loved her and she'd told him she loved him. Then he'd offered a compromise. Not willing to lose him, she'd jumped at it. She'd thought she could wait but waiting wasn't her nature. She had to admit, however, the exploring her fantasies part was kind of fun.

She'd given him a week.

And now here she stood.

Had he heard her? The words had felt like a whisper on her lips. She was scared to look up. When had she looked down?

Suddenly his hand appeared before her eyes and his knuckle moved to under her chin. He dipped her head back until they were locked in a staring match. His eyes held laughter. A grin curved his sensual lips.

She'd never get over how gorgeous this man was. And he was hers. She hoped.

"Francesca, isn't the man supposed to ask that question?"

She darted a glance to her left and then to her right. The dinner hour, especially at this time of year, brought out couples, companions…and lovers. For the first time ever, she'd used her connections and managed to snag reservations at the newest restaurant in town. Which was perfect for what she had planned. And she'd been planning for days. Did guys put in this much effort?

She had wanted to propose over a nice meal, with a glass of wine and candlelight, her confidence shining. They'd sit gazing into each other's eyes, wrapped in their own little cocoon. They'd hold hands across the table. Isn't that how it worked in the movies?

But she'd been so nervous she'd blurted it out on the sidewalk near the front entrance in amongst a herd of people waiting to get inside.

She clamped her eyes shut. Damn it. They'd just gotten out of the car. People were lined up ten feet away from them to get into the restaurant. Gabe hadn't even been facing her when the words spilled from her quivering lips.

She sighed. She seemed to be doing that a lot lately. "Normally, sure. But we're not normal." At least she wasn't.

He chuckled. "No, I guess we're not." He looked her up and down, in the same way he'd been doing since he picked her up. He loved making her sweat.

She loved when he made her sweat.

Frankie glanced down. "Do I look OK?" She knew it had been a mistake to wear a dress tonight. But she'd wanted to look nice.

It was the shoes. She couldn't walk for shit on heels. She should have worn a pair of ballet flats. Not as comfortable as work boots, but probably more appropriate with a pink dress.

Maybe he was going to say no.

"You look absolutely stunning."

She felt heat rise and flush her cheeks. She felt girly. She hated girly. But she loved Gabe.

"But it's not you, Francesca." He angled his head so he could look her in the eye.

She couldn't pull her gaze away from his earnest one. Not that she ever wanted to.

"You don't have to dress up for me, Frankie," he whispered.

Could love really swell your heart? Because her chest suddenly felt tight.

"I love you, Francesca. Just the way you are. I love you because of *who* you are." He shook his head. "I don't want you pretending to be anything else or anyone else." Gabe took her hands in his. "I don't want you changing for me."

Relief swept through her like a tsunami. She would do almost anything for this man, but she wasn't sure she could change her essence. She didn't know how to be anyone else. But Gabe made her want to try. He made he want to be the woman he dreamed of. Even if it wasn't comfortable for her.

"You're OK with me working?" she asked, anxious for his response.

"I wouldn't have it any other way." He smiled.

"You won't be expecting me to sit at home with dinner waiting on the table?"

He tossed his head back and laughed. "Only if you take some cooking lessons, sweetheart."

She tried to scowl, but he wasn't lying. She giggled. Giggled! Frankie never giggled. Then she turned serious. "Kids?"

"What about kids?" he asked.

"You want them."

"Someday," he clarified.

"Will you want me to quit my job and be a stay-at-home mom?"

"Do you want to do that, Francesca?"

She frowned. "I don't know," she replied in all honesty.

"Then I can't answer that for you. The choice will be yours when the time comes. If you want to stay home for a while, we'll work it out. If you want to go back to work right away, we'll work that out too."

"OK. What about you?" she asked.

"What about me?"

"You described your ideal woman to me. I'm not her, Gabe. What about me do you get out of this relationship?"

He stepped closer, crowding her. He slipped his arms around her waist and bent his head to press his lips firmly to hers.

Every person in the crowd surrounding them disappeared. It was just the two of them.

Then he pulled back just enough to see her face.

One good thing about heels, in this position she wasn't arched as far back as she'd be if she hadn't worn them.

"I get to spend every day and every night with you. I get to watch you succeed in business. I get to be your sounding board when you need one. I get to love you," he said.

"Is that enough?"

"That's all I need. I'm so sorry I didn't tell you that a long time ago, Frankie, because I've known for weeks that I loved you. I just didn't have the courage to say it until last week."

She tipped up onto the tips of her toes and nipped his chin. "Who gets to be the boss?"

He grinned that beautiful sexy grin. "I get your submission in the bedroom, sweetheart. You get to call the shots everywhere else."

"So we both get to be the boss."

He nudged her nose with his. "We both get to be the boss."

"So I guess that takes me back to my original question then."

"And what would that be?" He winked at her. He was teasing her.

If he thought she was still nervous, he was so, so wrong. She'd never been more sure of anything in her life.

With him standing before her, sharing the control with her, she had nothing to lose and everything to gain. This time when she looked up into his smiling face and asked, the words rang out nice and clear. "Gabe McBride. Will you marry me?"

"I thought you'd never ask."

## ABOUT THE AUTHOR

Shoes are her addiction, but books are her passion. Anne reads many genres of romance, but prefers to write sexy stories with a side of those sinful pleasures your mom never told you about—along with a happy ending, of course.

Anne juggles a full time job and a family. She's a Canadian who lives in Eastern Ontario with her wonderfully supportive husband, three awesome kids, Rocky the bearded dragon, and Lily the chocolate lab.

**Discover more about Anne Lange here:**

**Web Site**
http://authorannelange.com/

**Facebook**
https://www.facebook.com/AuthorAnneLange

**Twitter @Anne_Lange**
https://twitter.com/Anne_Lange

**Goodreads**
http://www.goodreads.com/author/show/6896566.Anne_Lange

**Sign up for Anne's Newsletter at**
http://authorannelange.com/newsletter/

**Join Anne's Fan Club at**
https://www.facebook.com/groups/982082321801793/

## ALSO BY ANNE LANGE

### FRIENDS WITH BENEFITS

THE VAULT SERIES
FRIENDS AND MORE

*Can sexual exploration lead to three times the bliss?*

Tyler had no idea his wife Angela's desires so closely matched his own. But when some unguarded pillow talk reveals her fantasy of two men at once, Tyler jumps at the chance to make her happy.

Enlisting the help of his best friend Connor, who'd shared some threesome adventures with him in the past, Tyler secretly hopes exploring Angela's fantasies will lead to his own personal desire—a permanent threesome with the two people he loves most in the world.

Connor can't believe it when his best friend asks him to seduce his wife. Then he meets Angela, and all the women in his past fade away. With Tyler's blessing, Connor sets out to melt Angela's reserve, and when Tyler joins the party, the three of them set the sheets on fire.

Angela is floored when her husband suggests they explore some of her fantasies—things she'd only read about but never in a million years thought she'd actually do. Sandwiched between Tyler and Connor, she's never felt so treasured, so protected, so loved.

But the reality proves much more complicated than the fantasy. She loves her husband, but she finds herself falling for his best friend too. That's not normal, is it? What will people think?

## HERS TO OWN

THE VAULT SERIES

THE MCBRIDE MEN: KADE

*He'll teach her to love her body...one spanking at a time.*

Brienna Morgan has worked hard to look good. Ten years ago she stuck to the shadows, watching the popular kids, wishing she could be one of them. But when they weren't calling her cruel names, nobody noticed the smart overweight girl with the glasses.

So when she braves her high school reunion and runs into Kade McBride, the boy she loved from afar, the last thing she wants is for him to remember her. It's bad enough she still sees that girl every time she looks in the mirror. But Kade does remember—and he makes it impossible for Brie to refuse to go out with him. She's not convinced it's a good idea, but she can't pass up the opportunity to be part of the in crowd.

Kade had no desire to go to his high school reunion. As far as he's concerned, he'd rather forget those days. Especially the day he screwed up and left his best friend to pay the ultimate price. But when he sees the gorgeous woman enter the gym, he's immediately drawn to her. Regardless of her claims that she's not the girl he thinks he remembers, Kade realizes maybe he's been given a second chance to right at least one wrong from his past. And he's determined not to throw this opportunity away, even if he has to tie Brienna to a spanking bench to prove his point.

## WICKED INDULGENCE

THE VAULT SERIES

FRIENDS AND MORE

*Two men. One woman. How wonderful wicked can be.*

Jamie Logan prefers one-night stands to the risk of hurting someone he loves. He's not willing to repeat the past. Years ago, his naïve attempts at dominance left his girlfriend bruised and frightened. Then, almost overnight and without a good-bye, she left town and he hasn't seen or heard from her—until four months ago.

Daniel Oliver wants something more. As members of the prestigious BDSM club known as The Vault, and co-owners of a veterinary clinic, he hopes that one day he and Jamie will find that perfect woman to share, not just at the club, but forever. He never thought she'd walk through their door. Or ask for his best friend.

Finally rid of her abusive ex and living on her own terms, Melissa Stanford has done everything she can to protect the only man she's ever loved. Only she never counted on Daniel, a man who ignites enough sizzle in her body to compete with her passion for her first love. In order for them to be happy, she must find a way to convince Jamie that he was never the monster he though himself to be.

A|L
hotRom publishing

73014244R00175

Made in the USA
Columbia, SC
04 July 2017